Healing on the Land
By Melissa Baker

Published by   he Way Publishing

First Edition – 2025

ISBN: 978-1-7642101-1-9

For enquiries, contact:

admin@thewaypublishing.com.au

Follow us on Facebook: facebook.com/thewaypublishingAus[1]

Dedication

To God—
Thank You for being my refuge, my strength, and my ever-present help.
For never leaving, even in my brokenness.
For whispering inspiration when I had none left,
and for turning ashes into beauty, again and again.
This story is Yours.
To Nick—
Your unwavering support, your steadiness,
and your love have been my anchor through every storm.
Thank you for believing in me, always.
To Hannah and Ella—
My precious girls, you are the light that teaches me
what courage, resilience, and joy truly look like.
You are my inspiration, every single day.
This is for you.
With all my heart.
To Dad and Emily—
Thank you for your love, your help, and your ongoing support.
Your quiet strength has meant more than words can say.
With all my heart,
—Melissa Baker

Dear Reader,

This book was written with tenderness, truth, and trembling hands.
It is a story woven from ashes and hope—about what it means to
survive, to heal, and to be seen by love that doesn't walk away.
But before you turn the page, I want to gently let you know:
Some parts of this story may be hard to read.
It contains references to domestic violence, emotional abuse, sexual
coercion, PTSD, and suicidal ideation. These themes are handled
with care and purpose, never for shock, but always to tell the
truth—because truth matters. And because, for many, these
experiences are not fiction.
If you are in a place where these topics feel too close or too heavy,
please honour what you need. You are not weak for stepping back.
You are brave for knowing your limits.
This book is not just about pain. It's about the God who stays. It's
about redemption, found family, sacred beginnings, and the wild,
healing grace that meets us in the wreckage.
If you are living in the midst of grief or fear, I want you to know this
with every fibre of my being:
You are not alone.
You are not too far gone.
You are not invisible.
You are not unloved.
And there is help.
If you or someone you know needs support, here are some 24/7
services in Australia:

- **1800RESPECT** (Domestic, family and sexual violence

4

support): **1800 737 732**
- **Lifeline Australia** (Mental health and crisis support): **13 11 14**
  - **Beyond Blue** (Anxiety, depression and suicide prevention): **1300 22 4636**
- **Kids Helpline** (For young people aged 5–25): **1800 55 1800**

You are worthy of a safe life. A full life. A story that is still being written.
Thank you for choosing to read this one.
With love and gentleness,
Melissa

Chapter 1: The Weight of Loss

"The Lord is close to the broken-hearted and saves those who are crushed in spirit." — Psalm 34:18

The wind carried a low hum across the rolling hills, rustling the golden heads of wheat that stretched to the horizon. James stood at the edge of the old verandah, arms folded. He still had yesterday's mud caked on his boots. Beside him sat Bear, his loyal German Shepherd—alert, still, sensing something heavier than weather.

Today marked three years since the call. He could still hear the officer's voice—young, unsure, painfully careful. The voice that knew it was about to splinter someone's world.

James had struggled to keep up as the officer described the scene at Ellie's house. The words blurred into one long ache until the officer paused and lowered his voice.

"Mr Harding........ I'm so sorry to tell you this. But Ellie is gone."

His sister. His bright, reckless, stubborn-hearted sister. Dead—not by illness or accident, but by the hands of the man who once swore to love her.

James closed his eyes, and there it was again—uninvited, unrelenting. The memory slid into his mind with the precision of a blade, familiar in its rhythm but jagged in its sting. His fingers curled around the weathered railing of the porch, knuckles whitening, wood creaking in protest. A sharp sting pierced his palm as a splinter drove beneath the skin, but he welcomed the pain—it was simpler than the ache of the memory he was trying to leave behind."

He hadn't saved her.

He had offered her everything—his voice hoarse from begging, his arms outstretched with hope, his heart cracked wide open.

Come home, El. You don't have to stay with him. You can come back to the farm with me.

But every time, she met him with that quiet, practiced calm that masked the chaos. She smoothed over the jagged truth.

"He's just tired," she would say, brushing a strand of hair behind her ear like it didn't tremble.

"It was just the one time." Or "He is trying." That one always gutted him. As if effort was enough.

He swallowed hard, the weight of what wasn't said pressing like a stone against his chest.

James felt it rise again—that heat in his chest. Not the kind that kicked in doors or shouted down walls. This was quieter. Older. The kind that settled behind his ribs and refused to leave.

Grief had many masks. Today, it wore fury. He sat with it—jaw tight, hands still.

As a Christian, he knew the words. Forgive. Let it go. Vengeance is the Lord's.

He'd said those words himself once. Believed them with his whole heart. But now?

The words seemed to hold little meaning for him in his grief. He still had faith. He still prayed. But belief felt different now. Like walking with a limp. Like arriving at a familiar house and finding all the furniture rearranged.

God was still there but, James just didn't know where to sit anymore.

He sighed and looked up. A lone magpie traced a wide circle overhead. Its wings caught the last of the light—black and silver and bone-white where the feathers flashed. It didn't land. Just kept circling.

That's what it's like, Jame thought. This thing with Ellie. It doesn't crash down anymore—it just circles. Comes back whenever the sky is quiet enough.

He watched the bird drift above the paddock. Always there. Always returning.

James let out a long breath through his teeth. Beside him, Bear shifted and leaned gently into his boot, warm and wordless. James reached down, brushing his fingers across the dog's shoulder. Not for comfort. Just contact.

In that moment, a Ute engine rumbled up the long gravel drive. James didn't move. He knew that sound. Neil.

The Ute stopped beside the shed, engine ticking as it cooled. The driver's door creaked. A moment later, boots approached the house.

"Hey James, nice to see you." The voice was familiar—rough like gravel, but warm.

Neil Clarke. Old neighbour, who'd been farming three paddocks down since before James had facial hair.

James didn't answer at first. Neil climbed the stairs slowly, one step at a time. He carried a cardboard box balanced on one hip.

"Margaret sent food," Neil said. "Said she was tired of waiting for you to come 'round." James glanced sideways. Neil set the box down by the screen door.

"She put in some roast lamb, bread rolls and her weird lemon slice that tastes like dish soap but somehow still works." James smiled faintly.

"She still uses that tin with the dent in it?" "Claims it's the reason it holds together."

They stood in silence for a moment, with the wind curling around them, wheat rustling below like a crowd of quiet mourners.

"She remembered, you know," Neil said. James looked up. "Ellie," Neil clarified.

James swallowed but didn't speak.

"You've got everything you need for today?" Neil asked.

"I'm fine." James replied.

"That wasn't the question."

James looked out at the field. "I got work. That helps." Neil didn't argue. Just nodded, hands in his coat pockets.

"You ever think about letting folks help more?" James glanced at the box. "I did. I let you drive food here." Neil gave a half-smile.

"That's a start." "Well," Neil said, stepping back. "Marg says she'll bring more next week—unless you show your face at church." James gave him a look. "Her words, not mine."

Neil headed back to the Ute. "You're not alone, son. Even when you want to be.

Well, I've got to head out now—off to see Tom. Marg made a box for him too."

Inside, James unpacked the box in silence. Roast lamb wrapped in foil. Buttered bread rolls. A Tupperware container of something lemon-coloured with plastic wrap clinging too tightly.

He didn't touch any of it. He boiled water for tea.

Later, he stepped back onto the veranda, mug in hand. Bear followed, settling with a groaning sigh that made James's chest ache.

It was the sound of an animal who knew sorrow, even if he didn't name it. The sky had turned that shade of blue that feels holy. Like someone who still believed in comfort had painted it slowly and carefully.

James stared out at the fields, hands shoved deep in the pockets of his worn flannel coat. The crooked fence still leaned where the wind had taken it last winter, untouched, forgotten. Beyond it, the line of trees stood still and sun-bleached, their leaves whispering memories he wasn't ready to hear. That was where Ellie had once run barefoot through the long grass, laughter trailing behind her like music, daring him to catch her, always just out of reach.

His chest tightened. He closed his eyes.

"God," he said, the words trembling. "I miss her. I don't know what to do anymore. Please... please just show me the next step. Help me, Lord. Help this pain stop."

The silence pressed in. Heavy. Familiar.

He waited. Not for thunder. Not for miracles.

But for something—anything.

There were no visions. No burning bushes. No signs etched in the sky.

Only the quiet ache of longing.

And the hollow echo of a man who used to know how to pray.

He missed what it felt like to believe someone was listening.

Really listening.

Chapter 2: The City Encounter

"Do not neglect to show hospitality to strangers, for by doing so some have entertained angels without knowing it." — Hebrews 13:2

The highway rolled flat beneath James's tyres, the Ute humming steadily. His right hand rested on the wheel while his left drummed idly on the gearshift. On the seat beside him sat a folded list in Margaret's neat, cursive handwriting that read—rails, walker, cushion, shower chair—far more legible than his own writing.

Tom wouldn't ask for help. But Neil had rung that morning and said he'd found Tom, who had taken another fall and bruised his hip. "Stubborn as a post!" Neil had muttered. "He needs those rails. Won't admit it—but I think they'll help."

James didn't need convincing. Tom was church family. When one of theirs went down, someone showed up, it was as simple as that.

The city air hit like dust after rain. The longer he stayed in it, the tighter his shoulders pulled. It wasn't the crowds exactly—it was the closeness. The noise. The way no one made eye contact. He missed space. Dirt roads. Knowing who passed you by name.

After three supply stops and a reluctant pie from a servo with faded signage, James found himself near a train station, just across from a strip of old shops, their windows crusted with age.

A bakery nestled behind a chemist, with a crooked chalkboard out front that read: Jesus fed the 5,000. We can make a sandwich. He almost smiled.

Inside, the air smelled like burnt coffee beans and day-old cinnamon rolls. The waitress looked exhausted but kind. James ordered a flat white and carried it out to a metal bench facing the station.

He sipped slowly, watching foot traffic stream by. Teenagers. Suits. A young woman yelling into her phone. Life, raw and unbothered, rolled past like a tide that didn't care who slipped beneath it.

Then he heard it. A voice—low, tight, sharp.

James turned. Across the street, near the station entrance, a man had a woman by the arm—fingers dug in like claws. He leaned in, spitting words in her face. She didn't move. Her eyes were wide, vacant, fixed somewhere far away.

James stood before he even registered the motion. He crossed traffic—quickly but calm. Boots on pavement. Coffee left behind.

"LET HER GO!" he said, voice steady, loud enough to carry.

The man, early twenties. Wiry and full of anger, turned in response. "MIND YOUR OWN BUSINESS!!!" he snapped.

James stopped a few feet away. His voice didn't rise. "She clearly doesn't want you near her. That's reason enough for this to be my business!"

The man's eyes swept over James—his height, his build, the calm that radiated from him, unmistakable and unmoving. It wasn't fear. It was something heavier. He smirked, that instinctive curl of someone used to dominating. Then came the pause. A flicker of calculation—measuring risk. James didn't flinch. Didn't speak. He didn't have to. The smirk drained from the man's face, and his grip loosened.

The woman stumbled back. James caught her elbow instinctively, but she flinched as if it burned. "Easy," he murmured, pulling his hand away.

She backed against the wall; bag clutched to her chest. The man fled, melting into the crowd.

James turned toward her—slow, careful. "Are you alright?" He asked.

Her lips parted, then pressed shut. Her eyes darted left, then right—like a cornered animal, scanning for a way out, bracing for whatever might come next. "No police," she whispered. "Please."

"No police," James promised quietly, though confusion tangled in his chest. He didn't know what to do next. So, he did the only thing that seemed safe.

"There's a bench across the road," he said, nodding toward the bakery. "It's In the sun. You don't have to talk or stay long. Just... come and sit with me for a bit if you want?"

She blinked, uncertain. "What?"

He gestured again—gentle, unthreatening. "It's just a bench. That's all."

She didn't move, didn't answer—but she didn't run either.

James walked ahead without looking back, crossing to the bench and sitting down as if it were any other day. After a long moment, she followed.

She didn't sit. Just hovered a few feet away, clutching her bag like it was the last thing she could trust. Her eyes darted everywhere—faces, doorways, shifting shadows. Watching for threats.

"I'm James," he said, not looking her way. "Ruthie."

Her voice was hushed. Not timid—restrained. Like volume might bring punishment. She didn't meet his eyes. Just kept watching the street. Listening for danger in the quiet.

James recognised the look. Ellie had worn it once.

"You don't have to stay long," he said. "But you're welcome to stay here with me as long as you need."

The silence stretched. Eventually, she spoke again. "I don't know where I'm going. I thought about the train. But I didn't have a destination. I just needed to get away from him."

James nodded. "Do you have anyone? Family? Friends?"

She shook her head before he finished. "I haven't seen my dad since I was six. Grandparents are gone. My mum..." She paused, jaw clenched. "She didn't want a kid. Especially not me. Gave just enough to look like effort. Then disappeared."

Her hand tightened on the bag strap. "My friends..." she swallowed. "They warned me. Said Dylan was dangerous. Told me if I stayed, they couldn't keep pretending it was okay."

"I haven't heard from them in over a year."

James didn't interrupt. He just let the truth hang undisturbed. Fragile.

He wasn't the sort of man who knew how to fix people. But he knew how to fix things—fences, hinges, broken gates. Practical things.

Thinking for a moment, he said, "I know of a place you could stay."

"What do you mean?" she asked, confused.

"I know a shelter. Out near Croydon. I live a couple of hours away, and our local church is often collecting donations for it."

She tensed. "It's safe," he added. "It will just be a warm bed and a place to get something to eat for a while."

She was quiet for a long time.

The silence stretched—awkward, heavy.

Then finally, her voice, flat and uncertain:

"I guess I could catch a train... if you've got the address?"

James shook his head—calm, unhurried, gentle.

"No need. I'll drive you—it's on my way home."

He let the offer settle. Then, softer still:

"You're safe with me. I promise."

She didn't answer. Not right away.

Her fingers tightened around the strap of her bag until her hand trembled. Her eyes flicked back toward the station—dark, quiet, indifferent. Like it could vanish at any second and take her last shred of control with it.

She had no real options. Not safe ones.

Staying meant staying near the man who'd hurt her.

Going meant trusting a stranger.

Both paths held risk. Both lit up her nerves.

Still, something in James's voice—unshaken, kind—held her there.

She exhaled through her nose. Not relief—more like resignation. Or survival.

Then, a small nod.

"...Alright. Yeah."

It wasn't confidence. It wasn't peace.

But it was a decision.

And maybe, just maybe, the first step out of the wreckage.

Chapter 3: Lost Hope

"He heals the broken-hearted and binds up their wounds." — Psalm 147:3

The drive to Croydon was long and silent, thick with unspoken things. The sun sagged low over the western sky, smearing gold across the horizon like a last-ditch attempt to warm the day. Ruthie didn't speak. She sat with her arms tightly crossed over her backpack on her lap.

As the city thinned out behind them, the landscape changed. Glass gave way to graffiti and small Shopfronts.

The shelter emerged without fanfare—a concrete box on the corner of a forgotten street, with rust-streaked awnings and bars on every window. The kind of place that looked like it held more ghosts than people.

Two women sat smoking on the front steps. One could barely have been eighteen, the other had the kind of eyes that had already seen too much. They both watched the ute approach without any expression while exhaling smoke.

James parked across the street, engine rumbling low.

"Want me to come in?" he asked, voice soft.

Ruthie hesitated. Her grip on the bag tightened.

Then she nodded.

As James and Ruthie approached the shelter, he reached for the door and pulled it open. The hinges groaned in protest—a rusted wail that echoed off the bare concrete walls. Ruthie flinched. The sharp sting of bleach hit her nose immediately, thick in the air.

James held the door open as Ruthie stepped inside.

At the front desk stood a woman in a sagging grey hoodie. She looked young—no older than Ruthie—but her eyes told a different story: dark-rimmed, hollowed out by too many sleepless nights and too many desperate faces.

"We're full tonight," she said, voice brittle with regret. "I am sorry but, the waiting list is backed up until at least the weekend."

James looked over at Ruthie. She didn't react, but something flickered in her eyes. Disappointment, maybe. Or just another piece of hope quietly dying.

"I can give you Ballarat's number," the staffer offered, trying to sound helpful, "but—"

"That's three hours away," James interrupted, his frown deepening.

"I know. I'm sorry. Just... call them first. It's likely they're full too."

Ruthie didn't respond. She just turned and walked out, shoulders rigid.

Outside, the air was cold and sterile. Even the breeze felt indifferent. Ruthie stopped near the kerb; her backpack now clutched against her chest like armour. Her eyes stared straight ahead, unmoving.

James stood beside her, hands in his jacket pockets, saying nothing.

Behind them, the shelter door creaked again as it closed.

One of the girls on the stoop lit another cigarette with shaking hands. The other stared at the ground like it might open and swallow her.

James watched them. His jaw locked.

I wonder if Ellie ever stood outside a place like this, he thought. *Needing help. Getting told there was none.*

17

Maybe she had.

Maybe no one walked out with her.

He turned toward Ruthie.

"Look, Ruthie... I know this isn't ideal, and I'm really sorry there aren't any spots available. But I've got a place. It's nothing official—no program or anything like that. Just a quiet little cottage. It used to be my grandfather's."

She didn't respond. Didn't move. Just stared down at the bitumen, like it might offer the answers she couldn't find anywhere else.

"It's not much," James added gently. "But it's safe. Clean. Cosy. And it's yours, if you want it."

At last, she looked up, guarded. Her voice was low and rough.

"You're... offering for me to stay at your house?"

James shook his head. "No.... it's not mine, my house is nearby to the cottage. You'd have complete privacy. No one's been in it for years."

A pause. Then:

"Why me?"

She didn't sound angry. Just frayed. Confused.

James didn't look at her. His gaze went back to the stoop.

"I had a sister," he said, as he looked down at the ground. "Her name was Ellie."

James took a breath and then continued.

"She was in a similar situation to you, and she didn't make it out."

Ruthie didn't ask for details. She didn't need to. The way James said it was enough.

Her features shifted. Not soft, not gentle—but something opened. A recognition. A truth she wasn't expecting.

"I offered her help," he said. "Too late. I didn't see how bad it was until..."

He didn't finish the sentence. He didn't have to.

Silence stretched between them.

"You'd let me stay?" Ruthie asked. "Just like that?"

"Your own key," James said.

Her eyes narrowed, not in distrust but disbelief.

"People don't do things for nothing," she said. "They always want something."

"I don't," James said. Steady. Honest. No wavering.

Across the road, a door slammed. Ruthie flinched like she'd been struck, the sound ricocheting through her body.

"I don't want to be someone's project," she said, her voice brittle. "I'm not a broken thing you get to fix."

"You're not," James said, evenly.

"And I don't want your pity."

"It's not pity," James replied. "Just clean sheets. And bad lemon slice. That's all."

A breath of something like a laugh trembled through her lips. She didn't smile, not really—but something softened. A thawing at the edges.

She didn't say yes.

But she didn't turn away.

After a long moment, she nodded—barely more than a tilt of her chin.

"Okay," she whispered. "Just a couple of nights."

James crossed the road and opened the passenger door.

And for the first time that day, something unfamiliar stirred inside Ruthie—something that almost felt like hope.

Chapter 4: The Drive Out

"In peace I will lie down and sleep, for you alone, Lord, make me dwell in safety." — Psalm 4:8

The Ute rolled onto the highway just after five.

City lights faded fast behind them, dissolving into brush and rusted signs. The hum of the tyres settled into a steady rhythm—low, almost comforting. Ruthie sat rigid in the passenger seat, one hand on the door handle, the other pressed flat against her thigh like she had to hold herself in place.

She didn't say a word, and James just drove.

Wind curled through a crack in the window, cool against their skin. The silence wasn't awkward—it was deliberate. James knew better than to crowd the moment with noise.

An hour out of the city, James broke the silence.

"Should be a servo up ahead. You hungry?"

Ruthie hesitated. Then nodded once.

"A little."

He pulled off just past a crooked sign reading:

Peterson's Roadhouse — Best Coffee & Pies Since 1984

The car park was mostly empty. Fluorescent lights buzzed above the windows.

Inside, the air was cold and stale.

Fridges hummed. A deep fryer crackled behind the counter. Somewhere overhead, a speaker played pop songs from ten years ago—loud and echoing.

Ruthie stopped just inside the doorway.

Her pupils narrowed. Shoulders lifted. She scanned the room like someone checking for exits, not specials.

"You okay?" James asked gently, his voice low.

She didn't respond.

But she stepped inside.

James moved with her—not intruding, just steady and near, like a shadow offering comfort.

He nodded toward the chalkboard sign above the counter; its white lettering smudged at the edges. Pie, chips and drink for ten dollars, it read. James tipped his head in its direction. "Sound alright to you?"

Ruthie gave a quiet nod.

Behind the counter stood a young cashier—barely out of high school, with weary eyes and a posture that sagged under the weight of long shifts. His disinterest was almost tangible, worn like part of his uniform.

He hardly looked up as James and Ruthie approached to order.

The total blinked onto the screen, and Ruthie was already reaching for her purse. She pulled out a small handful of coins—scattered silvers, a couple of golds. Her fingers worked quickly, lips moving as she counted under her breath.

"I've got it," James said, reaching into his back pocket.

"No, I can pay" Ruthie replied quickly, already placing two coins on the counter.

But before she could gather the rest, James gently cut in.

"It's okay, I will get this one and you can get the next one."

Ruthie paused, her thumb resting on a worn fifty-cent piece. The metal felt cool against her skin, but his words settled warmer—unexpected, kind, and quietly steady.

Then, reluctantly, she nodded and slipped the coins back into her purse.

The boy handed James his change with a look that said he had noticed nothing unusual.

But Ruthie's cheeks were flushed.

They took their food to a metal bench bolted to the floor near the window.

Ruthie picked at her food more than she ate it, nudging chips around the plate with the edge of her fork.

The overhead lights buzzed too loudly and cast everything in a harsh, sterile glow. The plastic seat beneath her felt icy against her thighs. Every clang of cutlery or sudden scrape of a chair made her flinch, shoulders tightening as if bracing for impact.

"You don't have to finish it all if you don't want," James said softly, watching her with quiet concern.

"I'm fine, James." Ruthie replied.

"You're not."

His words weren't sharp—just true. They settled between them with the weight of something known.

She glanced up at him then. Her eyes were tired, rimmed with shadows. There was no defence in her face—just honesty.

"No," she whispered. "But I'm trying."

James gave a small nod, steady and sure.

"You don't need to try around me."

Then Ruthie turned and stared out the wide glass window. After a long moment, she said, just above a whisper:

"I honestly thought leaving would feel more freeing, like I'd finally be able to stand up straight without fear of being knocked down. But it doesn't feel like that at all."

James didn't interrupt.

She kept talking. Voice low. Almost clinical.

"It feels like I stole something. Like he's going to show up any minute and make me give it back."

James shook his head gently.

"You stole nothing, Ruthie! You only reclaimed what was always yours."

Ruthie just shrugged, falling quiet again. She looked down at her arms, where bruises were already deepening in colour—evidence of a day that had marked her in more ways than one. There weren't words big enough for the fear and guilt swirling inside her, so she let the silence speak instead as they finished their meal and headed back to the ute.

Back in the ute, Ruthie settled a little deeper in her seat. Still upright. Still alert. But her grip on the door handle loosened.

The land widened the further they drove. Ruthie had never been this far outside the city.

Trees lined the road—dark silhouettes against a starlit sky.

James slowed near a weathered mailbox with peeling paint.

"We are almost there, not long now."

Ruthie didn't speak.

But she breathed—one long, full breath—as James turned onto the gravel drive.

A house came into view slowly.

Whitewashed timber. A porch with a lean. One front window lit warmly against the hush of night.

James parked and cut the engine.

In the sudden quiet, the low chirp of crickets rose.

Bear bounded to the driver's side as the ute came to a stop, nose pressed forward, investigating not just James's return but the unfamiliar scent of an unknown visitor. His whole body vibrated with barely contained excitement, tail thudding against the dirt in slow, eager sweeps. He didn't bark—just bounced on his paws, eyes shining with anticipation, making it clear he'd spent the whole day waiting for James to come home.

Ruthie didn't move.

She sat motionless, eyes fixed on the wide-open land beyond the window. No traffic. No voices. Only endless paddocks stretching toward the horizon.

She turned to James.

"Do you live here?"

He nodded.

"Yeah. That one's mine," James said, nodding toward the timber house nestled among the trees. "Your cottage is just a few metres behind it. You can see the side of it, just there." He said as he tilted his head slightly, motioning with a subtle gesture toward the smaller building tucked just out of view, its edge barely visible beyond the main house.

A wave of unease crept over Ruthie as the silence settled in. The vastness of the land, the absence of neighbours, the complete stillness—it all pressed in at once. She hadn't realised just how far removed they were from anything or anyone.

She turned to James, the flicker of fear unmistakable in her eyes. "Um... it's really lovely," she said, her voice soft, trying to steady herself. "And I'm so grateful you're letting me stay here. I just... to be honest, I didn't realise how far out you lived. It's a little more isolated than I expected."

James nodded, his voice gentle. "Yeah, I get that. Especially coming from the city—it's a big shift. But Ruthie, you're safe here. I promise you that."

He held her gaze for a moment longer, steady and sincere.

She didn't answer, but her fingers tightened on the door handle, knuckles whitening. Fear and doubt washed over her—sudden and cold—the realisation hitting.

Still, after a long, hesitant beat, she drew a shaky breath, pulled the handle, and stepped out of the ute.

Her shoes crunched on the gravel as she walked toward the porch slowly, like each footstep had to negotiate with the earth before committing.

The silence here wasn't peaceful yet. Not to her.

It was too complete.

Too alone

James greeted Bear, then followed behind at a respectful distance. When they reached the door, he opened it without speaking and stepped inside.

The space was dim and hushed. The air carried a coolness that felt clean, with hints of lavender, wood soap, and the sharp green breath of eucalyptus.

Ruthie hovered just inside the threshold, eyes scanning—corners, windows, doorframes. The scan you learn through fear and terror.

James pointed gently.

"Towels are in the wardrobe. Tea above the stove."

She didn't move.

Bear, meanwhile, had padded up the steps and now sat just outside the doorway. Ears relaxed. Eyes on her. His tail thumped once—low, calm. Not eager. Just steady.

Ruthie looked at him.

Her shoulders dropped—just slightly. But enough to notice.

"Are you okay with dogs?" James asked, tone light.

She gave a small nod, eyes still on Bear.

James gave a quiet command, and Bear responded instantly—trotting over like he'd been waiting for permission. He pressed his head gently against her side.

Ruthie crouched—hesitantly at first. Then she let her hand move through his thick fur. Bear leaned into the touch, offered one slow lick to her wrist, then stayed close—a comforting anchor.

Something in her posture eased.

James watched them.

"He likes you," he said. "Doesn't hand that out to just anyone."

He paused. Then added:

"He can stay with you tonight, if that feels better. Or I can take him back to the house."

Ruthie hesitated, hand still on Bear's neck.

"...He can stay," she said, just above a whisper.

James nodded.

"He'll guard the door better than I or any lock could, anyway."

She didn't smile.

But something on her face softened.

James took a step back toward the door.

"There's a key on the table. Lock it, leave it, throw it in the bush. It's yours while you're here."

She didn't speak.

Didn't have to.

James lingered a moment longer, then tipped his head slightly.

"Been a big day. I'll let you get some rest."

He stepped back—careful not to crowd the moment.

Then, he pulled the door closed behind him.

No creak.

No slam.

Just the soft finality of wood meeting wood.

Chapter 5: A Fragile Peace

"Come to me, all you who are weary and burdened, and I will give you rest." — Matthew 11:28

That night, Ruthie struggled with the quiet.

She drifted through the cottage, searching for something—anything—to ground her, but everything about the place felt foreign. Even the calm felt alien, like something borrowed from someone else's life. The fear, however, didn't leave. If anything, it sat heavier on her chest, whispering that safety was a trick, that the next bad thing was lurking just out of sight.

Ruthie had never known real calm. Not as a child—her mother too distracted, always bending herself to please whatever boyfriend was around, making sure he didn't walk out the door. Not with Dylan, either, where quiet was just the pause before the next violent explosion.

She paced the floor, bare feet finding every creak and knot in the boards. Her hands fidgeted with anything she touched. She kept checking the locks, glancing over her shoulder, listening for a raised voice that never came.

When she finally crawled into bed, sleep only came in fragments—two hours, maybe three—but even that was different. No shouting. No doors slamming. Just Bear, curled at the base of her bed.

When she stirred in the early morning gloom, Bear lifted his head, blinked at her, then sighed and drifted back to sleep, as if to say, *It's safe now. You can rest.*

For a while, she laid there, watching the ceiling. She was exhausted, but for the first time in years, the exhaustion felt clean—untainted by adrenaline.

Eventually, Ruthie made her way to the kitchen. She fixed herself a cup of tea and carried the chipped mug outside, barefoot on the cool boards of the porch. The land stretched out in front of her—acres of dew-soaked grass and distant trees, the mist still lifting with the sun. No traffic. No neighbours peering through curtains.

It should have been peaceful, but the quiet was too complete. It made her feel exposed.

Her hands wrapped tighter around the mug as she sat on the top step, letting the silence seep in. It felt like sitting at the edge of a world she wasn't sure she belonged to.

Around midmorning, James came up from the lower paddock—hat pulled low, sleeves rolled, dust clinging to his boots. He raised a hand in greeting but didn't speak until he reached the porch.

"Hey, Ruthie..." He said, voice low and steady. "Nice to see you up. How did you sleep?"

She offered a small smile, still wrapped in sleep and silence. "Hey, thank you again for letting me stay. I slept better than I expected."

He stepped up onto the porch, resting one hand on the post. "Glad to hear it. It's no trouble. I just wanted you to feel safe here."

He paused, brushing a streak of dirt from his jeans. "I'm heading into town soon—quick stop at the hardware store. And Naomi's."

Ruthie looked up from her mug, blinking. "Naomi's?"

He smiled, easy and familiar. "A little bookshop tucked off the main road. Shelves to the ceiling, barely any room to walk. The best part's the coffee. "

"That sounds nice," she said, voice soft.

"You're welcome to tag along," James added, not pressing, just leaving the offer there. "Only if you feel up to it."

She hesitated, fingers tightening slightly around her mug. She wanted to say no. Wanted to say she needed more time, more quiet. But that old reflex kicked in—the one that made her say yes when she wanted to say no. The one that feared seeming ungrateful, or difficult, or disappointing.

"Sure," she said, nodding lightly. "I'll come."

James gave a small, satisfied nod, unaware of the war inside her. "Alright then. I'll give you ten minutes to get ready—and then you can meet me by the Ute and we can head into town."

As he stepped away, Ruthie stayed still for a moment, staring into the trees. She already felt the tightness in her chest, the weight of being agreeable. But she also felt something else—an odd flicker of hope.

She grabbed her bag, heart thumping, and climbed into the passenger seat, stiffer than she meant to be, her bag clutched tight in her lap. Even though there was nowhere left to run, she found it difficult to break her old habit of being ready to escape.

James didn't comment, just started the Ute, cracked the windows, and let the breeze carry eucalyptus through the cab.

As James drove, neither of them spoke. Ruthie spent the journey quietly taking in her surroundings, her eyes darting from window to mirror, tracking every passing car and shadow. Even here, on open roads, she stayed hypervigilant—always mapping exits, scanning for threats, bracing herself to run if she had to.

It was a habit she'd learned too well: survival as second nature.

Town was a single main street, the sort of place you could blink and miss. A red post-box, a sun-bleached petrol station, an old pub, and between a hairdresser and a pet shop, a little bookshop with Naomi's Books & Brew stencilled on the window in curling white paint.

A bell chimed when they stepped inside. Ruthie flinched at the sound, but no one stared. Inside, it smelled of lemon oil and something sweet baking. Shelves reached toward the ceiling, packed with books that looked like they'd lived a hundred lives. An armchair sagged in the corner, threadbare but welcoming. At the back, a tiny counter held a chalkboard menu and a battered coffee machine.

A woman in her fifties with sharp eyes and a silver braid looked up from behind the counter and smiled at James.

"Morning, James. I see you brought more than safety equipment back from the city."

James chuckled. "This i s R uthie," h e s aid, n odding i n her direction.

"Glad you came in," Naomi replied, her eyes kind. "The books will be grateful."

Ruthie managed a flicker of a smile—just enough to count. She slipped away down an aisle, fingertips d rifting al ong th e spines, lingering on a shelf marked Lightly Loved. She picked out a worn paperback—a book she'd read under the doona with a torch at twelve, hiding from the world.

She held it to her chest as if it might vanish if she let go.

Meanwhile, Naomi motioned James over to the counter. Her voice dropped, gentler now.

"Your message surprised me. I didn't think you'd offer her the cottage."

James hesitated. He and Naomi went back nearly a decade. There was an ease with her, an unspoken knowing—they'd both lost things they didn't talk about. They simply understood.

"She flinched at the bell," Naomi said, eyes soft.

"She flinches at everything," James admitted. Not unkindly—just stating the truth. "But she came."

They both glanced down the aisle to where Ruthie stood, straight-backed and quiet, hands gentle on the book.

Naomi held James's gaze for a long moment.

"You're doing a good thing. But you know this won't be quick—or easy."

"It never is, Naomi." His voice was quiet, almost lost in the shop's hush. "Learning to breathe again after holding it for so long… that takes time. We both know that."

A slow smile touched Naomi's lips.

"Good. Because that girl looks like she's been holding her breath for years."

When Ruthie returned to the counter, she was still holding the book—thumb brushing the edge, caught between hope and panic.

"Found something you like?" James asked.

She looked up, startled. "How much is it?"

James shrugged. "Doesn't matter. We'll put it on the tab."

Naomi called from behind the counter, smirking. "But you don't have a tab."

James didn't miss a beat. "Well, no better time to start one."

Ruthie hesitated, torn between politeness and a lifetime of going without. Before she could object, Naomi said warmly,

"It's already on your tab, love. No need to fuss today."

Ruthie didn't quite smile. She just nodded, clutching the book tighter.

"Thank you," she whispered.

As they stepped outside, a man came striding up—tall, all swagger and charm, with a confidence that didn't quite fit the sleepy quiet of the street.

Before James could say a word, the man was already there, grinning like he owned the place.

"Well, well—who's this stunning creature?"

James moved instantly, stepping in front of Ruthie with a calm but unmistakable firmness.

"Not now, Micah!"

Ruthie froze. Her breath caught, muscles tightening. Her eyes darted toward the street, scanning for a way out.

Micah, either oblivious or pretending to be, leaned in with a wink. "Easy, love. Just being friendly. James, you can't keep her all to yourself—aren't you going to introduce us?"

James stepped forward, his voice cold and clipped.

"Walk away, Micah."

But Micah only smirked, stepping a little closer, ignoring the warning in James's tone.

"Don't listen to him, sweetheart. He's all rules and routine. I'm the fun one."

"That's enough," James snapped, voice now edged with threat. "I won't tell you again. Not today, get lost!"

Micah finally stilled, catching the shift in the air. The easy grin faltered. He raised both hands in mock surrender, backing off with a dramatic sigh and a sloppy salute.

"Alright, alright. Message received."

He turned with a lazy whistle and wandered off down the street, swagger intact.

James exhaled, then turned to Ruthie, his shoulders softening.

"Sorry about him. He means well, in his own twisted way—but he never knows when to stop talking and take a hint."

Ruthie nodded faintly, still gripping her book as if it were armour. Her heart thundered in her chest.

But as they walked back toward the Ute, the ground beneath her felt steadier. Something had shifted—a thread of safety stitching itself quietly into place.

And for the first time, the day didn't feel ruled by fear. It felt like maybe, just maybe, there was room for something more.

Chapter 6: Just for a Few Things

"The Lord is gracious and righteous; our God is full of compassion. The Lord protects the unwary; when I was brought low, he saved me." — Psalm 116:5–6

On the drive back to the farm, Ruthie sat in silence, staring out the window as the road blurred beneath them. That flicker of safety she'd felt in town—James stepping in, standing between her and the world—had begun to twist into something more complicated.

Confusion. Doubt. A quiet dread.

It would be so easy to pretend this was safety. To imagine she belonged here, to let herself be lulled by kindness and borrowed comfort. But she knew better. This wasn't her home. She had nothing—no claim to this land, this man, or the steady silence between them. She couldn't quiet the rising tide of fear and anxiety, and without thinking, she turned to James—reaching not with words, but with eyes full of questions she couldn't yet name.

"Thank you," she said at last, the words nearly swallowed by the hum of the tyres. "For everything. For giving me a place to sleep last night. For breakfast. For... the bookshop. I'll pay you back. I mean it."

James didn't look over. Didn't offer some awkward reassurance. He just nodded, eyes on the road, like he'd been thanked for things his whole life and never once kept a tally.

Ruthie hesitated, fingers tightening around the book in her lap.

"I wasn't planning to stay long," she murmured, barely more than a breath.

James didn't respond. Didn't argue or try to change her mind. He simply let the words settle between them—unanswered, unjudged.

And somehow, that said more than any protest ever could.

A flock of galahs burst up from the roadside, sudden and pink. Ruthie's gaze followed them, heart aching.

"I don't want to put you out," she tried again, voice thinning. "You've already done more than anyone else has. It's not fair."

James kept his eyes on the road. "You're not putting me out. Stay as long as you need."

Something in Ruthie's chest tightened, her hands squeezing the book until her fingers hurt. The silence threatened to swallow her. All the words she'd tried to bury tumbled out, sharp as glass.

"I need to go back," she blurted. "I can't stay here like this. I have nothing, James. I left with a backpack and a half-dead phone. Everything else—my clothes, my ID, even my bank card—gone. I panicked. Just ran."

"We'll get you what you need," James said, voice calm.

Ruthie's breath rattled in her throat. "Don't say that like it's simple. It's not. I can't keep taking from you. I'm not a stray dog you found by the side of the road." Her voice cracked, the anger flickering in and out like a faulty light. "Just because you helped me—just because you pulled me out—doesn't mean I owe you anything. I'm not a... a project. Or a pity case."

James didn't flinch. He just let her anger come, the way you'd let a summer storm pass.

She hugged her book tighter, voice raw. "I won't sleep with you!! You can't just think I'll come here and be a plaything for you, just because you're all alone out here."

The words hit the tight space between them like a slap—louder than she meant. She wanted to take them back and also needed them to be said.

James took one hand off the wheel and ran it through his hair, jaw clenched. "I never said I wanted anything from you. You don't owe me anything. I saw you needed help, so I helped. That's how I was raised."

Ruthie's anger collapsed as quickly as it had come. Tears stung her eyes, frustration and shame crowding in.

"Sorry. I'm sorry. I know you haven't—I just... no one's ever helped me and not wanted something in return. No one."

James's voice was softer now, but steady. "You don't owe me anything, Ruthie. Nothing."

She stared out the window, eyes burning, fighting the tears.

"You say that, but everyone says that—until they change their mind! I can't stay here, James! I break everything. Every friend, every home, every relationship—gone. My mum gave up, Dylan... well, you know what happened there. I'm the common thread. I must be!"

Her breathing quickened, panic threatening to spill over.

"Please just take me to the bus stop. I'm not asking for anything else. I can't breathe here. I need—"

She didn't finish. The words got stuck behind old scars.

"Alright. If that's what you want, I'll take you to the bus stop," James said quietly, his tone steady but unreadable.

Soon he pulled into the empty bus shelter at the edge of town, the old bench half-buried in weeds. Before the engine had even shut off, Ruthie had the door open. She stood outside, the breeze tangling her hair. The silence felt raw.

James got out and joined her on the bench, hands between his knees. He looked out at the road; eyes narrowed against the glare.

For a while, he said nothing. Just sat with her, letting her shake in her own skin.

"Look," he said at last, voice rough, "I'm not here to keep you. If you want to leave, I'll drive you anywhere. But I hope you're not heading back to Dylan. I can't stand the thought of you being hurt again."

Ruthie looked down, picking at a thread on her sleeve.

"I don't know where I'm going. I just know I can't stay. I feel like I'm made of bad luck! I have nothing—not even an ID! With Dylan, at least I was someone. Even if it was someone I hated."

James's face was tired and sad. "The bus only comes once a day. Four hours from now. I'll sit here with you, or I'll take you back to the farm until then. You call it."

He hesitated. Then his voice dropped lower.

"And for what it's worth... you were right. I had my own motives for offering you the cottage. My sister—Ellie. I couldn't save her from her husband. That eats at me every single day! I guess... I guess helping you was my way of trying to make the pain mean something. To believe it's not all pointless. That I'm not useless."

Ruthie's face softened, replaced by something else—sorrow, or maybe understanding. She wiped her eyes on her sleeve, sniffling.

"I'm sorry about your sister, James. No one should have to carry that."

He nodded, eyes far away. "Yeah, the pain never goes away.

Ruthie squeezed the book to her chest, looking impossibly young and lost.

"I just want to go back. Get my stuff. Maybe then I'll know what to do next."

James looked at her, really looked.

"Alright. We'll go in a couple of days. Get what you need. After that, I'll take you anywhere. Or you can come back here. Up to you."

She bit her lip, not trusting herself to speak, but managed a nod.

There was nothing neat or tidy about it. They both knew tomorrow would still be messy, but for now, just sitting side by side—ruined, hopeful, and hurting—was enough.

Chapter 7: Holding Her Breath

**"When you pass through the waters, I will be with you; and
when you pass through the rivers, they will not sweep over you."**
— Isaiah 43:2

A couple of days passed. Ruthie lingered mostly at the cottage, keeping her world small. Some days, she shared lunch with James on the porch. Sometimes, she helped with odd jobs—Bear padding after her like a shadow she could almost trust.

The fear, though, didn't lift. If anything, the nightmares clawed deeper. The flashbacks grew more vivid—old bruises surfacing in dreams, dread seeping into the edges of every quiet moment.

Then the day came—James was driving her back to the city to collect her things.

James said nothing on the way into the city. The Ute rolled softly over gravel, carrying them into the heart of Ruthie's dread. She sat folded in on herself, arms crossed tight. She watched the rear-view mirror obsessively—every car behind them a threat, every white sedan a ghost she couldn't shake.

James didn't press. Didn't ask what they were collecting, or why. He just drove—one hand loose on the wheel, the other steady. Bear sat upright in the tray, his fur whipped by the wind, body rigid with attention—almost like he understood how much Ruthie needed a sentry.

About halfway there, Ruthie finally spoke, voice flat and trembling.

"Dylan should be at work now."

"I still have a key, so I should be able to get in and out quickly."

James nodded, not needing to say more.

The city closed in around them. Suburbs thickened. Old memories pressed in, thickening the air. Ruthie pressed her palm to the glass, feeling herself shrink with every block.

She realised she was holding her breath—and let it out in a ragged, shaky exhale.

James glanced at her, the worry plain, but didn't push.

"You want me to do a drive-by first? Just in case his car's there?"

She nodded once, jaw clenched.

James followed her directions, creeping past the street with practised nonchalance. The driveway was empty. No white sedan. Only a tipped-over bin and a crate stuffed with old boxes. He circled the block once more, slowly.

Then he stopped across the road from the house, engine idling.

Ruthie reached for the door, every muscle screaming to run.

"Hey Ruthie before you go," James said.

She paused halfway out the car door.

"I will give you ten minutes," he said. "If you're not back, Bear and I are coming in after you! Alright?"

She nodded, throat tight. "Ten minutes will be enough."

Bear watched her go, ears perked, body low in the tray, as if ready to leap after her.

She crossed the street as if every step was a test of the ground's loyalty. Not fast—not slow—just wound tight. She scanned every window, every car, each shadow. When she reached the door, her hand shook as she slid the key in. The lock caught, then clicked.

The smell hit her before the memories. Dust. Stale takeaway. That cold tang of pine cleaner over old mistakes.

Inside, the front room looked mostly unchanged. A pair of boots by the door. Dylan's jacket was slung over a chair. She crept through the hall, heart battering her ribs.

But when she looked for her things—her bag, her clothes, even her worn slippers—they were gone. She opened drawers and cupboards with rising panic. Each room emptier than the last.

Her breathing sped. No photos. No notebooks. No little treasures tucked away. Nothing.

She ran to the backyard, hope burning in her throat.

That's when she saw it: a scorched heap of her things, blackened by flames, the unmistakable stench of smoke still clinging to the air. Dylan had burned them.

Something inside Ruthie snapped.

Rage boiled up—wild and useless. She hurled the empty laundry basket across the yard, tears streaming down her face. She stormed back inside, slamming doors, sobbing, yelling wordless sounds of loss and betrayal.

James, hearing the commotion, moved with purpose across the street. He didn't know what he'd find, but he didn't hesitate.

He stepped through the door to find Ruthie collapsed in a corner of the hallway, shaking and broken, fists pressed to her mouth to muffle the sound. She didn't look up.

He crouched beside her, not touching—just sharing the space.

"What happened?" he asked, voice gentle.

Ruthie tried to speak, but it came out as a sob. She pointed back at the backyard, where the remnants of her life smouldered in a black pile.

"He burned it. All of it. Everything that was mine—gone."

James closed his eyes for a moment, fury tightening his jaw. He stayed silent, letting her cry it out.

Then, slowly, he asked, "Is there anything left to save?"

She shrugged, eyes distant. "A few things... maybe. I haven't looked everywhere yet."

James met her gaze gently. "Then let's look. We'll find what we can—together."

Together, they searched the house—moving with purpose. They found a battered duffel bag with a change of clothes, some faded paperwork, and a photo that had slipped behind a dresser.

Ruthie stuffed it all into the small bag, hands shaking so hard she could barely zip it shut.

James carried her bag outside, wordless, holding the door open as she passed.

Back at the ute, Ruthie all but collapsed into the seat, dropping her bag at her feet. She buckled her seatbelt, fingers trembling on the latch, unable to stop shaking. Eyes forward, but she wasn't seeing anything.

James got in, started the engine, and pulled away from the kerb. They drove in silence for several blocks, neither able to speak over the grief and anger buzzing in the cab. The city slid away behind them. Only the sound of the road filled the air.

At a red light on the edge of the city, the ute eased to a stop. Outside, the faint hum of traffic pulsed in the distance, but inside the cab, the silence pressed in—heavy, full of everything neither of them had dared to say.

Then, finally, James spoke.

"Hey Ruthie, I just want to check; if you want to go back to the cottage?" he asked, voice even. "Or... is there somewhere else you need me to take you?"

Ruthie didn't answer. Not because she didn't know—but because saying it out loud felt to vulnerable. Too raw. Too exposing.

There was nowhere else. Not anymore. Dylan had burned what little she had left—her things, her plans, her pride. The illusion of having options had gone up in smoke with that heap of ash.

James waited, eyes steady on the road ahead. He didn't press. Didn't shift uncomfortably or fill the space with empty words. He just waited.

The light turned green.

Without a word, he turned the Ute toward the edge of town.

"I'll head home," he said quietly. "But if you change your mind, just tell me where to go."

Ruthie let out a breath she hadn't even realised she'd been holding a long, shuddering exhale that trembled at the edges. Her shoulders softened, the coil of tension loosening just enough to let air back in.

She kept her gaze on the window, watching the city give way to open fields, the landscape washing past in streaks of green and gold.

James didn't say anything, but he noticed. The way her posture shifted, the way something within her eased—just slightly.

It wasn't everything.

But it was something.

And for now, that was enough.

Chapter 8: Something Still in Her Hands

"The Lord is near to all who call on him, to all who call on him in truth." — Psalm 145:18

The drive back from the city was mostly silent, and it was a silence with edges—neither hard nor soft, just... there. Ruthie sat twisted toward the window, the duffel bag in the tray, proof that her whole life had shrunk down to a small, battered bag. She barely blinked at the familiar landscape rushing by, feeling every minute in her bones.

By the time James turned onto the last stretch of gravel, dusk had collapsed over the farm. The paddocks stretched away in golds and fading blues, the long shadows of fence posts trailing back behind them like tired ghosts. It looked peaceful—beautiful, even—but Ruthie could only feel the raw, hollow ache of loss. The way it hurt to hope for anything at all.

James parked. Ruthie opened the door before the engine cut off. She slid out with the book clutched to her chest, moving on autopilot. No words. No goodbyes or thank you—just a need to get away. From the way everything inside her felt split wide open.

Bear hopped down from the tray and padded quietly behind her, the gentle tap of his nails on the steps the only sound as she let herself into the cottage. She didn't look back.

She couldn't—not yet.

James followed at a distance, her bag in hand, setting it gently inside the door. He stood there for a moment, hat crushed between his hands, as if he might say something. Instead, he cleared his throat.

"I'm about to put some dinner on," he said, voice steady but soft. "You're welcome to join me, or I can leave a plate if you'd rather be alone."

Ruthie stood with her back to him, too hurt and exhausted to turn around.

James hovered a second longer—then, with a quiet nod she couldn't see, let the door fall closed behind him.

The room felt huge and empty. Ruthie dropped the bag and just stood there. The last of the sunlight spilled across the floorboards, gold and deep amber, making even the dust motes seem sacred for a moment.

She let herself collapse to the floor, knees giving out.

Opening the duffel, she stared at what remained: a worn jumper, a few crumpled papers, a toothbrush, and a photo—creased, half burned at one edge—of herself as a child, beaming at the camera.

That old grief rose again, sudden and sharp.

She pressed the photo to her lips and sobbed, low and desperate, clutching her knees to her chest.

The tears wouldn't stop. Not for a long time. Not until her throat ached and her chest was sore and her whole body felt hollowed out, as if the crying had wrung her dry.

Night came, slow and invisible, swallowing the gold. The air outside was still—no wind, no stars, just a heavy hush pressing against the cottage walls.

It was the silence that made everything inside echo louder.

A while later, James's voice broke through the quiet from the porch.

"Dinner's ready," he called, as she heard his boots crunching closer. "Nothing fancy. I'll just leave a plate by the door in case you'd rather eat alone. Or you can bring it up to the house, if you feel up to it."

Ruthie sat frozen, unable to answer, only listening to the retreat of his footsteps.

She saw the plate rest on the step—steam rising from it. Ruthie tried to decide what to do.

Even simple choices felt like cliffs these days.

After several minutes, she forced herself to move.

She stepped onto the porch, lifted the plate in both hands, the warmth almost shocking against her skin.

She stood at the threshold, torn between staying in her hole and risking something more.

For a long, uncertain moment, she stood frozen—staring at the food, caught in the eye of a quiet storm made of exhaustion, hunger, and a loneliness too deep to name.

Eventually, the weight of indecision became too heavy to carry. So she didn't decide—she just moved.

Ruthie walked—slow and unsteady—toward the main house, the plate wobbling in her trembling hands. At the door, she paused, her palm resting against the cool wood. Then, without a word, she stepped inside.

James was at the kitchen table, hands folded, eyes tracing the grain of the wood. He didn't look up, just nodded toward the empty chair.

"I'm glad you joined me," he said, his voice quiet but sure.

Ruthie sat down at the table and began eating, each bite a minor act of defiance against the sorrow that wanted to swallow her whole.

When she finished eating, Ruthie stood and turned to James. "Can I take your plate?"

"You don't need to do that," James replied gently.

"I want to. Please, let me," she insisted, her voice wavering. "I need to feel like I'm doing something, even if it's small. It feels like nothing compared to everything you've done for me. I just want you to know I'm grateful... even when I can't always show it."

James paused, meeting her eyes. "I don't need anything in return, Ruthie. I promise."

She offered a quiet smile and carried the dishes to the kitchen, methodically rinsing and stacking them. The simple rhythm of washing calmed her hands, which had only just stopped trembling.

After setting the final dish in the sink, Ruthie returned to the table. Her voice was soft.

"Thank you, James. For everything. I should get some sleep."

James nodded, warmth in his gaze. "It was my pleasure, Ruthie. Sweet dreams."

She gave him a small, genuine smile—one that didn't hide behind fear or politeness—and turned toward the door. The night air greeted her as she stepped outside, the cottage light glowing faintly in the distance.

Back inside the cottage, Ruthie moved slowly toward the bed, every step weighed down by the ache of the day. The silence settled around her like a blanket—one that didn't comfort so much as expose just how tired she truly was. She had lost everything. Her home. Her belongings. Her sense of safety. Fear had become a permanent shadow in her existence, something that curled up beside her no matter where she went.

But amid the wreckage, something unexpected had broken through—kindness. Gentle, steady, unwavering kindness that she had never known. James had been there—present, patient, and giving—yet never demanding anything in return. He kept reassuring her that she owed him nothing. And that... confused her.

Her old patterns, shaped by trauma and twisted by years of survival, whispered familiar lies: You have to repay kindness. He'll expect something eventually. You'll feel safer if you offer first. There was even a fleeting, familiar thought of heading back to the main house and offering her body as a form of repayment—because in her past, that kind of transaction felt more predictable than genuine grace. It was what she had known: give something, or risk it all being taken anyway.

But then—quiet, small, and almost impossible to trust—something inside her stirred. A flicker of belief. For the first time, she believed James when he said he didn't want anything from her. Not her body. Not her loyalty. Not her debt. Just... for her to be safe.

So she didn't go back to the main house.

She didn't bargain with her body. She didn't try to prove her worth.

Instead, she crawled beneath the blankets, and for the first time in her life, she allowed herself to receive kindness without sacrifice.

Chapter 9: The Invite

"I will refresh the weary and satisfy the faint."- **Jeremiah 31:25**

T he next morning crept in quietly. Light spilled through the cottage's east window, striping the wooden floor in soft gold. Ruthie was already awake, lying on her back and tracing the shifting patterns with tired eyes. She still woke before sunrise, anticipating danger in the pre-dawn darkness.

But there was nothing threatening here. No footsteps in the hallway, no slammed doors, no low voices rising to anger. Just the gentle snoring of Bear curled beside the bed, and the sound of the wind rustling through the trees outside.

For a long while, Ruthie simply lay there, letting herself believe in the stillness. It felt foreign, but not unwelcome. Then, slowly, she rose—moving quietly, more out of habit than need—and slipped into the soft rhythm of her morning routine. She washed her face, brushed her teeth, and tied her hair back, before setting the kettle to boil. Each movement was measured, almost ritualistic, as if repeating these small acts in the same familiar order might somehow keep the world from falling apart again.

Meanwhile, at the main house, James was sitting at the kitchen table, breakfast half-eaten and his mind somewhere far off, when he heard the crunch of tyres on gravel. He glanced out the window and saw a familiar little hatchback bumping up the drive.

He let out a sigh—equal parts exasperation and affection—at the unspoken truth that it could only be Margaret.

James pushed back his chair and went to the door. He barely had it open before Margaret was halfway up the steps, arms full—a loaf of fresh bread cradled like a newborn, her cheeks flushed from the morning chill.

"Morning, James!" she called, not waiting for an invitation.

James couldn't help but smile. "Margaret, so good to see you"

She breezed past him into the kitchen, setting the bread down and immediately scanning the room for signs of chaos or hunger. "Neil and I heard about your trip to the city with Ruthie—and Naomi filled me in, of course." She paused, fixing James with a look equal parts worry and warmth. "We've all been concerned. For both of you."

James leaned against the counter, rubbing the back of his neck. "It... didn't go well. I honestly don't know what to do next. Ruthie's lost nearly everything, and I'm just—" He stopped, struggling for words. "—I'm just trying not to make it worse."

Margaret softened, her face kind. "You're doing more than you realise, love. Sometimes just being there matters more than fixing anything."

She sliced the bread, the sound crisp in the quiet kitchen. "Maybe another trip into town would help. Let her see there's life beyond what she's lost. And James..." Margaret hesitated, then continued gently, "Maybe it's time to come back to church this Sunday. Not just for you, but for her. There's healing in being with family, even the family we choose."

James glanced away, conflicted. He missed his church community—missed the fellowship and feeling of belonging—but he wasn't sure Ruthie was ready to be asked. He didn't want to push her, not when she was still so raw.

Margaret pressed the loaf into his hands. "Think about it. Let her choose, but don't shut her out of the invitation. She might surprise you."

James nodded, tucking the warm bread under his arm. "I'll think about it, Margaret. Maybe a quiet trip into town first, to see how she goes."

Margaret's eyes sparkled with approval. "That's all you can do, love. Be gentle—with her, and with yourself."

With that, she kissed his cheek and bustled out the door, leaving the scent of fresh bread and encouragement behind.

James stood there for a moment, weighing her words, before heading off to see if Ruthie was up for another small step toward the world.

Mid-morning, James tapped lightly on the cottage doorframe. In his hands was a still-warm loaf of bread, wrapped in a faded tea towel.

Ruthie had heard his boots on the stairs and was already at the door when he looked up.

"Hey," she said, brushing a loose strand of hair behind her ear.

James held up the loaf. "Morning delivery. Margaret dropped it off—still nice and warm."

Ruthie's eyes lingered on the bread, then lifted to his face, guarded but curious.

He gave the loaf a small wave. "Only thing is—we're out of butter. Thought I'd make a quick run into town. Want to come?"

She raised an eyebrow, arms loosely crossed. "Are you bribing me to socialise with carbs?"

He shrugged, all innocence. "Worked on me."

A soft laugh slipped out of her—quiet, surprised. She didn't say yes, but she didn't say no either. Instead, she reached over to grab her book from the table and stepped outside, falling into pace beside him.

James didn't push. He just smiled, the kind that said he noticed... and appreciated the small 'yes' underneath her silence.

In town, Ruthie headed for the bookshop.

Naomi's bookshop was quieter today. The bell gave its same soft chime, but the air inside felt less expectant, more lived-in.

Naomi looked up from a pile of gardening books, glasses perched low on her nose.

"Good morning, fancy seeing you again," she said, "guess I didn't scare you off."

Ruthie offered a small smile but didn't speak.

James turned to her. "I'll head to the shop to get the butter and while I am there, I'll grab some extra feed for Bear." He tipped his head toward the shelves. "Do you want to stay here for a bit? I shouldn't be more than 10 minutes."

Ruthie nodded, grateful.

James gave a nod and headed for the general store.

Naomi didn't rush forward or fill the quiet.

She just watched Ruthie with a steady, open kind of stillness.

"Ruthie," she said.

"Do you drink tea?"

Ruthie blinked. "Um... yeah?"

Naomi was already walking. "Come on, then," she replied as she led Ruthie into the backroom.

The room smelled of old wood, cinnamon, and maybe sage. Sunlight slanted across the mismatched furniture, scratched and worn smooth by years of use.

Naomi poured hot water and set two mugs—one chipped, one stained with tea rings—in front of them. Ruthie sat carefully, as if she might knock something loose by accident.

Naomi settled into her chair with the ease of someone who'd survived enough storms to know not to rush.

After a minute, Naomi said lightly, "So, I asked James how things went in the city, but you're probably already learning—he's not much for talking, is he?"

Ruthie gave a faint, almost apologetic smile. "Not really."

Naomi's eyes sparkled with something knowing. "Didn't think so. Man's got a heart the size of a barn, but you need a crowbar to get more than three words out of him sometimes."

Ruthie wrapped her hands around her mug. The warmth steadied her a little. "It was... hard," she admitted. "I—" She hesitated, picking at the rim of the mug. "When we got there, all my things... My ex had burned them. Everything that was mine—gone. I just... I didn't expect it to hurt so much, even after everything else."

Naomi's expression softened, her own mug pausing mid-air. "That's a cruel loss, losing what's yours. I'm sorry, love."

Ruthie's eyes stayed down. "It felt like watching the last of my life go up in smoke. Like I had nothing left to prove I ever existed."

Naomi didn't offer quick comfort, just let Ruthie's words settle in the quiet.

"Ruthie, I'm so sorry you're walking through this. Truly. None of it is fair, and you never deserved the pain that's been dropped at your feet. But I need you to hear me—this isn't the end of your story. I know everything feels heavy and tangled right now, like it might never get better... but you are not alone. And your ex? He doesn't get to hold the pen anymore. He doesn't get to decide who you are or where your life goes from here."

Ruthie nodded, staring at the swirling steam in her cup.

"Are you a therapist or something?" she asked, a wry smile tugging at her lips.

"No, just a good listener.... and I have been around long enough to know a few things," Naomi smirked.

For a few moments, they sat in the gentle hush, the weight of shared understanding filling the space.

Then Naomi stood and crossed to a small shelf. She returned with a slim, dog-eared book, its blue binding faded almost to grey.

"Try this," she said. "It helped me once."

Ruthie accepted it, fingers tracing the soft spine. Inside the cover, a handwritten inscription read: To whoever needs it more than me. —N

"Thank you," Ruthie said quietly, truly meaning it.

Naomi tilted her head, her tone gentle. "You ever need air, or a chair, or someone who won't ask 'how are you'—I'm here most days."

Ruthie nodded, the offer feeling safer than she expected.

A few moments later, James reappeared, butter in one hand and two bags of feed in the other.

"Ready?" he asked.

Ruthie glanced at Naomi and then back at James. "Yeah. I'm ready."

Chapter 10: Fault Lines

"Even though I walk through the valley of the shadow of death, I will fear no evil, for you are with me; your rod and your staff, they comfort me."— Psalm 23:4

It started with a sound.

A door slammed—sharp, sudden, splitting the silence in two. But not here. Not the cottage.

In the dream, she was somewhere else. The floor was icy against her skin—bathroom tiles, unforgiving and cold. Ruthie sat with her back pressed to the tub, knees drawn tight to her chest, pyjama pants bunched beneath trembling hands. Her face buried against her knees, the fabric wet with silent tears she barely noticed.

On the other side of the door, Dylan's rage filled every corner of the house. He was screaming words she'd memorised, threats she couldn't forget.

"THIS ISN'T OVER RUTHIE! YOU'D BETTER OPEN THIS DOOR OR YOU'RE GOING TO REGRET IT!"

She pressed her palms over her ears, but the shouting only grew louder. The door shuddered beneath his fists, hinges rattling with each blow. The entire world shrank to the sound of banging—louder, louder—until wood splintered, the lock giving way, and—

She jolted awake, a scream tearing loose from her throat.

The cottage was still. The nightmare clung to her, sticky as cobwebs.

Her heart thundered against her ribs, breath coming in shallow gasps. Sweat slicked her skin, soaking the neckline of her shirt.

Bear, startled by her scream, had bounded to her side, barking—deep and frantic, ready to defend. He pressed his weight against her, warm and solid, a living shield between her and the shadows.

"It's okay," Ruthie whispered, though her voice shook so badly it sounded like someone else's. She reached for Bear, fingers sinking into his fur, anchoring herself to the present. "It's just a dream. I'm okay. We're okay."

But as she tried to steady her breathing, her whole body trembled with the memory.

Bear watched her another minute—chest heaving, eyes alert. Then, slowly, he lay back down putting his head on his paws. Ears still up.

He had believed her.

Even if she didn't.

Ruthie sat curled on her bed, knees tucked tight to her chest, the aftershocks of the nightmare still echoing through her body. Fear pressed down, heavy and unmoving, as if the dream had seeped into every corner of the room, into the very air she breathed.

She tried to slow her racing heart, listening for something—anything—to ground her to the present. Then she heard it: footsteps outside her window, steady and deliberate, the type of stride that belonged to someone who knew this place.

Ruthie's breath caught. She slid to the edge of the mattress, peering through the glass. James was crossing the yard, his shape cut in silhouette by the moonlight as he made his way toward the cottage.

She pushed the window open, hands trembling.

Before she could call out, his voice drifted up, rough around the edges, almost blending with the night.

"You alright?"

Ruthie nodded a little too quickly, hugging herself tighter. "Just... a bad dream."

After a moment, he spoke again. "Do you want some company?"

She hesitated, pride and fear tangling together. She wasn't used to asking for help, to letting anyone see her like this—raw and undone. But the need for comfort outweighed her old habits.

"Yes, please," she replied, surprised by how much she meant it—and how vulnerable it felt to say so out loud.

The words hung there, fragile but real.

A few moments later, James stood waiting by the door, his presence quiet and patient. Ruthie rose and let him in, her arms wrapped around herself for comfort. Together, they walked to the lounge. Ruthie sat on the couch, and James joined her—not too close, not too far—simply there, present and steady in the soft hush of the room.

He avoided pressing her for details and attempting to fix the unfixable. Instead, he sat in silence, offering the steady reassurance of someone simply willing to stay.

After a while, James spoke again.

"I still get them sometimes."

She looked at him confused.

"Dreams, or—moments I mean." He rubbed the back of his neck. "I'll be fixing a fence, and suddenly I hear Ellie's voice in the wind. Or I'll wake up swearing someone called my name."

He paused. Then added, quieter:

"Or worse—I dream of her alone. Life leaving her slow, scared, with no one there to stop it. Only someone hell-bent on hurting her."

He scratched behind Bear's ears, eyes far away.

"Pain and grief don't ask permission," he said. "It just rewires the house. Flicks the lights when it wants. Opens doors you thought you'd sealed."

Ruthie didn't respond right away.

"I hate that it still owns me," she said finally, voice like a frayed thread. "Even now."

"It doesn't own you," James replied. "It just left a mess. You're allowed to take your time cleaning it up."

She inhaled slowly.

Held it.

Let it out like something she'd been gripping too long.

"I am sorry I woke you, James."

"You didn't," he said. "Bear did."

"He's a good one. Doesn't let fear go unanswered."

They sat for a while longer.

Then Ruthie stood, careful. Not hurried. Not braced.

"I think I'll try again to get some sleep."

James nodded.

"Did you want me to wait on the couch for a while?"

"Thank you," she said. "But I think I will be okay. You need to get some more sleep too."

James rose from the couch, nodding.

"Yeah, you're right," he said. "I'm just glad you're safe. And I'm not far—if you need anything, just let me know." He offered her a gentle smile before heading to the door and making his way back to the main house.

Chapter 11: Naomi's Table

"Be devoted to one another in love. Honour one another above yourselves." — Romans 12:10

The invitation came folded in a reused envelope, the paper soft at the corners, the flap sealed with a bit of tape that had lost its stick.

Ruthie found it slipped under the cottage door around lunchtime, nestled between a breeze and Bear's curious nose.

The outside was blank. Inside, firm, looping handwriting, both precise and playful, formed the note.

Dear Ruthie,

I'd love for you to come by my place for dinner tonight—6:00 sharp.

Nothing fancy, a shared meal.

You don't need to bring anything but yourself.

With love,

Naomi

No address. Just the back of the letter covered in a pencilled map—arrows, landmarks, a crooked tree with a star beside it, and a little doodle of a teacup with steam curling into a heart.

Ruthie stared at it for a long time.

Her first instinct was to stay away. It was too soon—too raw, too complicated. The idea of showing up, of being seen, felt like standing naked in a room full of mirrors.

Kindness hadn't always been kind. Not in her world. It had come with expectations, with conditions, with the unspoken demand to perform gratitude—or worse, with silence that settled in afterward like dust on a wound, heavy and shaming.

Naomi's note had arrived in a plain envelope, but the words inside were anything but casual. Simple, yes. But not careless. Every line felt deliberate. Like it was written by someone who actually saw her. Someone who didn't just remember she existed but wanted her there.

Ruthie stared at the invitation, then slowly folded the paper along its crease and slipped it into her coat pocket. She couldn't tell which ache was worse—the sudden invitation to belong, or the realisation that someone had thought to include her.

She didn't decide then.

Instead, she opened her book and tried to read.

One page. Then again. Then again.

Four times she read the same lines, and not once did they register. The words blurred. Her eyes scanned them, but her heart was elsewhere—caught between the fragile hope of being wanted, and the old, familiar fear of what might follow if she believed it.

Every so often, she'd touch the note in her pocket like it might change if she held it long enough.

The hours drifted.

Then James showed up. He knocked once—lightly—then opened the screen door and leaned in.

"Just checking in," James said, his voice low and easy like always. "Wanted to see how you and Bear are doing... though I reckon I might've lost my dog for good."

Bear, curled up at Ruthie's feet, gave a lazy thump of his tail without lifting his head.

James chuckled softly. "Yep. Figures."

Ruthie looked up from her chair on the porch, the breeze brushing a strand of hair across her cheek. "He doesn't seem to leave my side" she said, her voice quieter than she meant it to be.

"Yeah, I noticed," James said, leaning against the post beside her. He folded his arms, eyes on Bear for a moment. "He's got a good sense for people. Always has. Picks his spot and stays loyal."

The silence stretched for a breath or two before he spoke again, more gently. "You alright?"

Ruthie hesitated. Something in her chest tightened—like her heart didn't trust itself to speak. Then she gave the faintest nod. "Yeah. Just, thinking."

She reached into the pocket of her hoodie and pulled out the folded note, holding it out to him with both hands like it weighed more than it should.

"Naomi sent this. Inviting me to dinner."

James took it, careful with the paper like it might tear. He unfolded it, smiled when he saw the hand-drawn map. "She's still drawing that teacup on everything, huh?"

He handed it back to her, their fingers almost brushing. "Are you going?"

She stared at the note for a moment before answering. "I don't know. I told myself no. But now... I can't stop thinking about it."

James nodded, not pushing. "If you decide to go, I can lend you the ute. Or drive you, if you'd rather. Whatever feels right to you. No pressure."

Ruthie glanced down at Bear, who blinked up at her like none of it was urgent. Like they had all the time in the world.

Her voice came out small. "I don't want to intrude."

James shook his head. "You wouldn't be. Naomi doesn't invite people she doesn't want at her table. She's got a gift for that and as for me you would never be intruding"

Ruthie unfolded the letter again, smoothing the worn crease with her thumb.

Then, instead of tucking it away, she placed it gently on the table beside her mug.

Not hidden. Not dismissed.

Just... there. Waiting.

5:55 pm arrived. Ruthie stood before Naomi's weather-worn cottage, framed by wild bush roses and thyme pots—equal parts tangled and thriving. Her hands trembled as she raised one to knock.

But before her knuckles touched wood, the door swung open.

Naomi filled the doorway, apron dusted with flour, braid over one shoulder, and the smell of something warm and real drifting out behind her.

"Good, I am glad you came!" Naomi said, eyes twinkling.

Ruthie blinked, thrown by the welcome. She fumbled to grab a jar of jam from her bag—unopened, awkwardly wrapped in a tea towel from the cottage pantry. She thrust it forward. "I... I didn't make this. But I wanted to bring a gift. I hope you like Jam."

Naomi took the gift, her brow lifting with surprise. "A present?" she said, a warm smile tugging at her lips. "You didn't have to do that—but thank you. That's really thoughtful."

Ruthie followed Naomi into the small dining room, where a table had been set for two—mismatched plates, a faded linen runner, and a simple jar of wildflowers at the centre. The setting was a little haphazard, but beautiful in its own way—like it had been arranged for comfort, not show.

"Take a seat; I'll be right back," Naomi said, disappearing into the kitchen.

Ruthie sat gingerly, breathing in the mouth-watering aroma of roasted vegetables and freshly baked bread that drifted through the house.

Naomi soon returned, balancing a large wooden board with a warm, crusty loaf of bread and a small crockpot. She set them down between them, smiling.

"Hope you've brought your appetite."

With practiced hands, she sliced thick slabs of bread and ladled steaming soup into their bowls before sitting across from Ruthie.

Ruthie hesitated at first, lifting her spoon and breathing in the steam. The smell was rich and earthy, both familiar and strange. She sipped carefully, then closed her eyes, letting the warmth settle deep inside her.

"This is delicious," she murmured, almost surprised at the comfort she found in something so simple.

They ate together. Ruthie savoured every spoonful, tearing off hunks of bread to soak up the last drops, grateful for a meal that made her feel—if only for a moment—safe and looked after.

When she finally set her spoon down, Naomi grinned.

"James must not be feeding you well out there—no one's ever finished my soup that fast."

Ruthie looked up. "Thank you, Naomi. That was the best soup I've had in a long time." Her voice was quiet, but there was no mistaking the gratitude behind it.

Naomi's face lit up with a warm smile. "I'm glad you liked it, love."

Without another word, Naomi slipped out of the room, her footsteps soft down the hallway. She soon returned, carrying a large, colourful tote bag, the fabric bulging with lumpy shapes. She set it gently beside Ruthie's chair; her smile gentle but a little nervous, as if wanting the gesture to be just right.

"I thought you could use a few things," Naomi said. "Some are mine, some are from the ladies at church. Everyone wanted to help."

Ruthie tugged the bag open, revealing a stack of carefully folded clothes: shirts, jeans, soft jumpers, even a set of pyjamas and a woollen scarf.

For a second, Ruthie just stared, her throat tightening. Then, her hands dove into the bag, running over the fabric. These weren't just clothes—they were a lifeline, proof that people had thought about her, cared enough to give.

She sobbed. The type of tears she couldn't hold back or swallow down, the kind that cracked her open.

"Thank you," she whispered, voice ragged. "Thank you, I... I don't even have words."

Naomi, without fanfare, pulled her into a hug.

Ruthie went, arms wrapping around Naomi, clinging like she might never let go. For a moment, all she could do was cry and let herself be held.

When Ruthie finally pulled away, wiping her eyes, Naomi squeezed her shoulders.

"I know it might feel strange," Naomi said gently, her voice steady. "But around here, Ruthie... people like helping others. It's just how we are."

Ruthie didn't reply right away. The two of them stood there in that tender moment.

Later, after they'd shared warm slices of homemade apple pie and the plates sat empty between them, Ruthie moved to stand, ready to leave.

But Naomi reached for something first—a small parcel, wrapped in brown paper and tied with simple string. She pressed it into Ruthie's hands.

"Just a little something," she said.

Ruthie turned the parcel over in her hands, fingers tracing the edges of the string like it might come undone if she breathed too hard. She didn't unwrap it—couldn't yet. Just held it close, like it might steady her.

"Thank you," she said quietly, her voice catching in her throat. "For dinner... for the present... and the clothes."

The last word barely made it out. Her voice broke, thin and splintered with the weight of it all—gratitude, disbelief, the ache of being seen when she hadn't expected to be.

Naomi just nodded, eyes warm and certain.

"It was my pleasure. You're welcome here, Ruthie anytime. Remember that!"

Outside, the sky had faded to bruised purple. Ruthie made her way back to the cottage, heart aching, hands clutching the parcel and the bag of clothes as if she might lose them at any moment. The warmth of Naomi's home lingered with her long after the night closed in.

Back in the cottage, she sat on the bed with the bag of clothes beside her, the parcel in her lap. She untied the string, finding a thick slice of spiced apple cake, a book of poetry, and a square of folded paper in Naomi's steady handwriting:

"Ruthie, I hope you know this—you don't have to be whole to be worthy of care. Even in the ruins, we are all deserving of love and care."

Ruthie pressed the note to her chest, eyes stinging with the weight of it. For the first time in years, she let herself believe it—not fully, not without doubt—but enough to feel the flicker of something she'd nearly forgotten: the possibility of being lovable, even as she was.

Just for tonight, she didn't feel like a burden. Or a mess to be fixed.

She felt... seen. Cared for.

And in the quiet glow of that moment, something tender stirred in her—

a small, aching kind of hope.

Chapter 12: A Crack in the Frame

"A friend loves at all times, and a brother is born for adversity."
— Proverbs 17:17

Ruthie stood in the main house kitchen, gently drying dishes while James sat at the table nearby, hunched over a stack of invoices from the week's stock sales. The room was warm and lived-in, filled with the comforting scents of fresh coffee, toasted bread, and a hint of woodsmoke drifting in from the fireplace.

Bear lay sprawled under the table, tail flicking lazily, eyes sharp and hopeful—ever watchful for a wayward crumb.

A sharp, rapid-fire knock rattled the front door—confident and impatient, as if whoever was out there believed the house belonged to them. Bear shot up, tail wagging in great hopeful sweeps.

James gave Ruthie a crooked smile, equal parts warning and amusement.

"Brace yourself, Ruthie," James said, glancing toward the window. "That's not the postie—I think Micah's found his way over."

Ruthie dried her hands on a tea towel as James walked to the door.

When he pulled it open, the air filled with a distinct energy—a tall man with a wild mop of hair and a smile that looked like it had gotten him out of more trouble than into it.

"About time, mate! I thought you'd moved out to the back paddock for good, since you haven't replied to any of my messages."

James's face shifted to mock sternness.

"What are you doing here, Micah?"

Micah didn't miss a beat.

"I talked to Naomi. Heard I made a right mess of things last week." He glanced at Ruthie, then back at James, sheepish but grinning. "I'm sorry, for the other day. You know what I am like, never know when to take a hint."

Micah held up his hands, then winked at Ruthie.

"Come on, mate, let me in. I brought peace offerings."

James rolled his eyes, but there was fondness in it.

"Alright, but don't be yourself, okay?" His voice was half-joke, half-warning.

He turned to Ruthie.

"Dont worry Ruthie, he's really only here for the food."

"Guilty as charged!" Micah said cheerfully, rummaging in his coat pockets. "But I come bearing gifts—some of Margaret's jam drops and, believe it or not, the council paperwork you've dodged for a month, James."

He dumped a folder and a container on the table, then immediately snagged a chocolate biscuit on the table.

Bear sniffed at Micah's boots, tail thumping with approval. Micah bent to ruffle Bear's ears.

"Hey, mate; You missed me?"

James and Micah fell into easy banter, tossing insults and laughter back and forth about camping disasters, footy teams, and who could brew the best cup of coffee.

Ruthie watched, surprised to see James so animated—more relaxed, more himself than she'd ever seen him. She smiled too, the mood infectious.

"Fancy a game of cards while the old man here pretends to work?" Micah asked, producing a battered deck from his pocket with a magician's flair.

James looked up from the paperwork and smirked.

"Who is the old man, Micah?" James said with a grin on his face. "You'll be turning thirty well before me."

"Oh—and Micah," he added with a perfectly straight face, "try being nice for once. She doesn't know you cheat yet."

Micah grinned, unfazed.

"Come on mate. I only cheat when I'm losing, you know that."

They gathered around the table, laughter already stirring as Bear curled up contentedly at Ruthie's feet. Micah wasted no time launching into a dramatic retelling of James's infamous fishing disaster—how he'd fallen in twice, caught nothing, and managed to lose Micah's favourite lure in the process.

James, unbothered, fired back with equal flair, recounting Micah's ill-fated homebrew experiment that had left him with the worst hangover of his life—and a vow never to trust Micah's "fermentation methods" again.

Midway through the next round, James stood up and stretched.

"Back in a sec—I left the plans I need for this paperwork out in the shed," James said, heading for the front door.

As he walked out, Micah leaned slightly toward Ruthie, his tone softening just a touch.

"Been knockin' around with James for, what—seven years now? Bloke's one of the best there is. Solid as they come."

Ruthie looked at him, curiosity piqued.

"He's pulled me outta more scrapes than I care to admit—never asked for a thing. Just shows up, solid as a brick wall. Doesn't yap on about it either."

She nodded slowly, listening.

At that point, Micah's grin slipped just a touch.

"But he's different since Ellie. Bit shut off, y'know? Still bends over backwards for everyone else, but won't let anyone do the same for him. He cares for so many people, but hell—he's rubbish at being looked after."

Before Ruthie could respond, the door creaked open and James returned, giving Micah a sideways look.

"What lies are you filling her head with now?" he asked, voice light but knowing.

"Just telling her the truth for once, mate," Micah replied, grinning.

James rolled his eyes and flopped back into his chair.

For a while, Ruthie simply listened again, the laughter smoothing the rough edges inside her. Every joke, every friendly jab, eased her guard a little further. For the first time in a long time, the world felt a little less broken and a little more possible.

When the paperwork was signed and the cards finally put away, Micah stretched and grinned.

"All right, you two behave. Ruthie don't let him talk you into thinking he's some gourmet chef. I tried to teach him, but there's only so much one can do."

James groaned.

"You're such a liar."

Micah tipped an imaginary hat to Ruthie.

"Don't let this bloke scare you off."

With a final wave, he bounded out to his dusty truck, whistling off-key.

James watched him go, a genuine smile lingering at the corner of his mouth—a rare crack in the frame.

And in that quiet moment, Ruthie realised that healing didn't always arrive all at once—sometimes, it tiptoed in through laughter.

Chapter 13: A Name in the Margin

"You keep track of all my sorrows. You have collected all my tears in your bottle. You have recorded each one in your book."
— Psalm 56:8

Days slipped by, and a kind of rhythm wove itself around the three of them—Ruthie, James, and Bear. There was nothing official about it, no agreements or routines scribbled on calendars, but the pattern held all the same. Quiet mornings, the distant hum of work around the paddocks, Bear snoring in the sun, and the soft, comforting presence of knowing someone else was nearby.

But this week had left Ruthie feeling low, a heaviness trailing her like a shadow she couldn't shake. Next week would mark her 23rd birthday. Birthdays had always been a source of distress growing up—usually forgotten, leaving wounds that felt irreversible. With Dylan , they often ended in arguments. This year, Ruthie had tried her best to ignore it, but it was harder than she'd expected.

Wednesday came around—Wednesdays had become their town day. Not because anyone had declared it so, but because, somehow, it just felt right and gave the week shape.

So, like she had the Wednesday before—and the one before that—Ruthie heard the familiar knock on her cottage door mid-morning. The sound made her heart lift a little, even before she knew why.

James stood there, his usual steadiness wrapped in a navy flannel. He held a thermos in one hand and keys in the other, Bear's head peeking around his legs, hopeful as ever.

"Shop run. You in?" James asked, as if the answer could ever really be no.

She nodded, grabbing her bag and boots.

The drive into town had become predictable in a way that felt right, comfortable—a chance to settle into silence without feeling alone. Bear rode in the tray, tail thumping against the metal, ears flapping in the wind, tongue lolling out in pure joy.

Once at town they stopped first at the general store. Ruthie picked out tea bags, a new tin of sauce, and an impulse packet of liquorice. James tossed a sack of flour into the trolley and traded wisecracks with the clerk.

Then they ducked into Naomi's bookshop, the bell above the door chiming with a hopeful note. Inside, the light was soft and golden, slanting through rain-streaked windows.

Naomi was half-buried behind a stack of atlases, peering over the top with a knowing smile.

"Hey, you both. Ah, must be Wednesday?" she teased.

James tapped the doorframe in reply.

"Off to the feed store. I'll be back."

Alone in the shop, Ruthie wandered the aisles. Her fingers traced the spines of old novels and battered mysteries, moving without purpose—half-hoping, half-hiding. She wasn't really looking for anything in particular, but the act of searching soothed her.

Naomi appeared at her side, as quietly as a thought. She drifted into Ruthie's orbit, scanning the same shelf, not needing to say anything at first.

For a long moment, they stood like that—shoulders almost touching, eyes roaming titles, just sharing the gentle hush of the shop.

Then:

"So," Naomi said, her voice light but edged with understanding, "what's hanging around your shoulders today?"

Ruthie let out a breath, half-laugh, half-sigh.

"Is it that obvious?"

"Only a little. Books rarely get that much petting unless someone's looking for comfort."

A hint of a smile played on Ruthie's lips. She let her hand fall away from the shelf, crossing her arms, feeling a little exposed.

"I don't know," she admitted quietly. "This week's just... off. Like something's circling, but I can't quite see what it is."

Naomi nodded, her expression gentle.

"Something coming up?"

Ruthie shook her head, automatic at first.

"Not really. Nothing I'm looking forward to."

Naomi tilted her head.

"Oh, I see. That's not quite the same as nothing happening."

Ruthie hesitated. She thought about brushing it off, spinning some story or changing the subject. But Naomi didn't push, just waited—patient, letting the silence be a safe place to rest.

After a moment, Ruthie's voice slipped out, low and careful.

"It's my birthday next week."

She kept her gaze fixed on a worn copy of Wuthering Heights, the cracked spine a comfort in its imperfection.

The pause that followed felt endless, and Ruthie instantly regretted saying anything at all.

But Naomi just nodded—no questions, no fuss.

"That'll do it."

Ruthie blinked, uncertain.

"What?"

Naomi's lips curved.

"That feeling—the circling, the restlessness. Like the air's sideways and no one else has noticed. Birthdays will do that—especially the quiet ones."

Ruthie let out a shaky laugh, the sound thin and edged with vulnerability.

"That's exactly how it feels," she said quietly. "Truth is... I haven't really told anyone. Not even James."

Naomi didn't press, didn't ask. She just nodded—slow, understanding—like she already knew more than words could explain.

"Doesn't matter if anyone knows. It still weighs on you."

Stillness wrapped around them again, this time warmer—less lonely. For the first time all week, Ruthie felt the heaviness on her shoulders ease, the knot inside her loosening a little.

Chapter 14 – The Morning Of

"He brought me out into a spacious place; He rescued me because He delighted in me." — Psalm 18:19

The morning of Ruthie's birthday arrived without ceremony. No candles. No music. No one knocking with flowers or cake. Just the usual quiet, and the wind, wriggling across the paddocks.

She woke early—out of habit more than hope.

The sky outside her window was undecided, caught between a sullen gold and a stubborn grey. A thin slice of light crept across the floorboards, cutting a perfect line between her bed and the door.

She sat on the edge of the mattress, wrapped in the cardigan Naomi had given her. One foot tucked under the covers, the other pressed flat to the cool timber—half in, half out of the day.

She didn't move for a long while.

Eventually, she dressed slowly. Made tea. Tidied the cottage. Not because she expected anyone, but because doing something was easier than feeling everything.

Then—a knock.

Naomi stood on the porch, cheeks pink from the wind, holding a brown paper parcel tied with soft green ribbon.

"You're up early for someone trying to fly under the birthday radar," she said.

Ruthie blinked.

"You remembered?"

"Of course," Naomi replied, offering the parcel without fuss.

"Open it when it feels right."

Then she turned and walked away, leaving Ruthie holding the gift, the wind tugging at her sleeves.

Later, with Bear at her feet and tea warming her hands, Ruthie finally opened the package. Inside was a well-loved Bible, its cover soft with wear, wrapped gently in tissue paper. Tucked into the front cover was a small note in Naomi's careful handwriting:

For the days you forget, you're known.

The words landed somewhere deep inside her, like a stone skipping across still water.

Ruthie had never owned a Bible. Never really believed there might be a God who saw her. She wanted to open it, to read something, anything—but she didn't know where to start. The pages felt sacred and unfamiliar all at once.

But somehow, just having it near—this quiet, steady presence—felt like enough.

This gift, so unexpected and undeserved, was the first thing all day that made the ache in her chest feel seen. Held. Maybe even a little less alone.

That evening, as the light outside began to fade into soft gold, Ruthie stood in the kitchen, lost in thought. Her fingers gently traced the worn gold lettering on the Bible's cover, the familiar warmth of the tea in her hands grounding her.

Then Bear barked—sharp and sudden—snapping her back to the present.

A moment later, she heard it: laughter floating in from the driveway, the crunch of gravel under boots, and a loud, whispered "Shh!" Before a knock at the door.

Ruthie opened it slowly, surprised to find James standing on the porch with a hopeful, uncertain smile. Behind him stood Naomi, Margaret, Neil—and Micah, holding a fistful of droopy balloons.

"Hope we're not too late," James said. "You up for a little company?"

Ruthie blinked, caught between confusion and emotion.

"What's all this?"

Margaret didn't wait for an answer. She swooped in, wrapping Ruthie in a firm hug and pressing a bakery box into her arms.

"You didn't think we'd let your birthday slip by, did you?"

Naomi offered a fresh bouquet of flowers. Neil raised a tin of tea in greeting. Micah grinned, a bit sheepish, and added,

"Now I am here the party can start."

Soon, the cottage was glowing—filled with warmth. Margaret set out plates and snacks, Naomi moved with gentle authority in the kitchen, and Neil busied himself with the kettle. Micah strung balloons from the curtain rod using string that clearly wasn't designed for the job—but held anyway.

They gathered around the table, the atmosphere easy and alive. James took the seat beside Ruthie, his presence steady. He caught her eye now and then—little moments that anchored her whenever the noise began to swirl too much.

The meal was filled with laughter and stories, gentle teasing, and the kind of chaos that felt like family.

When the cake came out, they sang. Off-key, overlapping, imperfect.

Ruthie closed her eyes and blew out the candles, a pink flush blooming on her cheeks.

A silent wish hovered in her heart:

Let me belong. Let this last.

After cake came gifts.

Naomi gave her a hand-knitted scarf.

Neil presented a walking guidebook, well-thumbed and loved.

"Figured you might like to explore the place now it's home," he said.

Margaret handed over a tin of lemon slice—"For emergencies. You always need some lemon slice on hand" she declared.

Micah passed her a deck of cards.

"For beating James's fair and square," he said with a grin.

Then, a little awkwardly, James slid a small, lumpy package across the table. The wrapping was crooked. Tape everywhere. Corners bulging.

"I, uh... didn't have help wrapping it," he muttered.

"But... hope you like it."

Ruthie unwrapped it carefully. Inside was a delicate locket on a fine chain, a tiny wildflower pressed inside the glass.

Her breath caught. She looked up at James, eyes wide and shining.

"It's... perfect."

He shrugged, pretending not to notice how quiet the room had gone.

But he didn't look away.

And neither did she.

For a moment, everything else softened—the warm chatter, the flicker of candlelight, Bear's tail thumping lazily against the floor. Around them, the others had the grace to busy themselves: Margaret poured more tea, Naomi refolded a napkin that didn't need folding, Neil began quietly discussing hiking trails with Micah.

The locket glowed faintly in the light, resting against Ruthie's palm.

"Where'd you find it?" she asked softly, her voice a hush between them.

James smiled.

"I made it. Found the flower out near the ridge. Thought it looked like something you'd notice, even if no one else did."

Her throat tightened.

"I would've."

Ruthie and James lingered there in the quiet, neither rushing to fill the silence—just letting the moment settle between them, tender and unspoken.

Later, after the warmth of the evening began to settle—after second helpings, half-told stories, and laughter that eventually gave way to yawns—the others slowly took their leave. Naomi kissed Ruthie on the cheek with a soft, lingering squeeze of her hand. Margaret wrapped her in one last heartfelt hug, murmuring something about stopping by tomorrow. Neil gave a silent nod on his way out the door, and Micah paused dramatically at the top step to salute Bear with mock solemnity, muttering about forming an alliance against James.

James was the last to go. He stood in the doorway for a moment, eyes catching Ruthie's like he had more to say but didn't quite know how. Then he simply smiled—a quiet, knowing smile—and tipped his hat.

"I'll see you in the morning," he said.

The door clicked shut behind him, and the cottage fell into a gentle hush.

Ruthie lingered there in the stillness; hands wrapped around the tea she hadn't finished. The locket hung warm and steady against her collarbone, like a small heartbeat. A reminder of all the quiet kindness threaded through the evening.

She stood and stepped toward the window.

Up at the main house, the porch light was still on—casting a soft golden halo over the steps, glowing like a lighthouse in the dark.

She watched it for a long time. Not because she needed to.

But because it was there. And that was enough.

Moments later Ruthie decided to head to the main house. She knocked gently on the door. James answered, surprised but pleased.

"I just... wanted to say thank you," she said, fingers brushing the chain at her neck.

"For the locket. And the party. All of it."

James stepped aside.

"It was my pleasure. Why don't you come in and sit with me a while?"

She nodded, stepping past him into the familiar warmth of the house. The fireplace crackled quietly, casting a soft amber glow over the living room. James motioned to the couch, and she took a seat near the fireplace. He sat beside her—not too close, but close enough that their shoulders almost touched.

They sat for a while together. Bear padded in and settled at their feet. Outside, the night deepened. Inside, the silence was easy—unforced.

James glanced over.

"Did you have a good birthday?"

Ruthie smiled faintly, eyes flicking to the fire.

"I think it's the first one that's ever felt like it was really mine."

He exhaled slowly, shoulders loosening.

"I'm glad."

She turned toward him, expression soft.

"The locket... it was perfect."

"I wasn't sure if it would be too much," he admitted.

"No, it was just right."

They sat there, letting the fire warm the silence between them. The moment didn't need to be explained.

They simply were—together, whole, even if just for that breath in time.

Chapter 15 – The Edge of the Field

"Return to the Lord your God, for He is gracious and compassionate, slow to anger and abounding in love." — Joel 2:13

The day after Ruthie's birthday, James woke with something unfamiliar humming under his skin.

Not the familiar feelings of grief and dread that frequented his mind, since Ellie's passing.

This was different.

Something that made his breath hitch and his eyes blur for a second before he smiled into the silence.

Hope.

Real, unshaken, tender hope.

Sunlight spilled soft and golden across the paddocks, brushing the hills with morning light. For a brief, suspended moment, he let it reach him. He lay there longer than usual, arms folded behind his head, a small smile playing at the corners of his mouth.

He replayed her laughter. The glow in her eyes when she unwrapped the locket. The way she hadn't looked away when he'd said she was safe.

It felt good.

Too good.

And that's when it hit.

The heat behind his ribs turned sharp. The smile fell.

He sat up abruptly, swinging his legs over the edge of the bed like he could outrun the feeling.

He didn't deserve to feel this way. Not after Ellie.

Not when he hadn't saved her.

It crept in like it always did—low and poisonous—the voice that told him he was unworthy of peace, of anything good.

He dressed in silence and went to work checking the water tanks and feeding the animals. He went through the motions like muscle memory could drown out the noise.

But every task snagged. His thoughts moved too fast and his body lagged behind.

Everything looked the same—paddocks wide and gold, the gate's familiar groan, windmills casting slow shadows across dry earth. But it all felt off. Hollow.

He paused at the edge of the ridge, hand resting on the same fencepost where he'd picked the wildflower for Ruthie's locket. For a heartbeat, the memory of her face warmed him again.

And then the guilt flooded back, with force.

Later, with sweat on his brow and dust in his throat, James crouched by a section of broken fence near the back paddock. His hands worked steadily, twisting wire, driving in nails. It was the kind of job he could do without thinking.

Which was the problem.

Because all he could think—over and over, louder than the wind:

If Ellie can't be better—can't come back, can't laugh again—then I don't deserve to be happy.

The final nail hit harder than it needed to.

The wood split beneath his hammer-a sharp crack that echoed too loud.

James stared at it.

Then, a sound broke through the silence.

He turned at the crunch of tyres on gravel.

A dusty ute pulled in slow. The engine shuddered, then stilled.

Pastor Luke.

James hadn't seen him in months—not since he'd last slipped into the back pew, head low, leaving before the final prayer.

Luke always spotted him anyway.

Luke stepped out of the Ute, slow and deliberate. Like someone approaching a spooked horse—or a grieving friend who didn't know whether to bolt or break.

One hand rested on the door. The other held a thermos. A sun-bleached Bible sat on the dash like it had lived there forever.

"Morning," Luke said, voice worn smooth with years.

James nodded.

"Morning Luke."

Luke didn't rush. Just stepped forward until his boots touched the edge of James's shadow.

Luke studied him—not with pity, but with that steady look James had known since he was seventeen. The same look Luke gave him the day James stood at his father's funeral, too proud to cry, too angry to pray.

"We have missed you at church. I must say mate, you are looking a little tired today."

James offered a half-smile that didn't reach his eyes.

"I am a bit tired, to be honest."

Luke unscrewed the thermos and poured some into the lid.

"Margaret's coffee. Not that weak church blend you always hated."

James took it. Sipped. Let the warmth settle where nothing else had.

Luke crossed his arms, gaze drifting toward the ridge.

"You've been absent a while and I have been worried about you."

"I've been busy." James replied. "It's hard sometimes to find the time".

Luke hummed.

"Grief fills the calendar whether or not you schedule it."

James didn't answer.

"I didn't come to drag you back to the pews," Luke said gently. "I came to ask how your heart's holding."

The words cracked something open.

James turned the lid slowly in his hands.

"Look, Luke. I know God's there. I still believe in him. But since Ellie..."

He trailed off. The words failed.

Luke didn't push. Just waited—the way good shepherds do.

Finally, he said,

"Since Ellie, you've been out in the field."

James looked up.

"Not at the house. Not on the road. Just... somewhere in the middle. Not lost, not found. Not running but not coming home either. Just stuck. Tired. Still. Like you don't know whether to take another step or sink into the dirt."

James let out a breath he didn't know he was holding.

"You always know how to hit the nail on the head."

Luke nodded, slow and quiet.

"I've been in that field, too before James."

James didn't speak. He didn't need to. Luke had a way of seeing people.

It wasn't that James had run from God.

He'd just... stopped walking to God.

Luke glanced toward the cottage.

"I heard you've got a guest. Ruthie?"

James nodded.

"Yeah. She's been through the ringer to say the least."

Luke didn't ask for details. He never did.

"She doesn't talk much about it. But I see it—the way she double-checks locks and the way she jumps at sounds. Makes me want to fix it for her.... like I couldn't for Ellie."

Luke shook his head softly.

"You can't fix people James, you know that better than anyone. She needs someone who won't leave. Someone who stays, even when it's hard. She doesn't need an answer. She needs a witness."

James looked down at the dust stirring beneath his boot.

"So, what, I just... stay close?"

Luke smiled.

"Keep the porch light on, James. That's what God does for us when we've lost our way. He doesn't chase, doesn't force—He just stands still, steady, holding the light so we can find our way home."

James's voice cracked.

"I know God's good and that he is always there for us. But I have to tell you, since Ellie..." He paused, swallowing.

"It's like I'm standing here with empty hands, and I don't know what He wants from me. The porch light feels too far away—like I can see it, but I don't know how to reach it."

Luke let the quiet breath. Then said:

"You think He wants a performance? A list? James... you're not a tradesman knocking on the door with proof of work. You're a son. Sons don't bring receipts. They just come home."

James blinked. His shoulders dropped.

"But I'm still so angry and lost!"

Luke didn't flinch.

"You think God can't handle your anger?"

James gave a bitter half-laugh.

"Sometimes I think I should be afraid of it."

Luke stepped closer, placing a weathered hand on his shoulder.

"Grief shouts. But truth whispers louder—if you listen long enough. God's not pacing, James. He's on the porch. Lights still on. Still waiting."

James blinked, eyes stinging.

"What if I don't remember the way?"

Luke looked to the horizon.

"You don't need to. You just need to start walking and God will do the rest. That is how healing begins"

Silence settled between them, rich and real.

Luke finally glanced toward the Ute.

"I've got a few more stops today so I better head off. But you know where to find me."

He turned, hand on the door.

"If you need anything, James. I am here for you."

Long after Luke's Ute rumbled down the track and disappeared into the gum-lined horizon, James stood alone on the porch. The coffee in his hands had gone cold, forgotten. The paddocks stretched out before him, still and familiar, unchanged in every way that mattered.

But something inside him had moved.

He couldn't name it—not yet. Only that it was real, and it was stirring.

Pastor Luke's visit hadn't settled anything. If anything, it had shaken loose things James thought he'd buried—questions, longings, the ache of something more. And now, in the quiet aftermath, it all felt a little too much. A little too close.

Like God had knocked, and James wasn't sure if he was ready to open the door again.

Chapter 16 – The Weight of Silence

"To bestow on them a crown of beauty instead of ashes, the oil of joy instead of mourning..." - *Isaiah 61:3*

Ruthie hadn't spoken to James in days.

Each morning, she found herself watching—eyes scanning the paddocks beyond the window, hoping for a sign he might be headed her way. But there was no soft knock on the door. No quiet check-in. No shared coffee or small joke to fill the space between them.

She'd see him, sometimes—walking across the property, always brisk, always looking ahead like he was late for something. He didn't glance her way. Didn't linger. It felt deliberate, like he was trying not to be interrupted. Like he didn't want to be seen.

And each time, something inside her pulled tighter.

Had she said something wrong? Was it what she shared on her birthday? Too much, too soon? She replayed the night again and again in her mind—rewinding every word, dissecting every glance, trying to locate the moment it all went off course. Searching for the sentence that made him withdraw.

Maybe her story—the weight of it, the mess—had tipped some invisible scale. Maybe James had finally decided she was too much. Or not enough.

She tried to remind herself she was used to this. Loneliness wasn't new. She'd survived years of it, worn it like a second skin. But this quiet... this silence... it felt different.

It wasn't just the absence of sound.

It was the presence of ache.

It pooled in the corners of the room, pressed against her ribs, made her chest feel tight and her breath shallow. This kind of silence didn't just echo. It bruised.

There was one brief flicker of something else—a moment she caught him near the barn, sleeves rolled, hammer in hand. Sweat on his brow. Focused. Real. For a heartbeat, her hope lit like a match. If she could just get close enough, maybe he'd see her. Maybe she'd know that everything between them was still okay.

She stepped toward him slowly, hesitant but trying. But when he noticed her, he didn't smile.

His shoulders tensed. His jaw clenched.

"Sorry, Ruthie," he said, not unkind—but not warm either. His voice was clipped, too careful. "I'm just... really busy at the moment. Do you mind if we catch up later? I just need space at the moment."

He didn't wait for her to answer.

Just turned away.

And that—that—was the part that stung the most.

Because it wasn't a slammed door or cruel words. It was gentler than that.

But it still felt like rejection.

The kind that doesn't leave marks on the skin.

Just the soul.

She spent the rest of the day moving through the cottage like a ghost.

Peeling carrots. Slicing onions. Lining up potatoes. Her hands worked on autopilot. Light spilled across the floor, catching in the dust, painting gold on the tiles. She pressed her bare feet into the cool surface, trying to feel something—anything—beneath her.

Just then, she caught it—the bitter scent of garlic rising from the pan, sharp and acrid.

The bitter scent hit her like a slap.

And suddenly, she wasn't in the cottage anymore.

She was back in an old memory. A different kitchen. Colder. Darker.

Dylan liked the cold—said it kept the mould out. Said it made people move faster. He always said a lot of things that weren't true.

In this memory, she stood over the bench in that cold, dim kitchen—making pasta from scraps, stretching what little they had. She'd used the last clove of garlic, hoping the flavour might mask the emptiness of the meal, hoping it would be enough to keep the peace.

He walked in. Eyes swept over the stove. His jaw clenched.

Ruthie knew that look—too well. The look that meant it didn't matter what she'd done or how hard she'd tried. He was hunting for a reason to snap. To turn dinner into a battleground.

"What's this garbage. I thought I told you how much I hate eating pasta every night!!" His voice seething with anger.

She turned from the stove, wiping her hands on a tea towel. "It's all we had, Dylan. I'm sorry—"

He didn't let her finish.

"You're useless,"

he snapped, voice low and sharp.

"I don't ask for much. Just a decent, home-cooked meal. But no—you serve up the same slop every night like I'm not even worth the effort."

She swallowed hard and nodded, trying to steady her voice. "I'm sorry. I thought—"

He cut her off, not with shouting, but with silence first. The kind that crackled with warning.

Then came the words. Cold. Precise.

"You are always so stupid, Ruthie. If you had a brain cell it would be lonely."

She opened her mouth to respond, the apology trembling on her tongue.

"I just—"

But he was already closing the space between them.

His hand knocked the spoon from hers. It clattered to the floor.

She flinched. Trembled. But didn't step back. Not yet.

He moved closer. Voice like gravel in a storm.

"You are always trying to make me the bad guy. You are always the one pushing me to anger."

"I'm not!" Ruthie said in a raised tone.

His grip was sudden—hard, bruising.

"Don't you ever raise your voice at me!"

he hissed, the words slicing through the air like a whip.

Ruthie froze.

She hadn't even realised her tone had shifted—just a tremble of protest, a breath of defiance—but it was enough.

Her body instinctively tried to retreat, to fold in on itself, to disappear.

But he yanked her forward instead. Closer. The air between them vanished. His fingers dug into her arm like claws.

She couldn't breathe.

The heat of his anger pressed against her skin, sour and suffocating. She turned her face slightly, not daring to meet his eyes. It only made it worse when she had.

And then—he shoved her.

Hard.

Her back hit the edge of the hallway wall. Not enough to break her, but enough to bruise. Enough to remind her who held control.

She caught herself against the corner of the doorframe, her shoulder screaming. The silence that followed roared louder than the impact. He didn't speak. Didn't apologise. Just stood there, chest rising and falling too fast.

Ruthie didn't cry.

But, just then, the knife slipped from her hand.

The sharp clang of metal on tile snapped her back—back to the cottage, back to now. Her breath caught in her throat.

She looked down. A thin line of red was already blooming across her palm—just a small cut, but it was enough.

Enough to break the memory's grip.

Enough to remind her where she was.

Enough to feel it all.

The burnt garlic clung to the air now.

A scream rose up inside her—one she hadn't let loose in years.

Bear was there first, pressing his body to her shin. Steady. Real. Solid.

But it wasn't enough.

Not this time.

Her eyes landed on the garlic still in the pan.

Without thinking, she lifted the pan and hurled it across the room.

"I HATE YOU!!!" she screamed. "I HATE THAT YOU STILL LIVE IN HERE!!!! I HATE THAT A SMELL CAN STEAL EVERYTHING FROM!!!!"

She panted, chest heaving.

The words tore out of her, loud and guttural—part grief, part fury.

She collapsed to the floor, fists clenched, Bear's fur beneath her hands.

She didn't try to silence the memory. Didn't swallow the ache.

She let the mess be what it was.

She sat there for a long time, tangled in Bear's warmth, hands trembling, soul scraped raw.

Eventually, she rose.

Her hands still trembled, but her legs held.

The scent of lemon oil drifted through the cottage, chasing away the bitterness—not to forget, but to reclaim. To say: This is mine. You don't get to have this. Not this space. Not this breath. Not this day.

She crossed the room slowly, barefoot against the warm wooden floor, and reached for the small Bible Naomi had given her.

She'd looked at it every day since her birthday—run her fingers over the gold-embossed cover, traced the edges of the ribbon marker, even held it to her chest once when the nightmares lingered longer than usual.

But she hadn't opened it.

Not until now.

She didn't know where to start. The Bible felt both familiar and foreign in her hands—like a letter from someone she used to know but hadn't spoken to in years. So she didn't try to search. Didn't try to think.

She just let the pages fall open.

Her fingers trembled as she smoothed the crease. Her eyes drifted across the text, barely focusing—until they landed on a verse. And somehow, it was exactly what she hadn't known she was longing for.

Words about God's love—not for the perfect, the strong, or the composed.

But for the crushed. The broken. The ones barely holding on.

It wasn't fire and thunder. It wasn't judgment.

It was closeness. Nearness. A God who came close to those splintered by life.

She read the words again, slower this time, as if letting them settle in the cracks.

Something broke quietly inside her. Not like glass, but like a wall easing down brick by brick.

In the hush that followed, she whispered—not a vow, not a resolution. Just a prayer.

"God... help me!"

Chapter 17 – The Porch Light

"Even the darkness will not be dark to You; the night will shine like the day, for darkness is as light to You." — Psalm 139:12

I t was late afternoon when James knocked on the cottage door.

Not a light tap. Not the easy rhythm of habit.

This knock was different.

The kind that made Ruthie freeze mid-motion.

She had been folding laundry, steadying herself with the familiar scent of clean fabric. But the knock pulled her attention.

Her feet moved before her thoughts could catch up. Slow. Measured. Each step through the quiet cottage felt heavier than the last. She reached the door. Fingers curled around the knob. Paused. Then turned.

James stood there. Hat in hand. Shoulders rounded, like he was bracing himself for what was about to come.

"Hi." he said, voice almost hoarse.

"Hey," she replied, cautious but not cold.

They stood like that for a breath too long. Neither knowing where to begin.

"I should've come sooner Ruthie, look I am so sorry about the other day," James said finally, his voice low. "I have just... been stuck in my own head. I am so sorry."

Ruthie nodded slightly, then stepped aside.

He entered, but the warmth didn't follow—not at first. The cottage smelled of rosemary and stew, the kind of scent that normally soothed the body after a long day. But now, the air felt tight. Suspended.

James stood in the middle of it all like he didn't know where to land.

"Coffee?" she asked, softer this time.

"Only if it's strong," he said, offering a half-smile that didn't quite reach his eyes.

She poured a fresh mug and set it down in front of him, the ceramic clinking lightly against the wood. But James didn't reach for it.

His eyes lingered—not on the coffee, but on her hand. The bandage. His brows pinched.

"What happened?" he asked, his voice low but urgent.

Ruthie's body tensed like a wire pulled tight. She pulled her hand back slightly, instinctively.

"It's silly, really," she said, trying to shrug it off. "I slipped and nicked myself with the knife."

James sat up straighter. "Is it deep? Do you need stitches? Should I take you to the doctor?"

She shook her head quickly. "No, nothing like that. Just a small cut."

She hesitated, then added, quieter, "It was nothing. I was just chopping veggies... and my mind wandered. I wasn't paying attention, and the knife only made a small cut."

James tilted his head slightly; concern etched across his face. "I am sorry. Were you distracted because of me?"

Ruthie didn't answer right away. Her eyes flicked to the floor. Her fingers fidgeted with the edge of the tea towel on the bench.

"No," she said finally. "It wasn't that, James."

"It was more than wandering. It was... a flashback, back to a memory I would like to forget."

She swallowed, hard.

"One minute I was in this kitchen. Safe. Here. The next... I wasn't. I was back there. His kitchen. My old one. The garlic burned, and it was like my whole body remembered before my brain did. I was standing in the same place, but everything smelled like fear."

James went still. Like her words struck something deep in him.

"I get it," he said.

Her eyes lifted to meet his. "You do?"

He nodded slowly. "More than you know."

She searched his face—really looked—and there it was. The weight. The ache with history. The kind of grief you carry in your bones.

Ruthie took a shaky breath.

"That day... when you said, 'not today' and walked away," she said gently, "it hurt."

James's gaze dropped.

"It felt like I'd said too much. Like you regretted letting me into your world."

He gripped the coffee mug tightly. His knuckles turned white.

"I didn't mean to shut you out," he said, his voice cracking under the weight. "I just—I didn't know what to do with what I was feeling. I wasn't pushing you away... I was pushing everything away. Myself. The grief. The shame."

He let out a breath like he'd been holding it for days.

"I told you about Ellie, but not all of it. Not the parts I still carry. Some days it is all too much. Some nights it all rushes back especially the night she died."

His hands came up to cover his face for a second, shoulders hunched as if trying to fold himself inward.

"I was supposed to be her safe place. I was meant to see it. But I was so damn busy fixing fences, checking troughs, pretending everything was fine, to notice the pain she was in. I failed her."

He looked up again, tears streaking his cheeks.

"When she died, I blamed the world. But deep down? I blamed myself. I still do!"

Ruthie didn't say anything. She didn't need to. She just reached across the table and gently placed her hand over his.

"And then," he continued.

"On your birthday, I felt... different. Lighter. And that terrified me. Because I didn't think I deserved to feel okay. Not after what happened to her."

A tear slid down Ruthie's cheek, but she didn't wipe it away.

"You're not a failure, James," she said quietly, firmly. "You're a man with a broken heart, doing the best he can. And even in the short time I've known you, I've seen who you are. Steady. Kind. Brave, even when it hurts."

She squeezed his hand softly.

"I don't believe for a second that you failed Ellie. You loved her. You would've done anything for her."

James exhaled—long, slow—and something in his posture shifted. A burden easing, even if only slightly.

"You carry so much," she whispered. "So much that was never yours to carry alone."

He looked at her, really looked at her, like her words were reaching into places no one else had touched in years. His eyes shimmered with something raw. Not just pain. Hope.

"I think..." he began slowly, his voice barely more than gravel, "I just need to know I can keep you safe."

Ruthie's gaze didn't waver.

"You don't have to save me, James," she said, voice tender but steady. "I'm not asking for a hero. I just need to know you won't vanish without a word. That you won't leave me wondering if I did something wrong."

He looked down at their hands, fingers still loosely threaded. Her thumb brushed against his, gentle as breath.

When his eyes lifted again, there was something sacred in his expression—like a vow without the need for words.

"I won't," he said. This time, his voice didn't shake. "You never need to worry again Ruthie. I will never do that again."

Chapter 18 – Light Between the Fences

"Behold, I am doing a new thing; now it springs up—do you not perceive it?" — Isaiah 43:19

The morning after their shared confessions, the farm felt different.

Something had changed.

Grief still hung in the air, but it no longer ruled it.

Instead, a hush had settled—almost reverent, as if the land itself was waiting to see what might bloom after so much breaking.

Between them, truths had been laid bare—

pain given a name, regrets spoken into the open air.

And in return, there was no judgment.

Only gentleness.

A quiet kind of grace.

James had risen before dawn, like always.

But this time, his boots didn't take him straight to the barn.

Instead, they lingered on the gravel outside Ruthie's cottage, pacing slow half-steps, waiting for movement from the cottage.

At exactly seven, James lifted a hand and knocked gently on the old timber doorframe, the sound muffled by morning fog.

The door creaked open a moment later. Ruthie stood there, curls tangled from sleep, eyes swollen with the weight of dreams not yet shaken off. She blinked at him slowly, her body still catching up to consciousness.

"Hope you don't mind an early call," James said, lifting a battered thermos in one hand, two tin mugs hooked through his fingers.

She looked at him, lips parted in a question she hadn't decided to ask.

"Will you come on a walk with me?" he added, his voice quieter now. "There's something I want to show you."

She rubbed at one eye, stepping forward into the cool air. Her flannel sleeves hung past her wrists, and her bare toes curled against the cold wood of the porch.

"Depends," she said, her voice husky and low. "What's in the thermos?"

"Strong coffee." He offered with a small, sheepish grin.

That earned a faint smile. Just a flicker, but real.

"Then I guess I can come on a walk with you."

Relief passed over his features like the morning breeze—soft, almost imperceptible, but there. He handed her a mug, warmth seeping through her fingers.

They stepped off the porch and crossed the dew-drenched paddock, boots side by side, heading towards what waited for them at the edge of the morning.

James didn't say a word. He simply led—quiet and steady—as if inviting her into something sacred. His presence was gentle, almost reverent, like he was guiding her through a threshold where words might break the holiness of the moment.

They walked in silence, the crisp morning air brushing past them as they reached one of the last farm gates. Beyond it, the barn stood bathed in soft light, its timber worn and warm with memory. James paused, resting a hand on the gate before turning to Ruthie.

His eyes met hers, calm and searching. "Have you ever..." he began, voice low and tender, "have you ever seen a newborn foal?"

Ruthie shook her head.

"Only in movies."

"Well," he murmured, pushing open the gate to the south pasture, "then this might be worth your morning."

Inside the old shelter, Belle stood over her newborn.

The foal was still damp, legs too long for its body, trembling with the effort of learning to stand.

Ruthie stopped just inside the doorway, breath caught in her throat.

There was something holy about it. The vision of new life that was unfolding right in front of her.

"She's beautiful," Ruthie breathed, barely louder than a thought.

"He," James said gently, a smile ghosting across his lips. "He, was born just before dawn."

They stood together in the golden hush of the barn, the scent of straw.

The foal nudged at Belle's flank, wobbled, and collapsed into the straw with a soft thud. His limbs were still unsure, his coat damp and trembling. Then, with a quiet insistence, he tried again—rising, faltering, standing. Life, fresh and fragile, determined to begin.

Ruthie drew a shaky breath. "I can't believe it," she whispered. "It's... incredible. Watching them, having this moment together."

James didn't answer right away. His eyes weren't on the foal anymore.

They were on her.

The way her lips parted in awe, the way her shoulders had softened, as though even her scars had stilled for a second. Her whole body seemed to lean into the quiet, into the sacredness of it all—as if any sudden movement might startle the moment away.

James felt something shift inside him.

Not loud or dramatic.

But deep.

Like a lock clicking open in the dark.

He saw her—not just her outline or her face—but her essence. The woman who had survived things she never should have had to.

The one standing next to him in the straw, eyes full of wonder, letting herself feel again.

For the first time in a long time, he wasn't just witnessing someone else's healing.

He was feeling his own.

And maybe that's what made his next gesture feel so tender it hurt.

He reached out slowly—no rush, no demand—and brushed a loose strand of hair from her cheek. His fingers trembled slightly. The touch was light, reverent.

To Ruthie, it landed like thunder.

Not in sound, but in meaning.

Her breath caught. Not out of fear. But recognition.

Of what it meant to be touched like that—not owned, not handled, not reduced—but seen.

Truly seen.

And still chosen.

She didn't look away. Didn't retreat into the silence like she once would have.

She held his gaze.

Steady. Brave.

And in that fragile moment, something stirred.

Not a roar. Not a rush. But a flicker.

The smallest ember of trust, glowing in the ashes.

She let it burn.

James let his hand fall back to his side, fingers curling slightly, as though trying to hold on to something intangible. His throat was tight, thick with words he didn't know how to say—words he wasn't sure he had the right to speak aloud. The moment between them had cracked something open, and he wasn't certain what would spill out if he lingered too long.

A part of him wanted to stay there, rooted in the hush, memorising the way her eyes softened and held his. But another part—the one that had learned restraint, that had stitched control over emotion like armour—whispered that it was too much, too fast. That if he didn't step away, he might say or do something he couldn't take back.

He drew in a slow, grounding breath and looked away, blinking hard.

"Alright," he murmured, voice low and uneven. "Let's get you back inside... before you catch a chill."

It wasn't the cold he feared.

It was the warmth.

And what it might mean if he let himself reach for it.

But Ruthie didn't move. Her gaze lingered on his face, her voice trembling just enough to betray the tenderness behind it.

"James?"

He turned to her, thermos cradled like something breakable in his hands.

"Yeah?"

"Thank you!"

His brow creased. "For what?"

"For just... being you." Her words came soft but sure, as though she was still learning how to speak from a place that hadn't always felt safe.

James swallowed hard, emotion pressing behind his ribs like a wave held back.

"But, Ruthie..." he said, voice rough with something honest, "I should be the one thanking you."

He looked at her then—not with guarded affection, but with everything in him stripped bare.

"For seeing me," he said. "Not the version I try to show everyone else. You see what's underneath."

Ruthie's eyes shone, not with tears, but something deeper.

In the stillness that followed, words became unnecessary.

The moment said everything.

James exhaled—a breath so full it felt like release.

"I've carried so much for so long," he admitted. "I forgot what it was like to have someone out here with me."

Ruthie took a single step closer. Close enough for the cold to slip between them. Close enough for warmth to rise.

A pause bloomed between them—quiet, weighty, beautiful.

Not empty.

But full.

Full of what could be.

Full of healing, still in motion.

And as the sun crept higher, frost melting to dew, and the newborn foal took another shaky step, something unseen—yet undeniable—took root between them.

Chapter 19 – The Knock That Shouldn't Have Come

"But the Lord is faithful, and he will strengthen you and protect you from the evil one."

— 2 Thessalonians 3:3

The moment they'd shared the day before didn't blaze like fire—it settled like embers. Quiet. Glowing. A warmth Ruthie carried in her chest that made everything else feel just a little less sharp.

Since then, she hadn't known what to do with herself.

James hadn't messaged. Hadn't come by. Not a single word.

Part of her was grateful. The silence gave her space to breathe, to not unravel completely.

But the other part—the aching, trembling part—had hoped.

For something.

A knock. A sign.

Proof that the way his gaze had lingered on her wasn't just mercy or pity—but something real. Something mutual.

Maybe she'd made it all up.

Maybe she'd wanted it too much.

Maybe she was too broken to be chosen.

Each thought struck like a match, igniting the self-doubt she thought she'd buried.

And Ruthie—still learning how to steady herself again—felt them all as they smouldered through her chest.

So when Naomi texted,

"Hey, can you help me unpack books today? Just a couple of boxes, I promise," she didn't hesitate.

Naomi was safe. Funny. Steady.

And today, the idea of something as simple as stacking books felt like salvation—like something she could control, something that wouldn't collapse beneath her.

She gathered her things and made her way toward the barn to tell James.

When she reached the doorway of the barn, she hesitated. The light inside was low, slanting through the wooden slats in soft, golden streaks that danced in the dust-filled air.

As she stepped closer, her eyes adjusted—and there he was.

James.

He was there, turning toward her. Ruthie froze—caught between breath and heartbeat, as if the world had narrowed to the space between them. She hovered in the doorway like someone unsure if the ground would hold, uncertain whether she was stepping into something sacred or something already slipping away.

His eyes met hers, and for a beat, neither moved.

Her heart kicked hard in her chest, sudden and wild. But she anchored herself in the weight of it, forced her lips into something resembling a smile—tentative, unsure, but real.

"Hey," she said softly, like a question and a wish wrapped in one.

He smiled back—slow and gentle, the kind of smile that carried things words couldn't.

The silence stretched between them, not uncomfortable but fragile.

"Naomi asked me to help at the bookshop today," Ruthie finally said.

"She was wondering if I would help with unpacking a few boxes."

James nodded and rubbed the back of his neck, voice a little hoarse.

"Sounds nice." He said.

I'm heading into town anyway. Meeting Micah about a supply order. I could give you a lift, if you wanted?" James offered.

Her eyebrows lifted.

"You don't have to go out of your way; I could drive myself if it's easier?"

"I want to," he said, calm but firm.

"Alright," she said, the word gentle but full. "Thanks."

James gave a quiet nod.

"I can be ready to go in ten minutes, if that's okay?" he asked, voice low, almost careful.

Ruthie met his gaze, something warm flickering behind her eyes. She nodded, the smallest smile touching her lips—less a gesture, more a letting down of walls.

When Ruthie arrived in town, she didn't linger. She headed straight for the bookshop.

The shop greeted her like a sanctuary.

Quiet. Sheltering.

The kind of place where the world felt manageable. Tape, books, shelves. Predictable steps.

Naomi hummed in the back room, her voice dancing between the pages.

The scent of paper and lemon oil wrapped around Ruthie as she found her rhythm.

The afternoon unfolded without incident. Ruthie slipped into a steady rhythm, unpacking box after box until six had been sorted, stacked, and shelved. She even found a few gems nestled in the mix—titles she hadn't read but already knew would end up on her growing wishlist.

She and Naomi paused for afternoon tea, settling at the small table near the front window. Steam curled from their mugs as they swapped stories about their favourite books and the characters who had stayed with them long after the final page. There was laughter—real and easy—and the kind of warmth that made Ruthie forget, for just a little while, how heavy things had been.

They were both wrapped in the ease of it—gentle conversation, the rustle of pages, the clink of spoons against ceramic. The kind of quiet company that doesn't demand anything, just is. The slow comfort of the day settled over them like a soft blanket.

The afternoon drifted on, and Ruthie kept her focus narrowed to the task in front of her—unpacking the last box with deliberate care, letting the quiet order of it soothe her nerves.

But just as she reached for the final stack of books,
everything shifted.

The soft ding of the bell above the bookshop door sliced through the stillness like a blade.

The peace she'd found—fragile and hard-won—shattered in an instant.

The air shifted. Heavy. Electric. Charged with something unseen but unmistakably wrong.

Her hand froze mid-air, a book half-raised toward the shelf.

A chill rippled through her skin, and every fine hair along her arms stood to attention, as if her body sensed the danger before her mind could name it.

Then she heard him.

"Miss me?"

She turned.

And in that instant, her world collapsed inward.

He stood in the doorway as if he'd never left.

Leaning against the frame like it was his. Like he was welcome.

Crisp shirt, freshly trimmed beard, posture too relaxed to be anything but rehearsed.

Dylan.

That same calculated smile stretched across his face—smooth and gleaming—like a porcelain mask too thin to hide the shadows writhing beneath.

Before Ruthie could gather a single thought, he began moving— slow, deliberate steps that sliced through the quiet like a threat made flesh.

"Ruthie," he purred, voice low and intimate. "Been looking for you."

Her throat seized. Her whole body went cold.

Across the room, Naomi stilled. Her eyes snapped from Ruthie to Dylan. Assessing the situation rapidly before interrupting.

"Umm.. Ruthie, just got to head to the back, be just a minute," Naomi said coolly, disappearing into the back with her phone already in hand.

Ruthie couldn't move.

Dylan took another step forward, slow and deliberate.

"You look good," he said, voice coiled like a snake. "Healthier."

Ruthie stepped back immediately, and her foot hit the edge of a box.

Dylan lifted his hands slowly, palms out, dripping with false innocence.

"I just want to talk," he said, voice smooth as oil. "That's all. Like old times."

But before he could take another step or let another poisoned word slip through that practiced smile—

The door slammed open with a force that made the walls tremble.

James and Micah burst through, called in by Naomi's urgent message.

They moved fast—boots thudding against timber, eyes scanning, every muscle coiled and ready.

There was no hesitation. No confusion.

Just a surge of protective energy that flooded the space like a storm front.

James didn't look at Dylan first.

He looked at Ruthie.

And in a heartbeat, he saw it all.

The way her hands trembled.

The way her breath had gone shallow.

The way every part of her screamed without making a sound.

His voice cut through the air like steel drawn in a storm.

"Back. Away. Now."

Dylan turned, jaw tightening, posture stiff with sudden threat.

"Well," he sneered, eyes flicking up and down James, "Fancy seeing you again. You really seem to be in my business these days."

James didn't blink.

"I said—back. Away."

Micah walked across the room without a word and positioned himself between Ruthie and Dylan like a wall made of flesh and fire.

It was at that point that Dylan's voice turned sharp.

"Don't tell me what to do! She is mine!"

"No!" Ruthie yelled. "I'm not his anything!'

Dylan's smile faltered and anger rose.

James stepped forward, voice still and unwavering.

"She doesn't want you here! So, you're going to leave. Now!"

"You're making a mistake," Dylan threatened.

But it was at that point that Naomi reappeared.

Carrying the long wooden pole, she used for reaching the high shelves. Her grip was firm. Her voice thunder in velvet.

"Get. Out!!"

Or I call the police."

Dylan looked around.

Naomi. Micah. James.

But it was Ruthie his eyes landed on last.

"You remember what I said?" he rasped. "About us being forever? You know I meant that."

Then, without another word, Dylan turned—

his jaw tight, shoulders rigid—and stormed out, the bell above the door giving one final, jarring chime as it slammed shut behind him.

And that was when Ruthie crumpled.

Her knees buckled beneath the weight of everything she'd been holding in,

and she folded into Micah's arms before she even realised, she was falling.

There were no words. No questions.

Just strong, steady arms gathering her in—

holding her together in that moment.

when she no longer had the strength to do it herself.

Chapter 20 – The Panic

"When I am afraid, I put my trust in You." — Psalm 56:3

Micah held Ruthie tightly.

One arm curved across her back, the other braced firm but gentle at her elbow—anchoring her to this moment, this place, this reality. Not restraining. Just reminding her she wasn't alone.

Her breath came in sharp, fractured bursts. Like glass shattering against ribs. Her eyes didn't blink, didn't move. They were locked on the door Dylan had just slipped through. As if it might swing open again.

James had followed him out the door. His jaw was clenched, fists curled—not out of rage, but as if trying to hold back every memory threatening to erupt. He didn't shout. Didn't lunge. But his presence spoke volumes. He positioned himself near the entrance, shoulders squared, silently daring Dylan to try stepping back inside.

He watched as Dylan's car skidded away and disappear down the road.

Only then did he turn back.

Naomi moved quietly—like a woman who had lived through her own apocalypse and survived it one breath at a time.

She moved with purpose and flipped the sign on the front door—CLOSED—with hands that trembled and fetched a worn blanket.

She didn't speak. She just placed the blanket over Ruthie, quiet and careful. Then she stepped back.

Micah adjusted his hold as Ruthie's lips parted.

"I need air," she rasped. The words were thin. Brittle.

He waited for her to move. Then followed—silent, steady, just a few paces behind—as she stepped into the blaze of the midday sun.

The light hit her like a slap. It was too much. Too loud. The sky too wide. The breeze too sharp. Everything felt enormous.

She stumbled past James and the bookshop window, boots scraping the gravel. Down the narrow alley behind it, her hand dragging along the warm brick wall, needing something solid, something unmoving.

Micah followed.

James didn't. Not yet. He was still standing guard at the door—shoulders set, eyes fixed on the road—prepared for the possibility that Dylan might change his mind and try to come back. He wasn't leaving his post until he was sure Ruthie was safe.

She dropped between two garbage bins, crouched low to the ground. Her whole body trembled as if the fear was vibrating through her bones. She cradled her head in her hands, fingers digging into her scalp, trying to press back the rising terror—trying to make herself small enough to disappear.

"He... found me," she whispered.

"I'm not safe anymore. I'm not safe anywhere." The words looped, stuck in her mind and replayed. A scratched record of terror spinning inside her chest.

She curled tighter, like she could disappear into concrete and sky.

Micah didn't touch her.

He crouched a few feet away, forearms resting on his knees. Present but unintrusive. Like a shadow made of compassion.

Ruthie lifted her head slowly. Her cheeks streaked with tears and her voice was thin and hollow.

"I... I felt safe," she said, voice trembling. "He only let me feel safe for five minutes... before taking it all away again."

Micah gave the smallest nod. "I'm sorry, mate... that really sucks!" he said, offering comfort in the only way he knew how.

And in that moment James appeared at the end of the alley, his shadow long in the harsh light. He didn't rush but slowly made his way down the alley.

"We need to get her home and away from here in case he comes back," he said with authority.

Micah stood and dusted his jeans with the flat of his palms. Then looked down to Ruthie, his voice gentler than before.

"You right to walk?"

Ruthie swallowed, her throat tight. Every part of her ached with the weight of memory. But she nodded.

Her legs trembled. But she moved towards James who had opened the passenger door of the Ute.

The drive home unfolded in near-total silence. No music. No small talk. Just the weight of what had happened hanging over them.

As soon as they pulled up to the farm, Ruthie stepped out without a word and James followed in silence.

She made her way to the cottage with a kind of haunted resolve. At the threshold, Ruthie paused. Her fingers brushed the weathered timber frame, grazing the familiar grain like it might steady her. The cottage looked the same—but it didn't feel the same. It felt... altered. Like stepping into a memory warped by time or grief.

She hovered there a moment longer before crossing the threshold. Bear padded in behind her, slow and deliberate, as if scanning for shadows only he could see. His flank brushed her leg, a quiet offering of presence.

James stayed at the door, watching her.

He noticed then—the blanket that had been wrapped around her shoulders had slipped off, trailed behind like something forgotten. He bent down and lifted it carefully and shook away the dust before stepping inside and draping it around her once more, gently. His knuckles grazed the hollow of her collarbone, and something in him cracked at how cold her skin felt.

Ruthie didn't flinch, but she didn't meet his eyes either. She just moved to the corner of the room and slid down the wall, back pressed to the cool plaster. Her knees drew up; arms wrapped around them. Her breath came in shallow bursts, but it came.

James crouched beside her—not touching, not intruding—just trying to anchor himself in the hush that had settled around them, offering his presence.

"He doesn't get to write the ending, Ruthie," he said, voice low—steady, but burning at the edges. "He doesn't get to decide what happens next."

She closed her eyes. A tremble passed through her—not of fear, but of release.

"I'm here," he added softly. "And if he ever comes near you again... he'll have to go through me first."

She said nothing.

Instead, she leaned into James—into the place where safety had taken root. His shoulder, solid and still, felt like home after a long winter. She folded herself into that quiet strength, into warmth steadier than fire, deeper than breath.

Wrapped in wool and silence, she let herself stay.

And he didn't move.

He stayed with her. Unmoving. Unwavering. Until the trembling softened, and the night finally let go.

James didn't speak right away. He simply adjusted the wool blanket around her shoulders, careful and slow, like tucking in something fragile but worth protecting. The kind of protection that didn't demand anything in return.

But his eyes never left her.

After a while, he broke the silence.

"Ruthie," he said gently, "I know you have a lot to process. But I would really like it if you would come stay up at the main house tonight."

He waited, then tried again, quieter this time. "I don't want you down here by yourself. Not after what happened."

Still, she didn't speak. Her fingers toyed with a loose thread on the edge of the blanket, eyes distant.

"I know you're used to handling things on your own," he added, voice steady but laced with a softness that tugged at something deep in her. "I know you've had to be strong in ways most people wouldn't understand. But you don't have to do that here. Not tonight. Not alone."

Her breath caught, a small sound in the dark.

"I've fixed up the guest room," he continued. "It's warm. Safe. Just down the hall from mine. I'll even leave the door open if that helps." His tone held no trace of pity—just care. A kind of reverence for her pain, not a rescue from it.

Ruthie turned her head slightly, eyes meeting his at last. They were rimmed red, but clear. Awake.

"I'm not weak," she said, the words almost a whisper.

James nodded. "I know."

Silence fell again.

Then, finally, she exhaled. Long. Hollowed out. Real.

"Okay, I will come stay at the main house" she murmured., nodding her head with a hint of surrender—not to him, but to the idea that she didn't have to hold her world together alone tonight.

Chapter 21 – Burn the Bridge

"Because of the Lord's great love we are not consumed, for his compassions never fail.
They are new every morning; great is Your faithfulness."—
Lamentations 3:22–23

After James had offered her the comfort she hadn't known how to ask for—but desperately needed—Ruthie remained in the stillness of the cottage a little longer. Something had shifted in her—not loudly, but deeply.

Without a word, she rose.

Her movements were slow, deliberate, but no longer heavy with dread. She crossed the small room, unzipped the duffel she'd left untouched for days, and began to pack. Not with panic. Not with haste. Just a quiet resolve.

She folded the blanket James had wrapped around her and laid it gently on the bed. Her hands lingered there for a moment. Then she took one final glance at the space—the worn bookshelf, the lamp with its frayed pull cord, the timber walls that had both sheltered.

And then she stepped out into the cool night, bag slung over one shoulder, James waiting at the garden path with Bear walking faithfully beside him.

They walked to the main house in silence, their footsteps soft over the gravel. The moon hung low, casting pale light on the farmhouse verandah, and the wind had stilled—as if the land itself was holding its breath.

Inside, the house was warm, lived-in, and welcoming without needing to try. James moved ahead of her with quiet intention—turning on a hallway light, then stepping into the spare room.

He didn't speak much.

Instead, he busied himself with small acts of care: smoothing the old quilt, adjusting the pillows with practiced hands, and tugging a soft woollen blanket from the cedar chest at the foot of the bed. His touch was gentle, his pace unhurried. Like he was tending to more than just a room.

Ruthie stood in the doorway, her bag strap clenched tightly in her hand. Her eyes swept the room—framed photographs on the dresser and a worn Bible resting on the bedside table.

"This was Ellie's room," James said gently, breaking the silence. "I haven't changed much. Hope that's okay."

His voice held no sorrow, only a quiet reverence. Like Ellie still lived there in some small way, and maybe always would.

Ruthie stepped forward, her throat thick. She reached out to trace her fingers along the edge of the dresser, pausing at the photo of a young woman with kind eyes and a smile that looked uncannily like James'.

"It's more than okay," she whispered.

James gave a small nod, eyes soft. "I reckon you would have both gotten on well."

A beat passed. Ruthie blinked against the weight of the moment.

He turned toward the door then. "I'll just be in the lounge. Take your time and when you are ready to come out and we can have some tea."

Ruthie hesitated.

Then, as he reached for the handle, she said quietly, "James?"

He stopped, turned.

"Thank you. For... being here with me. I don't know what I would have done without you."

The silence that followed was tender, sacred.

"I wouldn't want to be anywhere else," he replied.

And with that, he stepped out, leaving the door open just enough for the light to spill through.

Ruthie placed her bag down on the floor, then sat on the edge of the bed. She ran her hand over the quilt, over the soft memory of someone who had once called this room home.

And as the night deepened, for the first time in what felt like forever, she didn't feel watched. Or caged.

She just felt held.

Later, the fire in the lounge crackled low, casting long shadows across the floorboards.

Ruthie sat curled in the corner of the couch, legs tucked beneath her.

Bear lay across her feet—solid, warm, constant.

James sat nearby, elbows resting on his knees, his gaze fixed on the flickering flames. His mind churned with one thought—how to protect Ruthie. It was all he could think about.

"About earlier..." he began.

Ruthie didn't look up.

"I think we should speak to the police," James said, his voice low, cautious—like he was placing something fragile between them.

"You don't have to say much. But what happened at the shop..." he hesitated, jaw tightening, "it crossed a line."

Ruthie didn't answer.

The only sound in the room was the soft crackle of the fire and the gentle shift of the logs as they settled.

James glanced over at her, reading the silence not as resistance, but as reckoning.

"I remember how you were at the train station," he continued, softer now. "Back in the city. You weren't ready then. And maybe you're still not. But I can't not offer. Not after what happened today."

Still, she said nothing.

But her fingers curled slightly into the blanket draped across her lap. Her shoulders rose with a shaky breath. And then—finally—a small nod. Almost imperceptible. But it was there.

"I think I need to," she whispered, voice thin as smoke.

James exhaled slowly, like he'd been holding that breath since she first walked through the cottage door. Relief flickered across his features, quiet and steady.

"I'll take you first thing tomorrow," he said.

And in the hush that followed, something settled. Not resolved. Not yet.

But set in motion.

That night, Ruthie didn't sleep.

Instead, she sat curled on the woven rug in the guest room—Ellie's room—her knees drawn close, Bear's heavy head resting in her lap. One hand moved absently through his fur, over and over, like she was trying to ground herself to something real. The room was dim but not dark, lit by the faint flicker of firelight trailing down the hallway from the fireplace.

She stared at the door. Unblinking. Unsure.

Around 2 a.m., the weight in her chest finally pushed her upright.

She crossed to the wardrobe with quiet steps and pulled out the duffel—the same one she'd clutched when she ran. The same one that had sat untouched since she arrived. It still smelled faintly of antiseptic. Of fear. Of escape. Of not belonging anywhere long enough to unpack.

She zipped it slowly.

Bear stirred, lifting his head, and let out a low, questioning whine.

Ruthie paused. Met his eyes in the stillness.

And what she saw there—steady, sad, knowing.

When dawn finally crept across the paddocks, it came slow and soft—spilling light over dew-drenched grass like it was afraid to wake the world too fast.

Inside the cottage, Ruthie moved like a shadow. Wordless. Controlled. The duffel slung over her shoulder.

Each step echoed in her chest like a drumbeat she couldn't silence.

James was already outside.

He sat on the edge of the verandah, coffee in hand, the paper folded and untouched beside him. His flannel hung open over a worn tee, boots planted firm on the timber slats like he'd been sitting there all night. Waiting.

He looked up when the screen door creaked open.

Didn't speak.

Just watched her—quiet, steady—as she stepped into the light.

Ruthie froze a few feet from him. Her hand clenched tighter around the strap of her bag. Her mouth opened—then shut again.

Finally, she found her voice.

"I have to go," she said. Fragile. Fractured.

James straightened, his brow knitting with something that wasn't anger—but something close to grief.

"Where.. where are you going?"

"I can't stay here, James. Not after what happened."

Her voice cracked.

"I thought I could stay. But Dylan—he found me. And I can't risk anyone else getting hurt."

The words tumbled out like they'd been caged for hours, brittle and breathless.

James looked at her like he'd just been dropped into freezing water. Disoriented. Hurt. His coffee slipped from the arm of the chair and landed with a dull thud on the floorboards, forgotten.

"You're not putting anything on us," he said, his voice thick, rough around the edges. "We chose to care, and we want to care about you"

Ruthie stood at the edge of the porch like it was a cliff.

"I need to go," she said again, trembling now.

"Ruthie..."

She looked away. Couldn't bear his eyes on her.

Her shoulders pulled back—tight, rigid. Like that posture was the only thing keeping her from falling apart.

"I didn't choose this for you," she whispered.

"You didn't have to," James said. "That's what caring for someone is."

She flinched—not from the word, but from how deeply it landed.

"If I stay," she replied, "I'll ruin it. I'll be the reason Bear gets hurt. Or Naomi. Or you."

James took a step toward her—then stopped himself. Hands open. Careful.

"You can't leave," he said, pain slipping into the cracks of his voice. "You can't do this to me—I mean to us. We care about you."

She shook her head. Tears slipped past her lashes, fast and hot.

"I don't want to hurt anyone," she said, choking on the truth.!

"You're not, Ruthie!" he said. "But leaving—Ruthie, that's what will hurt."

She turned her face away, lips trembling.

"I care about you," James said, and this time the words cracked open something raw.

She stilled.

"I know you're scared. And you have every reason to be. But you're not alone anymore. You don't have to protect us by running. Let us protect you for once. Let us stand with you."

Her breath hitched.

"You don't understand!" her voice raising. "He doesn't stop. If I stay, he'll come back. He always does. And next time..."

She couldn't finish. The weight of the memory was too much.

"Next time someone won't walk away!"

James took another step, heart pounding, desperate to stop her from walking away.

"Ruthie—wait," he said, reaching toward her.

His hand hung in the space between them—hesitant, trembling. A bridge made of hope and fear.

She flinched.

Not at him.

At the ghosts that lived in the shape of a man's outstretched hand. At memories that didn't know the difference.

He froze, hand dropping, eyes wide with apology.

"I'm sorry," he said softly, lifting his hands in surrender, palms open—not to hold, just to show he wouldn't.

But she was already slipping away, her gaze clouded with something unreachable.

"I can't," she said.

From behind the screen door, Bear let out a low whine and pawed once at the timber—his own quiet protest.

Even he could feel what was being torn.

James stepped back, as if giving her space might bring her closer.

"I'm sorry," Ruthie said again, softer now. No longer shaking—just emptied.

Then she turned.

Duffel in hand. Shoulders hunched. Determined.

Every step down the path felt like a thread snapping—unravelling something sacred they hadn't even finished weaving.

James wanted so badly to run after her.

Every instinct screamed to chase her down that gravel path, to pull her into his arms, to say something—anything—that might anchor her to this place. To him. But his boots stayed rooted to the boards beneath him, legs stiff with restraint, heart pounding against the walls of his chest like it might shatter.

He knew.

He knew that chasing her would only drive her further away. That touching her now, even gently, would feel like a threat. That pressing her with words she wasn't ready to receive would undo every inch of safety they'd built together.

So, he stood there.

Torn between the ache of wanting to protect her and the truth that sometimes love meant letting someone walk away.

His hands curled into fists at his sides—helpless. His jaw clenched. His eyes burned.

There were a thousand things he could've said.

A hundred ways he could've begged.

But none of them would've mattered.

She wasn't running from him.

She was running from the war still waging inside her.

And he couldn't fight that battle for her.

Still... the word escaped him. Raw. Broken. Cracked straight from the centre of his chest.

"RUTHIE!!"

She didn't turn.

Didn't pause.

But he swore—for just a moment—her shoulders trembled. Like the sound of his voice had caught something deep inside her. Like maybe, even as she walked away, some part of her wanted to stay.

But she kept walking.

And James stood in the doorway long after she was gone, the morning sun warming his face as the ache in his chest settled in like an old wound reopening.

Chapter 22 – The Surrender

"But he said to me, 'My grace is sufficient for you, for my power is made perfect in weakness.' Therefore I will boast all the more gladly about my weaknesses, so that Christ's power may rest on me."— 2 Corinthians 12:9

James stood at the edge of the driveway long after Ruthie had vanished from sight. The morning sun lit the dust still suspended in the air where her footsteps had stirred it, but even that seemed to settle too quickly. The path she'd taken looked achingly empty now, as though the world itself had already erased her presence.

It should have been a beautiful morning.

The sky was streaked with soft peach and pale gold. Birds called from the gums. The paddocks glistened with dew.

But all James could see was the shape of her—shoulders hunched, bag slung low—disappearing down that long stretch of gravel. Another person he cared about, slipping through his hands.

And him, left behind.

He inhaled through his nose, slow and deliberate, trying to collect what little resolve he had left.

He turned back toward the house, each footstep on the gravel a drumbeat of grief.

The screen door slammed behind him with a clap so loud it startled him, reverberating through the weatherboard walls like a rifle shot echoing off a canyon.

Inside, it felt colder than it had before.

A ceramic mug sat near the sink, its rim marked with the faintest trace of her lipstick. Down the hallway, the softest wisp of lavender still hung in the air—her scent, lingering like a ghost that hadn't yet realised it was gone.

James froze.

He didn't make it to the kitchen.

A tidal wave of helpless fury and heartbreak.

He clenched his fists, knuckles bone-white, trying to wrestle it down.

But it surged anyway.

Fast.

Hot.

Wild.

With no warning, he exploded.

A stack of unopened mail flew across the kitchen bench like startled birds, paper raining to the floor. His elbow caught a ceramic bowl, which shattered on impact, shards ricocheting across the hardwood like tiny screams. He kicked a wooden chair with blind precision, and it fell with a splintering crack.

"Why?!" he roared.

The word tore from his chest like a primal howl—aimed at the ceiling, at God, at the silence that refused to answer.

His breathing was ragged. Panicked.

He braced himself on the table, but it didn't steady him. His legs buckled. He dropped to his knees, head low, hands fisted into his hair.

"No! Not again—please, God!" he cried out, voice breaking. "How is this happening again?!!"

And then, It came like a flood—unwelcome, unrelenting.

He wasn't just remembering. He was there again.

Back in the barnyard with Ellie, the scent of hay and iron and cattle dust clinging to the air.

It had been an ordinary Thursday.

Too ordinary.

He'd been getting the cattle ready for market—brushing dust from hides, checking tags, moving through the rhythm of work with sweat on his brow and no sense of what was coming. That was the cruelty of it. Nothing had felt off. Not at first.

Until Ellie arrived.

She'd pulled up in that battered sedan of hers, tyres crunching the gravel. He remembered wiping his hands on a rag and heading toward her with a smile. She'd stepped out holding a plastic bag of groceries and a thermos.

"I just thought you could use a break," she said, too breezy.

But her eyes didn't meet his.

And when he took the bag from her, his fingers brushed her forearm. That's when he saw it.

A bruise. Just below the elbow. Yellow at the edges, angry in the centre. The kind of mark that told a story without a single word.

He looked at her. Really looked.

Her hair was tucked beneath a cap, but the strands that escaped were limp, rushed. Her movements were stiff—like she was guarding something, or bracing.

"Are you okay?" he asked, trying to sound casual.

She gave a quick nod. Too quick.

"Yeah, just tired."

But she wouldn't hold his gaze.

He tried again. "El, did something happen?"

She didn't answer—just stepped past him, moving toward the fence like she hadn't heard the question. Her whole body had changed. Shut off. Pulled inward like someone folding in on themselves.

She made some half-hearted comment about the cattle, how fat they looked this season. He tried to laugh with her.

But it didn't reach either of them.

He wanted to push. To ask again. To insist. But something in her posture stopped him. That wall she could throw up with nothing more than a glance.

And so, he didn't press.

He told himself—if she needs help, she'll tell me.

He told himself—I'll go see her next week. Make time. Properly check in.

But he didn't.

And that was the last time he ever saw her.

Alive.

Back in the present, James staggered back like the memory had hit him in the chest.

His breath caught, ragged and thin.

Then it came—the fury. The grief. The unbearable knowing.

He grabbed the nearest thing—a handled mug left by the fireplace—and hurled it against the far wall. It shattered into a storm of ceramic shrapnel.

James let out a roar—not of anger alone, but of heartbreak, helplessness, fury all tangled into something uncontainable. He turned and struck the wall with his fist—once, then again—until his knuckles punched straight through the plaster.

White dust exploded outward. A clean hole gaped in the wall like an open wound. His chest heaved, each breath sharp and useless.

Bear barked sharply from across the room, tail low, ears back. He paced toward James, whining, pawing at his boot with urgency—trying to anchor him back to the moment.

But it was too late.

The rage had taken over. Not the kind that demanded destruction, but the kind born from despair. From the feeling of being powerless to stop the same story from repeating itself.

"I should've stopped her!" he shouted, voice hoarse. "I should've done something!"

Bear whined louder, nose nudging at James's hand.

But James didn't feel it. Couldn't feel anything.

His strength gave out all at once.

He collapsed.

Straight to his knees, forehead pressed to the floor. His body trembled with the force of a storm finally spent.

The sobs came, uninvited but unstoppable. He didn't hide them.

Didn't try to be strong.

Not anymore.

And then—

when the weight had all but crushed him, when the panic had hollowed him out—

stillness.

Not from outside.

From within.

Like the moment after a storm, when all the trees are dripping and quiet and broken branches lie in the grass—but something sacred hovers in the silence.

A holy kind of hush.

Not relief.

Not explanation.

Just presence.

Like God was kneeling there beside him, not offering answers—just being.

And that was enough.

James opened his eyes.

The house still bore the signs of his pain—broken porcelain, scattered papers, a toppled chair.

But something inside him had calmed.

He moved slowly now. Gently.

He turned toward the phone.

Calling meant surrendering his pride. Meant admitting he couldn't fix this alone. Meant opening his hands and trusting someone else to hold what he couldn't carry anymore.

He picked up the receiver.

Dialled.

"Naomi?" he rasped, barely louder than a breath.

A pause. Then her voice—sure, steady.

"James?"

"Ruthie left," he said. "I tried to stop her. I really did. She just kept saying how she had to leave to protect us"

His throat tightened.

Silence on the other end.

"I don't know where she went," he added. "But maybe you do. I don't think she wants me to follow her."

Another pause. Then Naomi's breath—gentle, like a thread stitching him back together.

"I'll find her," she said softly. "She'll be okay. I will find her."

James closed his eyes.

This time, when he exhaled, the weight eased.

"Thank you," he whispered.

Not just to Naomi.

But to the One who had never left the room.

Chapter 23 – The Search and the Song

"He will cover you with His feathers, and under His wings you will find refuge." — Psalm 91:4

R uthie walked until her legs ached and her lungs burned.
The gravel road wound like a silver scar through the bushland, its edges blurred by overgrown grass and the hush of eucalyptus leaves swaying in the wind. Sunlight dappled the ground in shifting patches, flickering like broken promises. She kept her eyes forward, never once glancing back.

Not at the cottage.

Not at the man who had looked at her like she was worth waiting for.

His voice still clung to her skin like morning mist. She couldn't scrub it off—not the softness in it, not the steadiness, not the ache of him trying to hold the door open without pulling her through.

But hope like that was dangerous.

Out here, the silence stretched wide and deep, swallowing everything. Every rustle in the underbrush sounded louder, sharper—like the world was holding its breath.

Freedom had always sounded noble.

But this didn't feel like freedom.

It felt like exile.

Like abandonment.

Like the wind itself didn't want to know her name.

She had no map. No plan. Just a worn backpack, a half-empty water bottle, and a heart pounding out one terrified refrain: Disappear before Dylan finds you again.

Because he would.

He always did.

The water ran out before the hour turned. The sun climbed higher, cruel and relentless. The road shimmered like it might melt. Her feet blistered in her boots. Her shoulders throbbed from the weight of the bag. Sweat trickled down her spine, and her breath came in short, hot bursts.

But she kept walking.

Not for herself—she never walked for herself.

She walked to keep them safe.

James.

Naomi.

Even Bear.

Dylan had found her once. He'd waited, watched, calculated.

He would find her again.

And this time... she wouldn't let him destroy anyone else.

Alone is safer, she told herself for the hundredth time.

But even as the thought echoed, it didn't ring true.

Not anymore.

Back at the bookstore Naomi knew she had to find her.

The moment she hung up with James, it struck—deep in her chest, clear as the morning bell of a mission. Not panic. Not even urgency. Just a knowing.

She moved fast but unflustered. Two muesli bars. A water bottle. Keys in one hand, prayer in the other.

She didn't bother with the radio. The silence helped her listen.

"Lord," she whispered as the road unfurled before her, "give me the words. Not mine—Yours. No more, no less."

The sun cut through the windshield in gold shafts.

And then—ten minutes out of town—she saw her.

A slender figure moving along the edge of the road, shoulders hunched against a weight no one else could see. Her movements were uneven, tired. Her shirt clung to her back with sweat. Her head was bowed like she was trying to disappear into the dust.

Naomi slowed to a stop on the side of the road and left the door open behind her—wide.

She stepped out onto the shoulder, dust rising around her boots. A napkin fluttered in one hand.

"Hey," Naomi called, her voice calm but unwavering—like sunlight breaking through storm clouds. "Fancy seeing you here."

Ruthie didn't turn.

Her eyes stayed pinned to the horizon, glassy and distant, but Naomi saw it—the tremble in her shoulders, the way her spine locked like armour, the breath she drew in sharp and tight, like a thread ready to snap.

"I had to leave," Ruthie said finally, her voice dry and crumbling, like leaves that had forgotten how to be green. "He'll come back. And I can't—won't—let anyone else get hurt."

Naomi didn't step forward.

She leaned against the bonnet of the car, arms folded, still and grounded, like a redgum weathered by time but never broken. Her stillness didn't demand anything—it offered safety.

"You're not the storm, sweetheart," she said gently.

"You're the one who's survived it."

Ruthie's jaw clenched. Tears threatened but held. Like they didn't have permission to fall.

"I'm the damage," she whispered. "Everything I touch breaks."

Naomi didn't flinch. Didn't rush to rescue. She simply stayed, her breath a quiet rhythm in the wide silence.

"James is wrecked," she said after a beat, voice low.

"Not because of what you've done.

Because he thinks he's lost you."

133

Ruthie flinched. "He shouldn't care."

Naomi gave a soft shrug. "Maybe not. But love doesn't always wait for permission. It just shows up—and stays."

The air between them thickened. Not heavy with judgment, but sacred with truth.

Naomi's next words came like a balm:

"You don't have to apologise for being loved."

That undid her.

Ruthie's knees folded, slow and helpless, as if the weight of every unshed tear, every night spent gripping fear like a shield, had finally caught up to her. She sank into the dust like something unravelled.

Naomi moved without a word. She crouched beside her—not to fix, not to rush, but to be. A steady presence.

She wrapped one arm around Ruthie, not like someone cradling what's broken—but like someone holding what's sacred.

"It's okay," she said. "You don't have to carry this alone anymore."

Ruthie gave the faintest nod.

It wasn't peace.

But it was surrender.

Naomi stayed there in the silence with her, like prayer made flesh.

Then, gently:

"I know what it's like."

Ruthie blinked through tears. "What?"

Naomi met her eyes with a gaze that didn't flinch.

"Different man. Same ache.

I remember the eggshells underfoot. The bags packed in the dark. The stillness after shouting, louder than the noise ever was."

She didn't say it for sympathy. She said it for solidarity.

"This land saved me".

Not because it was soft. But because it gave me space to remember who I was before fear taught me how to disappear."

Ruthie didn't answer.

She didn't need to.

Naomi's voice softened, reverent:

"That's why James told me about you.

He knew you didn't need rescuing.

You needed reminding."

Two women.

Different scars.

Same sacred knowing.

Naomi offered a small, steady smile. The kind born from ashes.

"I came here hollow.

But the Lord, the land, and the love I found...

they filled the places I thought were lost forever."

She nodded toward the car.

"Come on, Ruthie.

There's nothing for you out here but shadows.

But back there—there's light.

There's love.

There's hope."

Ruthie stayed in the dust for a long, shaking breath. The wind caught her hair. The earth beneath her held steady.

Then—slowly, deliberately—

she stood.

And walked to the passenger side.

The drive back was wordless.

Naomi just kept the car steady, eyes on the road.

When they pulled into the driveway, James was already outside.

Pacing slow, restless circles like a man trying to hold himself together with movement.

Bear barked once from the porch.

Then launched—full sprint—across the gravel, tail like a banner in the wind.

James froze.

His eyes caught on the passenger door.

Ruthie stepped out, slow and unsteady. Her legs wobbled, her hands trembled—but she didn't hide it.

Their eyes met.

James didn't rush forward.

He didn't speak.

He waited.

Ruthie swallowed hard.

"I'm scared," she said softly.

"I know," he replied, voice tight.

"But you don't have to be alone in it."

Naomi stepped back allowing space for them both.

Ruthie looked at James.

"I'm not good at this," she said.

"Me either. But I want to try. If you'll let me." James replied.

Chapter 24 – The Breach

"The Lord is a refuge for the oppressed, a stronghold in times of trouble." — Psalm 9:9

The car ride into town was thick with unspoken things.

Ruthie sat in the back seat, spine stiff, hands balled tightly in her lap. On one side, Bear leaned into her leg, sensing the tension and grounding her with his silent loyalty.

James eyes didn't leave the road. Beside him, Naomi sat quietly, hands folded in her lap, her expression unreadable but her presence steady.

No one had said the word police since breakfast.

Ruthie had nodded her consent earlier—after Naomi had sat beside her on the weather-worn front steps, gently outlining the process. The paperwork. The risks. The limits of what the law could promise. What it couldn't.

Now, the town's police station rose in front of them—an unassuming building of brick and quiet authority.

James pulled into the car park and turned off the engine.

No one moved.

They waited—for her.

Ruthie's throat was dry. She reached for the door handle but hesitated. Her reflection in the glass showed a woman she barely recognised—pale, tired, a shadow of the person she used to be.

"You're not alone," Naomi said softly, without looking back. Just a statement. Solid and still.

Ruthie nodded once.

Then opened the door.

Inside, the station felt sterile and too bright.

A uniformed officer looked up from the front desk, eyes flicking over the trio.

James stepped forward first, voice low and firm. "We're here to report a domestic violence situation. Her ex—Dylan. She's ready to make a statement."

The name hit the air like the crack of a whip.

Ruthie flinched.

The officer's expression didn't shift. "Come have a seat and we will see what we can do."

Ruthie followed him numbly, every step like wading through mud.

The questions began without ceremony—each one careful, clinical, and piercing.

"Have there been previous reports?"

"What's the history of the abuse?"

"Was it physical? Emotional? Financial?"

Ruthie answered, voice uneven. She gave facts, not feelings. Bullet points, not stories. Just enough to get through. Her fingers twisted the hem of her sleeve.

Behind her, James stood tall and tense, arms crossed, every muscle coiled. Naomi hovered to the side, her presence soft but alert. Now and then, she rested a hand on the back of Ruthie's chair, silent reassurance pulsing through her fingertips.

Each answer felt like peeling back skin.

James's breathing grew heavier, nostrils flared.

Naomi's eyes shimmered with unspoken memories of her own grief and rage flickering beneath the surface.

Finally, the officer looked up from his notepad.

"May I take a look at your phone, ma'am?"

Ruthie blinked. "Why?"

"It's routine," he said gently. "Sometimes abusers leave digital footprints. We check for spyware, tracking apps—anything that might compromise your safety."

Her heart pounded in her chest like it wanted out.

She hesitated, then offered the phone.

The officer connected it to a computer. The screen flashed, then mirrored her device.

Time seemed to slow.

She hadn't texted Dylan. She hadn't replied to him. She'd done everything right—but fear didn't care about right. It bloomed in her chest, wide and choking.

The officer scrolled.

Silent.

Methodical.

Then he stopped.

"Did you install this app?" he asked, pointing to a small icon on the screen—something so ordinary-looking it barely registered. A nondescript cloud symbol. Could've been weather. Could've been a calendar.

Ruthie frowned. "No. I've never seen that."

He tapped it.

The app opened to a grim interface—GPS logs. Movement patterns. Time-stamped entries charting her every step.

Not weather.

Tracking.

Her stomach dropped so fast it left her dizzy.

The officer's face darkened. "This is a live feed," he said. "The app has been getting your location in real time and sending it to whoever installed this".

Naomi gasped softly.

Jame struggled to control the anger rising inside of him. His hand clenching into a fist.

"Want me to delete it?" the officer asked Ruthie.

She instantly nodded.

A few taps, and it was gone from the screen. But the violation lingered.

"We'll file for an emergency AVO," the officer continued. "That gives you immediate legal protection. You won't need to appear in court unless things escalate."

He paused, meeting her eyes. "If he breaches it—even once—you contact us. Immediately. No second-guessing."

Naomi reached over and gently folded Ruthie's hand into hers. She didn't let go.

The officer stood. "We'll handle the rest from here."

The door of the Ute slammed with a heavy finality as they all moved back to the car.

The cabin was silent.

Ruthie stared out the window, Bear's fur warm against her leg.

Then, in a voice like breaking glass: "He knew where I was."

Naomi turned, unwavering. "He doesn't anymore. And we'll make sure it stays that way."

They reached the farm just after ten.

The day was still. Too still.

James stepped out first.

His boots hit the ground, but he didn't take another step.

He froze.

The front door wasn't ajar—it was wide open. Gaping.

A breath caught in his throat. His gut twisted, tight and hard like a warning.

Something was wrong.

"Stay in the truck," he barked, voice leaving no room for debate.

Bear leapt out beside him, alert and silent. The dog's head lowered, sniffing the air while James moved forward, eyes scanning every corner of the yard.

No movement.

But inside?

Carnage.

Drawers yanked from their slots. The mattress overturned. Plates shattered like brittle bones across the floor. Books ripped from shelves. Ruthie's clothes strewn like confetti.

It wasn't just vandalism.

It was personal.

James stood in the doorway, breath short, fists clenched.

Naomi sat frozen in the Ute, the blood draining from her face. Her instincts screamed—something was wrong. Her hand flew to her chest, pressing hard, as if she could still the thundering rhythm of her heart.

Then something inside her cracked.

The fear wasn't just for Ruthie—it was her own ghost rising up, the shadow of everything she hadn't faced. Panic surged like cold water down her spine.

By the time she caught her breath and turned—

Ruthie was already gone. The door swung open behind her.

Ruthie stepped onto the porch like a ghost, feet moving of their own accord. Her eyes widened as she took in the wreckage.

Her safe place—violated.

James was already on the phone to police, while Ruthie stepped over the shattered porcelain, careful not to cut her feet.

A book lay open near the window—its spine cracked, pages fluttering.

On one page, black ink scrawled across the paper in furious strokes:

I know where you are, Ruthie.

BTW, you mess up my house, I'll mess up yours.

No name. No signature.

But there was no mistaking it.

It was Dylan.

Naomi stood just inside the door, a tremor running through her shoulders.

Bear whined softly and pressed against Ruthie's leg.

James lowered the phone. "They're on their way."

Ruthie didn't speak.

But the message had already been received.

Loud and clear.

And for the first time since she ran, Ruthie wasn't just afraid.

She was furious.

Chapter 25 – What's Left Behind

"So do not fear, for I am with you; do not be dismayed, for I am your God. I will strengthen you and help you; I will uphold you with my righteous right hand."— Isaiah 41:10

The sirens finally came —two police cruisers pulling up as the midday sun bled across the dirt. Doors slammed like gunshots. Radios murmured static and clipped commands. The world kept turning, but Ruthie couldn't.

She stayed hunched on the porch with her arms locked around her ribs, as if her body might fall apart without the pressure. Her eyes were fixed on the door—the way it still hung open, the damage, the message. That house that once felt safe wasn't anymore. It had been touched. Tainted.

The officers worked quickly, with that smooth, rehearsed rhythm that only made her feel more exposed. They were kind, but this wasn't about kindness—it was protocol. One documented the damage, flash after flash of a camera catching the horror in sterile detail. Another knelt, dusting for prints near the jagged edge of the broken window, gloved hands moving through the wreckage like a silent judge.

To them, this was just another case. To Ruthie, it was a breach—a threat and a line crossed.

Naomi stood close, not speaking, but her presence was the only thing keeping Ruthie from slipping. She wasn't crying anymore. The tears had been replaced by something colder. Something sharper.

It felt like her skin didn't fit right. Like she was stretched too thin, nerves exposed, every sound scraping raw. Even the breeze felt cruel.

James kept pacing. He needed something to fix. But there wasn't a broken gate or loose hinge that could take away the anger he felt.

Naomi watched Ruthie in silence, her chest tightening with each minute that passed. There was something fragile in Ruthie's stillness—like a thread pulled too tight, about to snap. Or maybe... maybe that was Naomi's own reflection staring back at her. Maybe it was her own ache she saw mirrored in Ruthie's trembling hands and hollow stare.

She reached out, her hand trembling despite herself, and placed it gently on Ruthie's shoulder. The contact was tentative, almost reverent.

"Breathe, Ruthie."

"I am," she murmured, though it wasn't true. Every breath was borrowed. Shallow. Fragile.

From the back of the house, a voice called out: "Scratches on the screen door. We'll lift them—possible prints."

James was already moving. "Do you have enough to find him?" His voice was tight, controlled.

The lead officer gave a curt nod. "We'll try."

The police stayed another hour. They logged evidence. Took statements. With each question from the police Ruthie spoke as if reading from a script—monotone, detached. As though describing someone else's nightmare.

They couldn't give her safety back. But they gave her something else—documentation. Proof that it wasn't all in her head. That someone had crossed a line.

By the time they left, the sky had shifted to burnt orange, shadows long and stretched like old wounds.

James offered the spare room. The couch. Anywhere she wanted.

She couldn't choose. She just nodded.

Naomi kissed her cheek goodbye, her voice soft but her eyes fierce. Inside, she felt scraped thin—pulled in too many directions, with nothing left to give. Her own needs were pressing against her ribs, but there was no space to speak them. Not today. Today Ruthie needed her.

That night was quiet—but it wasn't peaceful.

The silence wasn't soft or soothing—it was swollen. Pressurised. Every corner of the house pulsed with the ghost of what had happened. Shadows stretched longer than they should have. The wind outside didn't howl, but it watched.

Bear lay between them on the couch, his big head resting across James's boot like a sentinel. His ears flicked at every creak of timber, every gust that rattled the windowpanes. He didn't sleep. Neither did they.

The television played on mute, a flickering collage of forgotten stories. The light danced across their faces—pale skin, tight shoulders, eyes too full to blink.

James sat rigid, elbows on knees, hands steepled like a prayer he couldn't finish. He'd done what he could—swept the glass into a bin, collected the papers, shut the broken door with nails and effort. But now, with nothing left to fix, he stared at the floor like it might give him an answer he hadn't asked for.

Ruthie sat beside him, not touching. Her hands gripped the edge of the couch cushion, white-knuckled. Her entire body was wired and brittle, like one wrong move would send her shattering.

She couldn't stop thinking about Dylan. About the moment she realised that if she had stayed, he would have killed her. Not might. Would.

And then—James.

That day at the station. The moment that rerouted her life like a gust of wind catching a falling leaf.

He had saved her. But how? And why?

And beneath it all, behind the ache and fear, something older stirred—something she hadn't dared voice until now.

Eventually, she turned toward him, voice thin as spider silk.

"Can I ask you something?"

He didn't move at first. Then a slow nod, his eyes still fixed on the floor.

"Why me?" she asked, barely audible. "That day. At the train station. Why did you help me and not anyone else?"

James turned, and for a moment, his eyes met hers—but they didn't settle. They drifted past her, into the shadows of memory.

He swallowed hard.

"To be honest..." His voice cracked dry in his throat. "I didn't think. I just saw you. And you looked—" He shook his head, jaw twitching. "You looked like someone being dragged to the edge. Someone who wasn't going to make it through the day. And I knew that look. Too well."

He rubbed his palms together—slow, rough, like trying to scrub something invisible off his skin.

"I just... thought maybe this time I could step in before it was too late. Maybe I could do something right. For once."

Ruthie's chest tightened. A sob pressed behind her ribs, but she held it in. Her voice wavered.

"James... what really happened to Ellie?"

The name landed between them like a dropped glass.

James went completely still.

Ruthie softened her voice, gently. "Did the police ever tell you?"

He let out a slow, shaky exhale. "Yeah, they did."

His throat worked around the next words.

"I even read the autopsy report. Took me six tries to get through it. But I made myself read it."

Ruthie didn't flinch. She didn't fill the silence. She let him decide.

And after a moment, he nodded—like a man who knew the telling would break something but told it anyway.

"According to the report... it was bad. Really bad. He didn't just hit her once. It was over and over. Head, face, chest. The injuries were... significant."

He swallowed hard, voice catching.

"It wasn't quick, either. She didn't go right away."

A pause.

"She suffered. For hours."

Ruthie covered her mouth with her hand.

James stared straight ahead. His voice turned thin. Hollow.

"He left her there. Didn't call anyone. Didn't even try to help. Just walked away and let her die."

His hands trembled. He gripped his knees like he needed something to anchor him.

"She fought back."

His voice caught on the last word.

"They found bruises. Scratch marks. Skin under her fingernails."

A beat of silence.

"She tried to fight. She didn't go quietly."

Ruthie's tears came silently, slipping down her cheeks like they belonged to someone else.

James wiped at his face with the heel of his hand.

"When I saw you that day—standing there like the ground had opened beneath your feet and no one even noticed—it felt like watching it all over again. And I thought, not again. Not on my watch. Not her."

Ruthie reached for his hand in the dark. Her fingers found his—cold, calloused, trembling.

The room was quiet again but no longer empty.

"What happened to him?" She asked.

James blinked, slowly, like he had to translate the question.

"Ellie's... husband?" She clarified.

He exhaled.

"Hung himself. Three weeks after the sentencing. In his cell."

The TV flickered, casting restless shadows across the floor, like ghosts circling but never settling.

For a long time, neither of them moved.

Ruthie's thumb gently traced over the ridge of James's knuckles. It wasn't much. But it was something—a soft place in the wreckage.

They didn't speak again that night.

Not because there was nothing left to say.

But because there was too much.

And in that space, held between flickering light and the weight of their shared grief, they stayed—quiet, broken, and healing.

Together.

Chapter 26 – The Night Naomi Fell

"Praise be to the God and Father of our Lord Jesus Christ, the Father of compassion and the God of all comfort, who comforts us in all our troubles..." - 2 Corinthians 1:3–4

The wind changed on a Friday.

Not the kind that flutters curtains or stirs gum leaves in lazy rhythm—but the kind that slices through denim and needles the skin as it passes. Ruthie felt it before she named it. A shift. A warning.

She kept herself busy that day—laundry on the line, sweeping grit from the porch, scrubbing at that old stain on the counter that never quite lifted. All the while, she told herself it was just a breeze.

But deep down, she knew better.

It had been days since the break-in. The police had called once, flat-voiced and vague: "We don't believe Dylan is still in the area." No reassurance. Just words.

Everyone was trying to return to normal, but Ruthie couldn't shake the feeling that Dylan's damage wasn't done—not even close.

James was out repairing the front gate, staying within earshot of the house, just in case.

When Ruthie wandered over, arms crossed against the wind, she asked gently, "Hey... have you heard from Naomi? I haven't heard from her in the last 24 hours. I sent a couple of messages... no reply."

James paused mid-twist of wire and looked up, brow furrowed.

"Nah, I don't think so," he said after a moment. "But I've got to head into town anyway—need more wire for the fence. If you're up for it, we could swing by the bookshop. She's probably just busy."

But when they arrived, the bookshop was shut tight.

No Back in Five sign. Just the faded placard that read CLOSED, swinging slightly in the wind.

The shutters were drawn. Lights off. Door locked—from the inside.

Naomi's ute sat in its usual crooked way—one tyre hugging the gravel, the other buried in overgrown grass.

James narrowed his eyes.

Ruthie pressed her palm against the glass. Still. Silent.

"I'll check around back," James muttered, already striding toward the alley.

The alley behind the shop was damp and musty and littered with empty boxes.

When James tried the handle of the back door, it creaked open.

"She never leaves this unlocked," he said.

Inside, the air hit them like a slap—thick, sour, and suffocating. The acrid stench of stale alcohol clung to the air.

James hesitated, then turned to her, jaw tight. "Wait outside," he said quietly—more out of habit than hope.

But Ruthie didn't move. Didn't listen. She followed him in, the soles of her boots sticking slightly to the warped linoleum as they passed the counter and stepped into the back room.

And then they saw her.

Naomi.

Slumped over the table in the break room, motionless. One arm dangled limp at her side. Her head rested on a crooked elbow, hair falling like a curtain across her face. Beside her, a bottle—half-empty, tipped, its contents trailing dark and sticky down the wood like a quiet confession.

James exhaled hard. "Oh, you've got to be kidding me," he muttered, voice thick with something between sadness and restrained anger.

Ruthie's brow furrowed. "What's going on?"

James hesitated. Then:

"She told you it's been hard, yeah? But what she probably didn't say is... Naomi's an alcoholic. She was sober—for five years, I think."

Ruthie's heart sank.

"See, James?" she said with a hint of anger in her voice. "Me being here is just... causing more trouble."

James turned to her sharply. "Ruthie—don't. Don't take this on as your fault, it's not. Naomi needs us right now. That's the only thing that matters."

She nodded, swallowing shame.

James stepping forward.

"Naomi?" James called.

No answer.

He stepped closer. "Naomi?"

She flinched, then jerked upright—eyes glassy, bloodshot. Mascara streaked her cheeks.

"Heey..." she slurred, voice thick.

"Whatcha doin' here?"

"The shop was closed. We just wanted to make sure you were okay," Ruthie said gently.

Naomi laughed—a brittle, jagged sound. "That's a dangerous question..."

She downed the last of the bottle before James could stop her.

"That's enough," James said, stepping forward and gently taking the bottle.

"No," she snapped, shoving at his chest.

"I'm fine. I just... needed a break."

"You're not fine," Ruthie said, voice trembling but sure. "But you don't have to do this alone. Please... come with us."

Naomi's fight drained slowly.

"You don't understand," she said.

"I had it together. I just... needed a small drink."

Her voice broke slightly.

"You don't know how hard I've been struggling."

Tears spilled freely now.

"Ruthie..."

Her voice cracked, barely holding together.

"Come on... you know it. There's no escaping the fear of your abuser."

She reached out—unsteady.

James stepped in, firm. "Naomi. That's enough, you can barely stand."

"No!" she cried, her voice sharp with fury.

"You don't get to tell mee what to do!"

She spun wildly, knocking over a stack of books. A paperback flew across the room like a wounded bird.

And then—she crumpled. Rage fled. Sobbed against the floor.

James didn't hesitate. He bent low and lifted her gently.

Naomi clung to him. One small sob escaped. But it held everything.

Ruthie opened the back door, the breeze curling in—cool, steady, unearned.

Grace, brushing gently against the wreckage.

James eased Naomi into the back seat with the same care he might have used for someone wounded. She resisted at first—muttering something sharp and incoherent—but her body sagged, heavy with exhaustion and whatever pain still churned inside her. Ruthie climbed in beside her, pulling the door shut with a soft click that felt far too final. She reached for the flannel she'd kept in the car, worn and smelling faintly of lavender and wood smoke, and wrapped it gently around Naomi's trembling shoulders.

Naomi didn't speak. But she didn't push it away either.

Her breathing began to slow—just a little.

The drive back to the farm passed in a hush. Only the soft whirr of tyres and Bear's low whine filled the space. The landscape outside blurred into night. Streetlights and silhouettes flickered past, indifferent to the storm they carried inside the car.

Back at the farmhouse, the night stretched long and heavy.

Naomi unraveled in waves.

It began with defiance—shoulders tight, jaw clenched, sarcasm biting through every word. But the sharp edges softened, and the heat of her fury gave way to something deeper. Rawer. The kind of sorrow that came from the marrow.

She wept—not neatly, not quietly, but in heaving, broken sobs that shook her body and soaked Ruthie's sleeve. She wept for the girl she used to be. For the woman she was now. For Ruthie. For herself. For all the days she had survived when she didn't want to. For the years she had pretended the world was safe just because she'd learned to smile.

Her rage came next. She cursed God aloud—swearing at the ceiling with a fury that startled even James. Her voice cracked with bitterness; her fists pounded the wooden table until her knuckles turned red. Then, all at once, her body collapsed inward like a building giving way. She slid from the chair and curled on the floor, arms wrapped around her knees, whispering desperate, choked prayers through the sobs.

"Please," she whimpered. "Please, God. Please don't leave me like this."

James turned away, jaw tight, heart cracking. Ruthie knelt beside her friend, her hand a gentle weight on Naomi's back.

They didn't offer platitudes. They didn't try to fix it.

They just stayed.

Naomi swayed between worlds—shouting, crying, then falling silent, as if grief had hollowed her out completely. Sometimes she curled into the corner of the couch like a frightened child. Other times she sat upright, eyes far away, as though watching ghosts move through the room.

And then, a few hours before dawn, she crumpled. Her body gave out mid-sentence, her head falling back against the cushion. Sleep took her in the way exhaustion sometimes does—with no warning, no grace. Just silence.

Her chest rose and fell in slow, even breaths.

Spent.

Silent.

James and Ruthie stood nearby, shoulder to shoulder in the quiet. They didn't speak, not yet. It was the first time in hours they had dared to exhale, the tension in their bodies slowly unspooling.

Naomi wasn't drinking.

She wasn't raging.

She wasn't trying to escape herself anymore.

She was still.

And for now, that was enough.

Chapter 27 – Ruin and Resurrection

"Come, let us return to the Lord. He has torn us to pieces but he will heal us; he has injured us, but he will bind up our wounds."— Hosea 6:1

D awn came grey and cold.

The light arrived reluctantly, filtered through a blanket of low clouds that pressed against the windows. The kind of dawn that carried no promises, only quiet acknowledgment that another day had come, whether they were ready for it or not.

Ruthie shifted in the armchair, her neck stiff and her back aching. One foot had fallen asleep, tingling now with pins and needles. Her eyes fluttered open, gritty with exhaustion. For a moment, she forgot where she was—then the chill in the room and the lump in her throat reminded her.

James stirred in the opposite chair, one hand tucked beneath his chin, the other still resting on the armrest where he'd last reached toward Naomi in the night. His boots sat heavily on the floor, knees spread, posture slouched by hours of uneasy half-sleep. A blanket had slipped halfway down his chest. Bear lay between them, chin on his paws, watching the door with quiet vigilance.

The room still smelled faintly of salt and sweat and sorrow. The air was dry, as if the grief had soaked up all the moisture.

Naomi hadn't moved much since she passed out. She lay curled on the couch like a wounded animal, flannel pulled high over her shoulders, hair tangled across her face. Her breaths came soft and steady—too steady. Like her body had decided to shut down completely in order to survive the night.

The hours had passed in fragments.

Moments blurred together. Ruthie couldn't remember when the kettle had last boiled or whether she'd cried again or only thought about it.

Outside, the world was waking.

But inside the house, everything still felt suspended. Held in that strange space between collapse and recovery.

Ruthie rubbed her arms, pulling the oversized cardigan tighter around her. She glanced at James, who had cracked one eye open and was now watching Naomi, his face unreadable.

"She's still out," Ruthie whispered, voice hoarse.

James nodded. "Probably for the best."

Neither of them said what they were thinking—that when she woke, the pain would come rushing back. That sometimes, sleep was the only kindness trauma allowed.

Ruthie stood slowly, stretching the ache from her back, then reached to gently adjust the blanket over Naomi's shoulder.

She didn't stir.

James then moved to the kitchen, fingers fumbling for the kettle While Ruthie went and slid some bread into the toaster.

Then came the sound.

A soft, guttural groan.

Naomi stirred, blinking against the morning light. Her face was a shadow of itself—pale, sallow, bruised beneath the eyes. Every movement looked like it hurt.

She sat up slowly, one hand bracing her forehead, the other trembling as she reached for the edge of the table.

Ruthie wordlessly slid a mug of coffee toward her, the steam rising between them.

They sat in stillness. No one rushed to fill it.

Then, in a voice dry and cracked from dehydration and shame, Naomi spoke.

"I'm so sorry." Her gaze didn't lift from the table. "I'm sorry you had to see me like that. I really thought I had it under control." Her voice broke. "That was my first mistake."

Ruthie reached for her hand—cool, unsteady—and squeezed.

"I'm sorry too," she whispered. "I'm sorry I brought all this here. That it hit you so hard you—"

"No," Naomi cut in, shaking her head, voice firmer now despite the quiver. "No one makes you drink. That's not how addiction works. I've lived with this demon long enough to know better. I picked up the bottle. That was me. My choice."

Tears shimmered at the corners of her eyes, but she didn't blink them away.

"I can only imagine what you must both think of me."

Ruthie's voice softened. "You're Naomi. The kindest, wisest woman I've ever met." Her voice cracked. "And I love you."

James leaned forward, rubbing a hand down his tired face. "Come on, mate—we've been through too much together. You've held me up when I had nothing left. This isn't about judgment. You're human. We all fall. What matters is that we get back up. Let's get some food into you, and then I'll drive you to see Pastor Luke. Sound good?"

Naomi nodded, eyes wet but no longer drowning.

James smiled faintly. "Love you, mate."

She exhaled through a broken smile. "Love you too."

After breakfast, they drove in near silence, the hum of the engine blending with the rustle of eucalyptus and the haunting cry of magpies along the fence line. The road was still damp from overnight mist, the gravel whispering under the tyres.

James turned into the familiar gravel lot beside the old country church. It stood quiet, humble—its white weatherboard exterior chipped by wind and time, the tin roof humming softly in the breeze. A simple wooden cross rose from the peak of the roof, steady against the open sky. The front steps creaked as the wind passed through, and the porch, lined with worn benches, looked like it had held generations of weary souls.

Sunlight filtered through clear glass windows trimmed in timber, casting clean light onto the entryway. There was no grandeur, no ceremony—just peace. Honest, unpolished peace. The kind that smelled like timber floors and old hymn books.

Ruthie hesitated at the threshold.

She had never stepped into a church before. Not as a child. Not even when she was searching for something she couldn't name. And yet... her feet moved. Not with confidence, but with a strange, quiet pull. Like the place was calling her home without words.

The scent met her first—aged timber warmed by the sun, faint traces of brewed coffee from a distant pot, and something older still... maybe hope. Maybe heartache. It lingered in the air like memory.

Worn floorboards creaked beneath her steps, echoing with the weight of years. The pews weren't grand—just simple timber, polished smooth by decades of sitting, kneeling, weeping.

She followed James and Noami down a narrow side hallway, the office door stood open.

Pastor Luke rose from behind a desk crowded with open Bibles, yellowing sermon notes, and a mug that read Grace Upon Grace. He was tall, broad-shouldered, with the kind of eyes that had cried with people in hospital rooms and held hands at gravesides.

"James," he greeted warmly. "And Naomi. It's good to see you."

Then he turned to Ruthie and smiled—not the way strangers smile, but like he'd already prayed for her without knowing her name.

"And you must be Ruthie. I've heard such beautiful things. Welcome."

Ruthie flushed, caught off guard by his sincerity. "Thank you. It's... good to meet you."

He motioned to a small circle of armchairs. "Come, sit."

Pastor Luke turned to Naomi, his tone shifting—softer, more reverent.

"I heard it's been a heavy few days."

Naomi gave a fragile nod. "I failed," she whispered. "I let everyone down and worse I let God down."

Her hands twisted in her lap, ashamed.

Pastor Luke leaned forward, elbows resting on his knees, voice thick with grace.

"Oh, Naomi. You know that's not true."

She looked up, her expression hollow and aching.

"God's love doesn't flinch," he said. "It's not shaken by our failure. It doesn't withdraw when we fall apart."

He paused, letting the weight of it settle.

"He knows how broken we are. And He still chose the cross. He still chose you. Not when you're perfect. Not when you've cleaned yourself up. Right here. In the ruin."

Naomi wept silently.

"You haven't shocked Him," he said, voice cracking slightly. "You haven't disappointed Him. You're His daughter. And nothing—nothing—can separate you from that love."

Ruthie sat still, barely breathing. The words soaked into places she hadn't let anyone touch.

Pastor Luke leaned back, gentle and sure.

"You're not a failure, Naomi. You're a testimony waiting to bloom."

Naomi broke. But it wasn't collapse. It was release.

James lowered his head. Ruthie reached for Naomi's hand.

And then—Pastor Luke began to pray.

Not in thunder. Not in polished cadence.

But in something raw and real.

The prayer trailed into silence, thick with something holy. Not the kind that needed incense or stained glass. Just presence. Undeniable and tender.

No one rushed to speak. Even the creak of the old walls seemed to hush, as though the church itself was listening.

Naomi sat crumpled but lighter, her tears still falling, but no longer from shame. Ruthie could feel her hand pulsing with life, not despair.

Pastor Luke didn't fill the quiet.

He let it stretch—gentle, unhurried—like someone who understood that healing didn't grow in noise.

When Naomi finally lifted her head, her voice was barely a rasp. "I don't even know where to start."

"You don't have to," he said gently. "Not all at once."

And then he waited again. No urgency. No expectation. Just presence.

After another long pause, he took out his small notebook and flipped it open, the pages soft with use.

"I've booked some one-on-one sessions for you, Naomi," he said, voice low and warm. "Over the next couple of days, if you feel ready. Nothing formal. Just space to talk, cry, breathe. We'll take it slow."

Naomi gave a small nod—tired, but real. It was the first decision she'd made all day.

"Okay," she said.

Luke smiled, soft and understanding. "Okay."

And with that, the silence settled again—but this time, it felt lighter.

The days that followed moved like healing—slow, uncertain, sacred.

Naomi stayed on the farm, wrapped in the rhythm of earth and sky. The stillness helped.

Pastor Luke visited each morning—sometimes with a Bible, sometimes just to sit.

Every evening, Margaret and Neil appeared with food—roasted root vegetables, warm broth, lentil pies, and bread that smelled like safety.

Naomi cried. Slept. Sat in silence. And, slowly, laughed again.

On the fourth morning, she stepped onto the porch, coffee in hand, and said, "I think I need to go back."

Ruthie looked up. James paused mid-task.

Naomi didn't waver.

"I need to return. To the bookshop. To my own space. My life."

James studied her. "Are you sure?"

Naomi nodded. "I'm not leaving empty. I'm leaving held. Held by prayer. By grace. By you two."

She looked at each of them. Her voice trembled, but her footing didn't.

"I needed a place to fall. And you gave me one. I won't forget that."

Ruthie reached for her hand. "You're braver than you think."

Naomi smiled, blinking against the morning light.

"I don't feel brave. But I feel... loved. And maybe that's the same thing."

They stood in the golden hush of morning, the paddocks stretching wide before them, the wind stirring gently through the gum trees.

And life, impossibly, began again.

Chapter 28 – The Waiting Place

"The Lord is good to those whose hope is in him, to the one who seeks him; it is good to wait quietly for the salvation of the Lord."— Lamentations 3:25–26

Naomi had returned to her little weatherboard cottage and the soft, familiar rhythm of the bookshop. It wasn't healing—not exactly—but it was something steady. Something she could hold onto when everything else felt too loose to grasp.

Ruthie and James checked in daily, never empty-handed—scones wrapped in tea towels, flowers from the paddock, a thermos of coffee still warm. Small, unspoken kindnesses offered without fanfare. It was care in its simplest form. And for Ruthie, it became more than care. It became an anchor.

Looking after Naomi gave Ruthie something to focus on. Something that pulled her forward. Pouring energy into someone else meant she didn't have to sit too long in the silence of her own mind, where fear lived like an echo.

She didn't have to ask the questions that crouched behind every door. Questions with sharp edges—about Dylan. About where he was. About when the next fracture might crack open beneath her feet.

Some mornings, she forgot.

Just for a moment, she believed the world was ordinary again.

Then the silence would remind her.

The house had been repaired. The broken glass swept. The door rehinged. The mattress replaced. But something still hummed beneath the surface. A picture frame just slightly crooked. A tightness under her ribs. A breath that stopped halfway and never quite made it home.

Healing didn't come in clean lines. It came in fragments—in haunted mornings, hollow evenings, in pretending she was okay because pretending was easier than falling apart.

And yet, slowly, life returned.

Bear began to match her rhythms again, his tail thumping against the floor when she crossed the room. The chickens came when she called. Margaret stopped by with bread and gentle company. Neil left tools and quiet encouragement. Micah brought his awkward humour like medicine he hoped she wouldn't notice.

Each evening ended with a call to Naomi—sometimes filled with words, sometimes with silence. But it mattered. Their rhythm wasn't loud.

But it was real.

One warm afternoon, Ruthie wandered the property alone. The breeze stirred the grass. The light turned gold. But inside her, thoughts still swirled—about Naomi, about Dylan, and about a deeper question that had begun to rise to the surface.

Something had started to shift weeks ago—since Pastor Luke had spoken life into Naomi's shame. Since Ruthie had opened the Bible and found not condemnation, but compassion. Not distance—but a God who drew near to pain.

She didn't understand it all. But she felt it.

Like a door cracking open somewhere deep inside her soul.

Drawn by something she couldn't name, Ruthie found herself walking toward the barn.

Inside, dust spun in the shafts of afternoon light. James was working, sleeves rolled up, brow furrowed. He looked up when she entered, but didn't speak.

He waited.

"James," she said finally.

She hesitated. "I know you believe in God... but I need to ask—how?"

She stepped closer. The scent of hay and warm earth grounded her.

"After everything," she whispered. "Ellie. Your dad. How do you still believe?"

James leaned against a timber beam, his posture loosening.

"Honestly?" he said, scratching at the back of his neck. "I do. But it's not easy. Some days it's a choice I make with clenched fists."

She listened, heart quiet.

"I've seen darkness," he said. "Not just pain—but evil. And the only thing that made sense of it... was knowing that for evil to exist then good had to exist as well."

He looked down.

"When Ellie was alive, my faith felt... clearer. She made it easier. But when she died, it got messy. I drifted. Still do sometimes."

Ruthie lowered herself onto a hay bale.

"I want to believe," she said. "But when I try, all I feel is doubt. Silence."

James nodded. "I've been there."

"I prayed the night I ran," she said, voice cracking. "Begged God to help me. Promised everything if He just made a way. And I thought maybe He did—maybe this farm, maybe you... were part of that answer."

She blinked hard. "But Dylan's still out there. The fear still comes. And it makes me wonder if God even heard me."

James knelt beside her.

"I asked the same thing when Ellie died," he said. "I stood over her grave asking why prayers weren't enough. Why the good ones get hurt. Why evil gets away with so much."

He looked toward the barn doors, where the sun dipped low behind the trees.

"I don't have all the answers. But I do know this—God doesn't promise we won't bleed. He promises we won't bleed alone."

He looked back at her, steady.

"And sometimes... when we're still enough, when the noise dies down, He comes close. Not always with answers. But with Himself."

Ruthie wiped at her eyes.

James's voice dropped low. "He's not asking for perfect faith. Just honesty. He already knows what's in your heart. He just wants you to bring it."

She stared at her hands.

"What if all I have is a whisper?"

"Then whisper," he said, his voice thick. "It's more than enough."

He swallowed hard. "I used to think faith was armour. That if I prayed hard enough, nothing could touch me."

He shook his head.

"But it's not armour. It's presence. It's choosing to believe that even when the world breaks wide open, God doesn't walk away."

Ruthie looked at him, eyes glassy.

"And that's enough for you?"

He gave a tired smile. "Not always. But it's enough to keep lighting a candle in the dark."

Her chin trembled. "I want to believe that. Even if the flame flickers."

James placed his hand near hers—not touching, just close enough to feel the warmth.

"If that's all you have," he said gently, "then maybe it's already enough."

And for the first time in days—

Since the fear.

Since the waiting began—

Ruthie took a breath that didn't burn.

By that Friday, the sky had softened—not just above her, but within her.

She was coming home.

Not just to the farm. Not just to her body. But to God.

Memories still clung like smoke after fire. Dylan's shadow hadn't vanished—it still lingered like a question mark in the back of her mind. But something was shifting. Not fast. But sure.

She read the Bible in the quiet hours before dawn.

She'd expected rules and reprimands. What she found instead was rebellion wrapped in compassion. A love that sat beside lepers. A Messiah who touched the untouchable. A God who didn't flinch at brokenness—but moved toward it.

It undid her.

This Jesus... He wasn't afraid of the dark.

And maybe—just maybe—He wasn't afraid of hers either.

She prayed now with honesty. No filter. No formality. And somewhere in the space between Scripture and tears, Ruthie found something stronger than survival.

She found the edges of renewal.

And James saw it.

In her stillness.

In her questions.

In the way she whispered God's name not like a burden—but like it soothed something raw inside her.

His own faith, dulled by time and grief, began to flicker again.

The world that had once felt like a battlefield now shimmered with quiet, sacred rhythms. Not perfect. Not painless. But steady. And in that steadiness, something inside Ruthie began to heal—not through grand moments or declarations, but through small, ordinary acts that grounded her in the present.

Ruthie had started working at the bookshop beside Naomi—just a few hours at first, a gentle re-entry into the world. It had been Naomi's idea.

"Come in. Help me shelve books. Drink tea. That's all," she'd said with a half-smile and a wink.

When Ruthie mentioned it to James, he was genuinely happy for her. She could see it in the way his eyes softened—how her excitement brought a lightness to his face. But he made one quiet request: that she take Bear with her. Not because he doubted her strength, but because knowing Bear was by her side brought him peace of mind.

So Bear became part of the daily rhythm—trotting beside her into the shop, settling under the counter, keeping quiet watch.

Ruthie shelved poetry with reverence, the tender lines soothing something inside her. She brewed tea for regulars who spoke in low voices and loved the smell of old pages. She dusted forgotten corners and alphabetised fiction with quiet satisfaction, grinning each time Naomi teased her for reorganising the cookbooks—again.

In those small, repetitive motions—placing a book on a shelf, wiping down the counter, pouring warm chai into mismatched mugs—Ruthie found something she hadn't felt in a long, long time.

Purpose.

The first time Naomi handed her an envelope with her name on it—her first pay—Ruthie stared at it in stunned silence. It wasn't about the money, though it helped. It was the weight of the moment. The ordinary sacredness of being trusted. Needed. Valued.

She took the envelope home and laid it on the table, fingers brushing the paper like it might vanish. That night, when the house was quiet and Bear had curled up at her feet, she lit a candle, opened her Bible, and whispered, "Thank You."

The words came easy—simple, soft, true.

She didn't have all the answers. She still carried fear. Still startled at unexpected sounds. But now, her days held shape. Her heart had a rhythm. And in the stillness of that rhythm, she began to hear God.

Not in thunder. Not in visions.

But in the rustle of pages and the smile of a stranger.

In the warm mug between her palms.

In the gentle joy of showing up and being seen.

Chapter 29: The Reckoning

"The Lord is my rock, my fortress and my deliverer; my God is my rock, in whom I take refuge..." - Psalm 18:2

The weeks passed—quiet, but significant.

Ruthie had been inching her way deeper into faith. Not in grand declarations or polished prayers, but in quiet, unsteady surrender. She opened her Bible each morning, not out of obligation, but hunger. At night, she whispered jagged prayers—sometimes only a breath, sometimes just His name.

It was enough—and it was renewing her. But it wasn't the only thing reshaping her days. Her work at the bookshop was giving form to the quiet restoration taking place within her.

She loved the bookshop. Its dusty corners, chipped mugs, and creaky floors gave her something solid to stand on. Naomi's warmth. The soft shuffle of browsing customers. The scent of worn pages. All of it stitched something steady back into her life.

She was rebuilding.

Until everything shattered.

Midday sunlight spilled across the bookshop floorboards. Soft jazz crackled from the old speakers. Naomi hummed off-key while reshelving mislabelled cookbooks.Her first day back for the week had passed without incident—quiet, uneventful. And that was exactly what she needed.

Ruthie moved with ease—recommending novels, smiling at teenagers hunting for fantasy trilogies, and gently teasing a grumpy crossword enthusiast into buying a local poetry chapbook with nothing more than an eyeroll over bad cover art.

Then 1:45 p.m. rolled around, Naomi slung her bag over her shoulder, keys jingling.

"Off to the bank. Back in twenty," she called. "Don't alphabetise yourself into a coma."

Ruthie grinned from behind the counter. "No promises."

The bell above the door jingled. Then silence.

She turned back to the returns pile—tattered poetry collections, dog-eared local histories.

She smiled. For a moment.

Then the clock hit 2:00.

Like always, she reached for the rubbish bag, tied it off, and stepped into the alley out back.

No tension.

No fear.

Just routine.

Inside, Bear stirred from his nap but didn't move—too drowsy in the patch of sun that warmed the shop floor.

The alley stretched out before her—narrow, hemmed in by weather-beaten brick walls and cracked concrete that bore the stains of time.

Ruthie stepped outside, her mind still lingering on the bookshop's warmth—the gentle music, Naomi's humming, the soft scratch of pencil as she'd been scribbling a book recommendation on a post-it.

Then she saw it.

A white car.

Sitting just beyond the back door. Silent. Unmoving.

Her breath snagged in her throat.

Her whole body went still, every nerve snapping to attention, tingling with the kind of knowing that comes before thought.

It was him.

The door of the car burst open so fast it made the air shudder. A figure unfolded from the driver's seat—familiar, dark, looming.

A shadow uncoiling.

Before she could react, before her brain could even form the word run, a hand clamped down over her mouth—rough, calloused, unyielding.

"Miss me?" Dylan's voice rasped against her ear, his breath hot and sour, curling across her skin like poison.

Panic detonated in her chest.

She thrashed. Kicked. Her elbow cracked hard into his side. He growled but held on, fists digging into her hair like claws.

Dylan grunted loudly as he dragged her backwards.

She screamed against his palm, muffled but furious, her whole body resisting.

The garbage bag slipped from her grasp and burst across the pavement—old newspapers, orange peels, torn packaging—scattering like confetti from a nightmare.

One of her shoes came off as she stumbled, her bare foot scraping against the rough concrete.

He wrenched the car door open with one hand, yanked her toward it with the other.

She shrieked, the sound tearing from her throat as she wrenched free of his grip. It was primal—raw—a cry that ripped through the air with desperate force. It didn't just come from her lungs; it came from somewhere deeper, somewhere ancient and afraid, echoing with everything she'd never been able to say until now.

Then the car door slammed shut.

A terrible click followed—final, unyielding.

Locked.

She scrambled for the handle, pulled with shaking fingers, desperation clawing at her throat. But it wouldn't open. No matter how hard she yanked, it stayed shut, trapping her inside.

Everything outside turned blurry behind the tinted windows—just smudges of colour and light. The world she'd just been part of was suddenly unreachable.

Dylan slid into the driver's seat without a word.

His eyes were dead.

The tyres screeched as he tore out of the alley.

And Ruthie—

Ruthie wasn't just afraid anymore.

She was stolen.

Inside the bookshop, Bear's whole body vibrated with panic. He barked—loud, guttural. He hurled his weight against the back door, claws raking at the wood, wild with rage and instinct.

Fifteen minutes later, Naomi stepped through the front door, her voice light.

"Sorry that took so long!" she called out, juggling her keys and shopping bag. "Neil was talking my ear off about the wheat crop again—"

She stopped mid-step.

The air had changed.

The quiet wasn't peaceful.

It was suffocating.

No humming.

No sound of shelving. No quiet laugh from behind the counter.

No Ruthie.

Naomi's smile fell away. She glanced around, her gut tightening. "Ruthie!?"

Nothing.

The silence felt wrong. Not empty—vacant.

She hurried toward the back, each step a little quicker than the last. Bear's barking grew louder, desperate, echoing through the corridor like an alarm.

She flung open the back door—and froze.

The bag Ruthie had been holding lay ripped open, limp like a warning flag.

And near the edge of the doorway, almost too easily missed, lay one of Ruthie's shoes.

Abandoned.

Naomi staggered back a step, the sight sinking in like ice water down her spine.

Her lungs seized.

"GOD... NO!," she yelled, eyes wide, chest trembling.

Bear shot past her like a bolt, teeth bared, barking down the alley with pure fury.

Naomi didn't hesitate.

She grabbed her phone, fingers fumbling but fast as she dialed triple zero. Her voice to the dispatcher was clipped, firm, automatic.

But inside?

Inside she was unraveling.

Because this wasn't a misunderstanding.

This wasn't Ruthie stepping out for a moment.

This was real.

And Ruthie—

Kind, brave and loving Ruthie—

Was gone.

Chapter 30: The Turning

"I sought the Lord, and he answered me and delivered me from all my fears." – Psalm 34:4

The road blurred past the window.

Trees became streaks. Signs unreadable.

Ruthie pressed herself into the passenger door, willing her body to vanish into the vinyl.

The silence in the car wasn't peace—it was suffocating.

Broken only by the tyres' roar and a persistent rattle in the dash.

And still, Dylan didn't look at her.

Until finally she asked, "wher...where are we.. g-going?" Her voice was no louder than the air between them—thin, brittle, shaped more by fear than breath.

Dylan's grip on the wheel tightened, knuckles pale against the leather. His leg bounced, erratic and restless—tension simmering just beneath the surface.

Then he looked at her. Not with love. Not even recognition. Just eyes—hollow, darkened by anger and something far more dangerous.

Ruthie didn't really need an answer. She already understood.

He wasn't heading toward a place. He was heading toward a feeling.

Control.

Dominance.

Retribution.

She studied him from the corner of her eye—the sharp angles of his face now distorted by rage, the barely contained tremor in his limbs. He was a live wire, fraying from the inside out. And she was strapped beside him, caught in the current.

He was unravelling.

And he wanted to pull her down with him.

"I didn't ask for this,"

he snapped, his voice jagged and brittle.

"You made me do it. You should've just shut up and stayed put."

Ruthie turned her head to the window, trying to steady her breath.

She counted the white lines flicking past on the roadside to anchor herself in the chaos before responding.

"I didn't leave to hurt you," she said, barely audible.

He scoffed—a sharp, ugly sound.

"You made me look like a monster."

"You did that yourself!!"

She said it louder this time, with more authority.

She knew the moment the words left her mouth that they wouldn't go without punishment.

His hand shot across the seat like a whip—fingers clawing into her hair. He yanked her violently.

The car veered, tyres screaming as they kissed the gravel shoulder.

Her heart slammed against her chest.

"Don't talk to me like that!"

He bellowed, voice breaking. Spit flecked his lips. His eyes—bloodshot, wide, wild—darted over her, through her.

His hand slammed her head against the window as he yelled—loud, furious, and incomprehensible. The words didn't matter. The violence did.

Making a loud cracking sound.

The sound echoed in her skull.

A white flash exploded behind her eyes.

The world blurred.

She tried to curl away, but the seatbelt locked her in place.

Trapped.

Then came the slap.

Hard and hot across her face.

It snapped her head sideways, knocked the taste from her mouth, and blurred her vision with tears she hadn't yet released.

Pain radiated outward like fire—across her jaw, down her chest, and into the already-bruised flesh of her ribs.

She trembled, fists clenched in her lap.

Then, without another glance her way, Dylan turned his attention back to the road. He fished a battered pack of cigarettes from his jacket pocket—only one left. He lit it with a snap of his lighter, smoke curling upward as he inhaled deeply. The car filled with the sharp tang of tobacco. His voice resumed, low and venomous, continuing his barrage of insults like it was the only language he knew.

Ruthie no longer heard the words. Inside, there was only pain, fear, and the blur of violence—flooded with questions:

Would she ever see James again?

Would she ever laugh with Naomi again?

Would she ever run her fingers through Bear's fur?

Hopelessness and helplessness swept over her. Her mind circled the thought that maybe... maybe this was the end.

But then—

A whisper.

A breath.

Not even words at first—just a sound shaped like surrender.

Her thoughts drifted to Jesus—softly at first, like a memory she hadn't known she needed.

Then came the words from the Gospel of Luke, chapter 12, verses 4 to 7:

"Do not be afraid of those who kill the body and after that can do no more..."

The truth struck her now, clearer than ever: Dylan could hurt her body, yes—but he couldn't touch her soul.

Even here, even now, she still had power.

Power in her choice.

Power in her prayer.

Power in her faith.

And in that moment, something within her lifted. A defiant whisper of hope.

She closed her eyes.

"God, help me.

Please don't leave me.

Please... hold me."

No lights split the sky. No sudden rescue.

But somewhere deep inside, the trembling began to still.

She wasn't alone. Not really. Not ever.

A hush wrapped around her soul—an invisible hand steadying her in the storm.

Dylan kept shouting. The car kept moving.

But the noise dulled.

She closed her eyes.

"God...... help me!" she said again.

This time, it wasn't a plea.

It was an invitation.

A cry for presence.

A declaration of defiance—not to Dylan, but to the darkness itself.

Up ahead, the road curved.

A blue sign flickered on the roadside:

SERVICE STATION – 1 KM

She opened her eyes.

Blood coated her lip.

Pain pulsed through her ribs.

But something steadier had settled in her spine—quiet, sure, immovable. A knowing had risen from somewhere deep inside her, anchored in resolve.

"I know you, Dylan," Ruthie said quietly, her voice stripped of fear but not of weight. It was steady, even—too even. "You don't mean this."

Her throat was dry, her heart hammering in her chest, but she kept her face soft. Careful. Controlled.

"I'm sorry I left," she said, the words tasting bitter in her mouth. "I know that must've felt like a betrayal to you."

"But, we can talk this through," she added, nodding slowly, as if she meant it. "We can work this out."

Ruthie didn't believe a word of what she was saying but, she needed him calm, and she needed time.

Dylan's eyes twitched, scanning her face for something—maybe sincerity, maybe fear. She didn't flinch.

"Right now..." she continued, tone almost coaxing, "you need a smoke. I can tell—you've gone through your last one."

She glanced toward the dash. No cigarette pack in sight. Just his twitchy fingers grasping the steering wheel, that restless energy she knew too well.

Dylan didn't respond.

She stared straight ahead, eyes locked on the cracked dashboard, willing her hands to stay still.

"There's a servo coming up, you can buy some smokes, and I can go to the bathroom and clean myself up."

He didn't answer.

She inhaled slowly. Then said, steady and deliberate:

"Listen. If I bleed in your car, they'll trace it. Or someone driving past might see and call the cops."

Her voice firm but not cruel.

"I know you're sorry. I know you don't want to look at me, like this the whole way... wherever it is we're going."

She turned her head, just slightly.

"Just, let me clean myself up."

He looked over.

His eyes scanned the damage—her swelling cheek, the cut on her lip, the red bruises forming just beneath her scarf.

A flicker of calculation passed over his face.

"You'll get two minutes. You try anything and I promise you will regret it,"

he snapped.

The servo loomed into view—buzzing with tired fluorescent lights, its cracked pavement stained with oil and wear. A rusted sign creaked in the wind.

Dylan pulled in hard. The car lurched as the tyres crunched over the pavement, parking crooked and close, angled like a trap reset.

He paused before opening his door and glanced at Ruthie, his eyes dark and cold.

"Don't even think about running,"

he said, voice low and venomous.

"The door's locked—and I know exactly where your little farmer and his friends live."

His words dripped with threat. Not anger. Not even warning.

Promise.

Then he stepped out, slammed the door shut, and locked it from the outside. The keys jingled in his fist with cruel certainty.

Through the glass, Ruthie watched him approach the shop attendant. His mouth moved—calm, almost friendly. Too smooth. Too practiced.

Ruthie tried to open the door, but it wouldn't budge. She quietly scanned the car, careful not to draw any suspicion from Dylan, who kept glancing back.

Moments later, he walked out with the bathroom key swinging from a stained blue tag, worn and chipped at the edges while sliding a pack of smokes into his pocket.

She sat frozen, hands trembling, heart pounding like it was trying to break through her ribs.

Click.

The door opened.

He didn't speak—just jerked his head toward the side of the building.

She stepped out, every movement deliberate. Her limbs screamed. Her ribs throbbed where his hands had bruised her. Her feet felt unsteady, like she was walking through deep water.

He shoved her into the bathroom.

"I'll be right outside the door, and I'll hear everything. Don't go doing anything stupid,"

he hissed, then slammed the door shut.

Fear had done its job.

As the door slammed shut, she collapsed.

Her knees hit the cold tile with a dull thud, and before she could stop it, a sob ripped free—quick, sharp, as if it had been waiting just beneath her ribs all along.

Not weakness.

Release.

After a minute, she stood up and caught her reflection in the mirror.

Her lip was split and raw.

A deep purple bruise was darkening along her cheek.

Her eyes, bloodshot and rimmed with tears, stared back at her—wide, shaken, but unbroken.

Still breathing.

Still standing.

"Lord, please," she whispered, gripping the edges of the sink as though it might anchor her. "Please show me the next step."

She scanned the small bathroom, her pulse pounding in her ears.

First, she turned to the toilet and stepped up cautiously onto the lid, her bare feet slipping slightly on the plastic surface. She reached toward the window above it—a narrow rectangle near the ceiling, glazed with privacy glass. She pressed her fingers against the latch. Locked. Even if it opened, it was barely wider than her shoulders. No way out. Not this way.

Her breath came faster as she stepped down again, glancing back toward the door. No sound from Dylan. Not yet.

She dropped to her knees and yanked open the cupboard beneath the sink, rummaging through a jumble of half-used cleaning supplies—sponges, gloves, a bottle of bleach. Nothing useful.

Then her eyes darted upward.

There—on the back of the door.

A laminated cleaning checklist hung from a metal clip, off centre slightly from when Dylan had slammed the door earlier.

She rose and stepped closer, her hands trembling.

She peeled the plastic back and slipped out the sheet of paper.

Wedged behind the cardboard: a cheap blue pen.

A single chance.

She steadied her hand against the wall and began to write in large, urgent letters:

Kidnapped. White car. Dylan Watts. Please help. Call police.

She paused, then underlined please and included the date.

Her heart pounded as she slid the paper back behind the plastic cover, smoothing it carefully so it stood out.

She stepped back, staring at the door like it might betray her.

The window was too high.

The door too solid.

But the words were there now—waiting. A whisper on paper. A cry for help.

Dylan stood just outside, the shadow of his boots visible beneath the gap.

Then—BANG.

His fist crashed against the door. Once. Twice. The frame rattled beneath the force.

Ruthie didn't flinch.

She wouldn't give him the satisfaction.

Instead, she smoothed her shirt with trembling fingers, willing her breath to stay steady. Her palm pressed once more against the cool porcelain sink—anchoring her, grounding her.

Then she turned the lock and opened the door.

And stepped out, praying the note would be enough…

He was on her instantly—rough fingers clamping around her arm.

His grip was like a chain, biting into bruises that hadn't yet formed.

He yanked her forward, then shoved past her into the bathroom, scanning the space for evidence she might have left behind.

Ruthie subtly wedged her foot against the door, keeping it from closing all the way. Praying he wouldn't look behind it.

Then—a sound.

Distant, but real.

She seized it like a lifeline.

"Someone's coming," she said, hoping it would serve as protection, a distraction—anything.

It worked.

He jolted into action, panic flickering behind his eyes.

He dragged her from the doorway like she was nothing.

Not human.

Not whole.

Back to the car. The gravel bit her feet through the thin soles of her shoes.

But inside her chest—where panic once ruled—something else was growing.

Resolve.

As Dylan shoved her back into the seat, she held one prayer close—like a match cradled in cupped hands:

Keep me brave.

Keep them looking.

Let the right eyes find that note.

Chapter 31: The Note

"For nothing is hidden that will not be made manifest, nor is anything secret that will not be known and come to light."
— Luke 8:17

Back on the farm, James was in the barn—sleeves rolled up to his elbows, arms streaked with grease. The afternoon sun cut through the gaps in the tin walls, catching on floating dust and the glint of spanners scattered across the bench.

The smell of diesel clung to his skin, mixing with sweat and old hay. He muttered under his breath, leaning deeper into the tractor's engine, trying to loosen a rusted bolt that refused to give.

Then—

BANG.

The sound of the door slamming open echoed like a gunshot across the quiet yard.

James froze, wrench in hand.

He looked up as the sounds of heavy footsteps got closer and then she appeared.

Naomi didn't knock. Didn't hesitate. She burst into the barn like the wind had chased her there—hair tangled, cheeks flushed, arms shaking as she stumbled to a stop.

"James!" she gasped, her voice cracking wide open.

The bolt in his hand slipped and clattered to the floor. His heart kicked into his throat. One look at her face—blanched, eyes too wide—and something in him lurched.

He was already moving.

"She's gone!" she cried.

James blinked. The words didn't make sense.

Gone, what do you mean?

His chest seized. "What happened—"

"I was only gone for twenty or thirty minutes," Naomi said in a rush, barely able to get the words out. "I came back and—she wasn't there. The door was open, the bin was knocked over, Bear was barking like mad. I screamed her name. I ran around the whole place. I found her shoe, James—just one—out by the driveway."

She was breathless now, voice torn and trembling. "I called the police. I—I don't know where she is. I don't know where he took her—"

James didn't wait to hear the rest.

He turned and ran—boots slamming into the gravel, heart hammering so loud he couldn't hear Naomi's sobs anymore. Only the blood rushing in his ears and the roar building in his chest.

He ran straight to the Ute.

"James!" Naomi shouted, chasing after him. "Wait for me—I'm coming!"

She wrenched open the passenger door and hurled herself in just as the ute jolted forward. No seatbelt. No plan. Just raw panic and the shared knowledge of who had done this.

Gravel shot out behind them as the wheels tore into the dirt road, fishtailing slightly on the bend.

James's hands gripped the wheel.

Naomi sat beside him, chest heaving, phone clenched in her lap.

The only sound between them was the growl of the engine and the terrible silence of not knowing where Ruthie was.

The farm disappeared in the rearview.

Fence lines blurred.

The wind scraped across the bonnet of James's ute as he veered around another blind bend. Loose gravel spat out beneath the tyres, slamming into the undercarriage, a cruel percussion keeping time with the thud of his heart. Dust billowed behind them in a ghostly trail.

Naomi sat rigid in the passenger seat, her fists clenched so tightly her knuckles looked bloodless. She stared straight ahead, eyes skimming the tree line, scanning for something—anything—out of place. A glimpse of movement. A flash of white. A shadow that might be her friend.

They had no leads. No destination. Just James's gut and the kind of dread that scratches behind your ribs like a warning from God Himself. It buzzed under James's skin, thick and inescapable.

They'd prayed out loud at first—frantic, fragmented. Then quieter. Now, just silent breath and unspoken pleas shared in the cramped space between hope and terror.

Fifty kilometres away, sunlight glanced off the windscreen of a marked patrol car cruising steadily along Highway 19. Two officers inside. It was meant to be a dull shift—delivering court documents. Names and charges that would blur by the end of the day.

Constable Jess Peterson rolled her shoulders and tilted her head, trying to ease a stubborn kink in her neck.

"Reckon there's anywhere half-decent to stop?" she asked, glancing at her partner. "Could really use a break."

Her partner didn't even look up from the road. "There's a servo coming up. Bit rough, but it'll do."

Jess nodded, her head heavy from hours on the highway. She needed a break. To stretch. To shake the flatline of nothingness this day had become.

The servo appeared like a memory someone forgot to bury—sun-faded roof, buckled signage, a single pump that looked like it might crumble under a stiff breeze.

Inside, the air was thick with stale oil and despair. The snack shelves were nearly bare—crushed bags of chips, limp jerky, a flickering pie warmer humming low in the corner.

Jess grabbed a bottle of water and some chocolate. Her movements were slow, automatic.

Then—just as she turned to leave—the sudden, undeniable pressure in her belly stopped her mid-step. An urge she hadn't noticed before surged through her like a jolt. It was more than just a bodily need. It felt placed. Timed. Like something—or Someone—was nudging her off course.

She decided to head to the bathroom, hoping it would relieve the pressure building inside her like a rising tide.

She followed the cracked pavement around the side of the building to the bathroom.

The door creaked open.

The room was grimy, unkempt. But it wasn't the mess that caught her eye.

A clipboard. Hanging on the wall by a bent nail.

It was just a cleaning roster. Smudged. Forgotten. Pen long gone.

But scrawled across the bottom, where someone shouldn't have been writing at all, were uneven, frantic letters:

Kidnapped. White car. Dylan Watts. Please help. Call police.

The date was today.

For one drawn breath, Jess went still.

Then training took over.

"Control, this is 421. I have a potential victim-initiated message at the Willowbend Service Station. Immediate response required. Confirm suspect as Dylan Watts. White sedan. Time unknown. We need full surveillance of Highway 19 and all exits. Over."

She snapped a photo, careful not to smudge the note and headed back into the servo to question the clerk.

Back in the Ute, James's hands were bone-white on the wheel, the Ute thundering forward. Naomi hadn't spoken in minutes; her phone held tightly in her lap. Her thumb hovered, occasionally tapping the screen, as though willing it to ring.

Then it did.

A sharp trill split the silence.

She jumped. Fumbled. Answered.

"Hello?"

"Senior Constable Harmer speaking. Am I speaking with Naomi?"

"Yes," she said, breath catching.

"You're listed as an emergency contact on a missing person's report for Ruthie Matthews. We have reason to believe she may have left a message for police at the Willowbend Service Station. One of our officers found a handwritten note in the women's bathroom. It names Dylan Watts as the abductor. Mentions a white sedan."

Naomi gasped, her hand flying to James's arm. His jaw clenched, already rigid. He didn't need to hear it—he already knew.

But then, with trembling fingers, Naomi pressed the speaker button. The voice on the other end filled the cab, making it real.

"The note is signed 'Ruthie,'" the constable said, voice steady but tense. "We're following up with the servo attendant now. He confirmed seeing a white car with tinted windows parked awkwardly at the rear of the property—timestamp places it about thirty to forty minutes before the note was found."

He paused, then continued, "We're calling to ask if you might know where they could be heading?"

Naomi glanced at James, who was now listening to the call.

"He'll take her back to the city," James said, his voice firm. "It's the only place he knows."

"That aligns with what we're seeing," the officer replied. "Anywhere else he might go? Anything at all that could help us narrow the search?"

James's mind whirred. God, help me remember. But the only clear picture was Ruthie—bound, hurting, terrified—and the rage boiled over again.

"No," he said at last. "But he won't stop unless you make him."

"We've deployed multiple units and are setting up roadblocks on all nearby highways," Harmer replied. "Please stay clear of the area. We'll keep you updated."

The call ended.

Naomi sat frozen. Then a sob ripped from her throat.

"She's alive," she said.

James's foot slammed down on the accelerator—he had a direction now, and nothing, not traffic, not time, not fear, was going to stop him from reaching Ruthie.

Chapter 32: Caught in the Light

"The light shines in the darkness, and the darkness has not overcome it."
— *John 1:5*

B ack in the car, every breath Ruthie drew was jagged with pain. Her face throbbed where he'd struck her.

Her ribs ached with every movement.

Even blinking felt like effort.

She didn't cry.

Not now.

Dylan kept his eyes fixed on the road, saying nothing. The cigarette burned fast between his fingers, and he lit another before the first had even died out—chain-smoking like it was the only thing holding him together.

Ruthie broke the quiet gently.

"I know there's still something good in you!" she said, voice raw. "Please... just stop! You don't have to do this!"

He didn't answer right away. His jaw twitched, the muscle pulsing beneath skin stretched taut with fury. His eyes, once warm and searching, had narrowed into cold slits of betrayal.

"I gave you everything. How could you leave me?"

"Dylan—" Ruthie's voice trembled as she tried to interject, her hands raised slightly in a silent plea for calm.

"Don't say another word!"

he hissed.

The car jolted as his grip tightened on the wheel, swerving slightly before correcting.

"Dylan, please," she said, desperation cracking through her tone. "Just listen—"

His hand shot up—not striking, but hovering—a cruel threat lingering in the air, his palm a silent warning.

Ruthie flinched and recoiled into her seat, breath caught in her throat.

Silence swallowed the space between them.

Thick.

Heavy.

Oppressive.

Only the low hum of the engine remained, and the sound of Ruthie's heart pounding like a drum inside her ribs.

She stared straight ahead, afraid to move.

Dylan's chest heaved beside her, breath ragged, shoulders trembling with rage barely held in check.

Something had snapped.

And now, they were both suspended in stillness—one heartbeat away from whatever would come next.

Then

The sound.

A distant wail.

Sirens.

Faint at first, then louder.

Closer.

Piercing through the hush of trees and the groan of tyres on bitumen.

Ruthie's fingers curled around the door handle on instinct.

Dylan's eyes shot to the rear-view mirror. Red and blue bled into the edges of the frame like a warning.

He swore under his breath—then louder.

"No, no, no,"

he growled, hitting the steering wheel.

Tyres screeched as he jerked the car across lanes without warning. Horns blared behind them.

"What have you done?"

he spat, rage bubbling beneath the surface.

"Did you do this? Let me tell you—this doesn't end with you walking out of this, Ruthie."

She didn't answer. She couldn't. Her voice had buried itself somewhere deep beneath her ribs.

Her gaze stayed forward. Locked. Steady. But inside, she was praying with every breath.

God, protect me. Keep me hidden. Keep me whole. Keep me alive. Please.

Dylan's foot slammed the accelerator like a war cry. The car jolted forward, the force shoving her back into the seat.

The sirens were right behind now—two police cars, maybe three. Lights danced through the trees like war drums, flashing red and blue.

He looked at her, eyes blazing, mouth twisted into something unrecognisable.

"You did this. All of this. If you'd just stayed... if you hadn't run your mouth, we could've fixed it."

Her lips pressed together. She wouldn't answer. Not now.

Not with the way his hands were trembling on the wheel.

Not with madness rising in his voice like a tide that wouldn't stop.

But her spirit—her spirit was on its knees, roaring into heaven.

Jesus, please be near. Please hold me. She prayed.

Suddenly, Dylan yanked the wheel left, veering off the main road and onto a side track lined with gravel and bone-dry weeds. The car jolted violently, dust exploding around them like a shroud.

The tyres fought for grip, spitting rocks in every direction. The undercarriage groaned in protest.

Dylan muttered some words, trying to convince himself he was in control.

He wasn't in control anymore.

He was cornered.

And cornered men break.

The car tore through the scrub, past brittle grass and dry gum trees that loomed like silent witnesses. A branch dragged across the passenger side, shrieking against the metal. Ruthie's shoulder slammed against the door, pain lancing through her side.

She didn't scream.

She prayed harder.

The sirens still howled, now fainter—but not gone.

Dylan swore again, louder this time.

Tears rimmed his eyes, but they weren't sorrow. They were something darker. Twisted. Desperate.

The road narrowed, winding like a snake through rising trees. Shadows thickened. The sky above blurred behind the treetops.

A new sound now—helicopter blades, distant but unmistakable.

He punched the steering wheel, the sound echoing in the confined space.

Dylan growled.

He jerked the car around a bend, a cloud of dirt rising behind them.

Then

The front tyre hit a rut. Too deep.

The nose of the car dipped violently.

The back end lifted.

Ruthie's breath caught in her throat as time seemed to lurch.

Dylan screamed something, but it was lost beneath the chaos—

The impact came without mercy.

The front tyre plunged into the rut, and in the next heartbeat, the car catapulted forward lifted, twisted, and thrown.

There was no time to scream.
No time to brace.
Only the sound.
A violent, unrelenting crash that ripped through the silence.
The vehicle flipped—once, twice—metal shrieking in protest.
A final, jarring slam.
And then—
Stillness.
Not peace.
Just the eerie, breathless pause after ruin.

Chapter 33: When the Sky Split Open

"He will cover you with His feathers, and under His wings you will find refuge; His faithfulness will be your shield and rampart."
— Psalm 91:4

The road smeared past in streaks of green and grey, but James saw none of it.

He wasn't chasing a car.

He was chasing the shape of his world—breaking loose in front of him.

Every nerve was lit. Every cell in his body screamed. The ute growled beneath him, rattling over dips in the bitumen, but he didn't care. He leaned forward like he could force the distance to shrink, his hands locked so tight around the wheel his skin had gone bloodless.

Wind shoved hard against the windows, but the storm was inside him.

Ruthie.

Her name pounded in his chest like a second heartbeat. Like thunder.

Every second was sand slipping too fast through desperate hands. Every curve of the road a knife edge.

Beside him, Naomi's eyes flicked between the road and the screen of her phone, lips moving in a trembling whisper.

"Jesus... cover her. Shelter her under Your wing. Please don't take her. Not now. Not like this."

They passed fence posts and power lines in a blur. A hawk lifted from the grass, wings stretching into the air—free, effortless, untouched by the violence below.

Then—something unnatural on the horizon.

A flicker of lights.

James leaned forward, eyes narrowing.

Red and blue lights.

Flashing. Pulsing.

The ute growled beneath him like a beast unleashed, shuddering with every push of his foot. Gravel exploded from beneath the tyres, spit out in burning arcs that rattled against the undercarriage like gunfire.

The lights ahead sharpened—red, blue, relentless. No longer a flicker.

His chest was a furnace. His soul already screaming the prayer his mouth couldn't shape.

"Please.. God! Please.. Just let me get to her. Let me get there in time!"

The road surged like a wave before them, rising to swallow the sky. And as they crested it—

Everything snapped into clarity.

Two. No—three police cars blocked the road, lights spinning in frantic pulses.

And just ahead—

A white sedan.

There.

Her.

James's throat clamped shut. He choked on breath. His heart thundered so hard it drowned out everything else.

"Ruthie!!" he rasped, barely audible. As if her name could break through space. Through time. Through death itself.

He mashed the pedal to the floor, but the ute was already stretched to its limit, engine screaming in protest. It couldn't go faster. Not now. Not when he needed it most.

But nothing else existed.

Not the road. Not the flashing lights.

Only Ruthie.

The white sedan jerked suddenly, veering off the gravel like a frightened animal. The turn was sharp—too sharp. Wild.

Desperate.

The tyres screamed as they lost contact, skidding sideways in a blur of dust and fear. The rear of the car clipped the edge of the embankment—metal on rock—then lifted, weightless for one frozen, harrowing second.

James watched, powerless, his scream still trapped in his lungs.

And then—

The car dropped.

The rear end clipped the embankment.

It lifted.

Suspended in the air for a single, silent breath.

Then.

Impact.

The car slammed down like judgement. Metal crunched and screamed. Earth split. Glass burst into the sky like shrapnel from a bomb.

Time didn't slow.

It broke.

James's scream exploded from a place beyond his body.

He didn't brake.

Didn't blink.

Didn't breathe.

The ute careened across the gravel. Naomi shrieked as it skidded, tail swinging like a whip. James jerked the wheel, slammed the brakes, threw the gear into park before the engine had even stopped growling.

He was out the door in a heartbeat.

Running.

Every step pounded like thunder through his body. Every breath was fire. His boots struck dirt, then gravel, then metal fragments. He dodged an officer's outstretched hand. Shoved past another yelling something he didn't register.

His world narrowed to one twisted, crumpled shell of a car.

He dropped to his knees beside the wreck, hands scraping on metal and glass.

And there—inside—

Ruthie.

She was crumpled like a discarded doll. Blood streaked across her temple, hair tangled and dark. Her face—barely recognisable beneath bruises and swelling. One arm was twisted at an unnatural angle, fingers curled like a child in sleep.

But this wasn't sleep.

This was death, knocking at the door.

"No!,—please, NO!" James reached into the mangled frame, the edge cutting into his arm, uncaring. His hand found hers—cold. Motionless.

Too still.

"God, please don't take her!" He pressed his forehead against the buckled window frame.

"I -can't-lose-her!"

The words cracked open his chest.

Tears broke free, hot and helpless, tracing lines down his cheeks as he clutched her fingers.

Then.

A flicker.

A twitch beneath his hand.

He froze.

Her fingers jerked again. Then stilled.

Then moved—deliberate. Faint.

Her lashes fluttered. Not open. Not yet.

But alive.

"Ruthie," he choked, inching closer. "I'm here. I've got you."

Her eyelids dragged open, heavy as iron. Dust and blood caked her lashes. Her eyes searched, unfocused, then found him.

"James..." It was barely a sound.

"My angel..."

He almost collapsed.

Her hand, shaking, brushed his cheek.

"I love you," she breathed, a ghost of a whisper.

And then—she exhaled.

And everything stilled.

Her hand slipped from his. Her head slumped.

Gone.

"RUTHIE?!"

His voice cracked the sky.

He gripped her hand, her shoulder, her face.

"No!, please, stay with me! Breathe. You have to breathe—"

Rough hands pulled at him.

"Sir!" a paramedic barked. "We need access!"

He didn't move.

Couldn't.

Then Naomi was behind him, tugging him gently.

"James—let them help."

His body obeyed before his mind did.

He stumbled back. Hands bloodied. Vision blurred.

Paramedics surged into the space, oxygen masks, trauma shears, muttered orders. A blur of urgent movement.

"Pulse faint—but she's still with us!"

James dropped where he stood. Breath catching. Ribcage aching.

Then—another voice.

But not hers.

Dylan.

Dragged from the front seat of the car by police. His shirt soaked in blood. Not dead.

Cursing.

Spitting.

Screaming.

Alive.

Still breathing after everything.

James turned.

His fury was wildfire.

He charged.

Officers leapt between them. "Sir—stand down!!"

He thrashed, fists swinging. Grief made him blind.

"James!"

Naomi saw what was happening and ran towards James.

Her arms wrapped around him, pulling him back from the edge.

"Don't lose yourself, James. Ruthie needs you!"

He stopped and collapsed before looking over at Ruthie.

They were lifting Ruthie now—her body wrapped, oxygen pressed to her face.

Her chest... moving.

Still here.

He stepped forward.

"I'm going with her!" He said as a demand not a request.

The paramedic nodded.

James climbed into the ambulance, barely fitting between the stretcher and the wall.

He reached for her hand—so fragile, still trembling.

"I've got you," he said.

And then—her thumb.

It pressed weakly into his palm.

That was everything to him in that moment.

The doors slammed shut.

The sirens howled.

And as the ambulance tore into the distance, James bowed his head beside her and breathed a single, shattered prayer.

"Thank You, God!"

Chapter 34: The Waiting Room

"The Lord is good to those whose hope is in him, to the one who seeks him; it is good to wait quietly for the salvation of the Lord."— Lamentations 3:25-26

The steady hum of noise filled the emergency waiting room—a cold, sterile chorus that underscored the ache of waiting.

James sat hunched in a brittle plastic chair, elbows braced against his knees, head bowed low. His fingers were stained with dirt and blood. His boots tracked dried gravel onto the white floor.

Beside him, Naomi sat rigid, her fingers trembling in her lap. Her foot tapped a restless, syncopated rhythm against the floor—erratic, fragile. A subtle metronome keeping time with her fear.

Neither of them spoke.

The silence was thick. Suffocating.

Images from earlier refused to fade.

The crumpled wreck.

The twisted metal.

The helplessness of standing by as she was lifted away.

And now...

They waited.

James jolted to his feet suddenly, like a puppet yanked by invisible strings. He paced three steps across the room, then sat down again just as fast—restless. Desperate.

He dragged his hands down his face, as if he could scrub the memory from his skin.

"She was right there," he whispered, voice hollow. "I was so close."

Naomi looked over at him, eyes damp but steady. Her voice came soft, anchored.

"And she still is, James."

He didn't answer. Just pressed his hands together, fingers interlocked tightly, like prayer was the only thing keeping him from unraveling entirely.

Then Naomi's phone buzzed in her pocket.

She jumped slightly, pulling it out with trembling hands.

It was a message from Neil.

Her throat caught as she read it, then she turned toward James slowly.

"Hey," she said gently. "There's something you need to know."

James barely looked up.

"When Bear ran—back at the bookshop—I couldn't go after him," Naomi said softly. "He bolted the moment I opened the back door after Dylan took Ruthie. I knew I needed to focus on calling the police and letting you know, and I couldn't follow Bear. But I did call Neil and Margaret once Ruthie was in the ambulance to see if they could find him."

She paused, her throat tight with emotion.

"They called Micah and Pastor Luke and some others in town. Everyone started searching—for Bear."

James's head snapped up. His heart stuttered. "Bear? Did they find him?"

Naomi nodded, tears brimming. "Yeah. They found him, James."

His mouth opened, but no words came.

"He was walking along the highway. Probably trying to find Ruthie, I'd imagine. Margaret said he looked worn out—limping, covered in dust—but he's okay. Just... determined. Like he was tracking her or something. They took him to the vet just to get checked over."

He sat back, overcome. The loyalty. The love.

Even Bear had been trying to bring her home.

And at that moment, the emergency room doors swung open.

A doctor stepped through in green scrubs, clipboard in hand, expression unreadable.

"Ruthie Matthews?"

James was on his feet instantly.

"Yes," he said, voice raw. "We're—with her. Please—tell me she's alive."

The doctor took a step closer, pausing with a breath before speaking.

"She's stable," he began, glancing between them with calm reassurance. "She's sustained two broken ribs, a fractured wrist, some facial bruising, and mild shock. She also has a mild concussion—nothing severe, but we'll monitor her closely for the next 24 hours."

He paused, letting the words settle, then added, with quiet awe, "She's conscious. Talking. And she's going to be okay."

He looked between them, voice steady but reverent now.

"It's a true miracle. Given the severity of the crash, she... she should've been far worse off. The fact that she survived it at all—let alone with injuries this minor—is extraordinary."

James's breath caught.

He hadn't realised he was holding it until it came out.

Naomi covered her mouth, tears spilling freely now.

"Thank You, God," James exhaled.

The doctor nodded solemnly. "We've had trauma cases with far less impact who didn't make it. Something—someone—was watching over her. I don't say that lightly."

A silence fell between them, thick with gratitude, disbelief, and the fragile weight of hope. James reached for Naomi's hand, his grip trembling.

Ruthie was alive.

Still here.

A miracle, indeed.

Naomi exhaled hard, collapsing forward slightly, her hand clinging to the seat's edge like it was the only solid thing in the room.

James closed his eyes. Just for a second. Then nodded, voice ragged.

"Can I see her?"

"She's asking for you," the doctor said gently. "One visitor, for now. She's groggy, but alert."

Naomi touched his arm. "Go," she said. "I'll be right here."

James hesitated. "You sure?"

She gave a soft smile. "You're the face she needs."

He followed the doctor through antiseptic-scented halls. Every footstep sounded louder now. His adrenaline had faded, but his heart thudded like a warning bell.

The doctor stopped outside a door. "She's a little disoriented. That's normal."

He nodded and stepped inside.

The room was dim. Machines beeped softly. Ruthie lay still, a bandage on her cheek, wrist braced, IV in her arm.

But her eyes—those eyes—opened when she heard the door creak.

She whispered. "James."

He crossed the room in three strides. Dropped into the chair beside her.

His hands hovered, then gently found hers.

"I'm here," he said. "I'm right here."

Tears slid down Ruthie's cheeks. "I thought... I wouldn't make it back."

"You did," he said, holding on tighter. "You're here. And you're safe now."

"Did they get him?"

James nodded. "They did. That note—Ruthie, it saved everything."

She looked toward the window. Her voice was quieter now. "I just kept praying. I didn't know if anyone would see it, but something told me it was going to be okay."

Chapter 35: After the Storm

"...the God of all grace, who called you to his eternal glory in Christ, after you have suffered a little while, will himself restore you and make you strong, firm and steadfast." — *1 Peter 5:10*

J ames didn't leave Ruthie's side.

Not for a moment.

He anchored himself to the cramped hospital room like his presence alone was holding her to this earth. Like if he stepped away—even for a breath—the fragile miracle keeping her alive might slip through his fingers.

The stiff vinyl chair beside her bed bore the imprint of his weight, a poor substitute for rest, but he didn't complain. He slept there in fits and starts, head tilted at impossible angles, neck aching, but always waking to check the steady rise and fall of her chest. Nurses slipping pillows behind his back and tucking thin hospital blankets around his shoulders like quiet blessings.

He didn't care about his discomfort.

Only her.

He watched her face constantly—searching for signs of pain, of improvement, of life returning. Her bruises darkened before they lightened. But colour, faint and slow, began returning to her cheeks. And her lips, once cracked and grey, softened into something like normal.

Naomi came and went like a gentle tide, bringing fresh clothes, hot takeaway coffee, and updates from the farm. "Bear's okay," she said on her second visit, pressing a hand to James's shoulder. "He's been lying by your front door, like he knows you'll come home with her."

James nodded but didn't look away from Ruthie.

He couldn't.

She drifted in and out of sleep for the first twenty-four hours, her body mending under the haze of painkillers and IV drips. And every time her lashes fluttered open, confused and heavy, she found him there. Still in the chair. Still watching. Still holding her hand as if his touch alone could keep her tethered.

On the second morning, she asked for her bible. It was barely a whisper—hoarse, dry—but full of clarity.

James blinked away sleep, sat up straighter. and then rummaged through the bag Naomi had left and pulled it out—worn leather cover, dog-eared pages. He placed it gently in her lap.

She held it like it was treasure.

Her fingers shook as she flipped through the pages. She found the bookmarked psalms and traced the words with her fingertip, tears gathering along her lashes.

"I was so scared," she admitted, voice trembling. "But I remembered... That God would not leave me."

James didn't speak. Just reached for her hand again and squeezed it.

Later, when her voice faded from exhaustion, he picked up the reading. Psalms. Isaiah. John. His voice low and steady, filling the space between the monitors and the beeping machines.

He didn't preach.

He just read.

And prayed quietly, sometimes out loud, sometimes with tears running down his face.

By the third evening, golden light spilled through the window like a gentle hand, brushing warmth against the sterile white walls. Ruthie was stronger now—eyes clearer, breath more steady. She shifted in the bed, head turning toward him as James rested his hand lightly over hers.

"You're here," he said softly, his voice catching.

She smiled, bruised and slow but real. "So are you."

Their fingers threaded together, the silence between them thick with things they weren't ready to say.

They didn't speak of Dylan.

Not yet.

Not of the crash, the ambulance, or the blood on the road.

But they spoke of second chances. Of life spared. Of days ahead.

In that small hospital room—between scripture and whispered prayers, between hospital sounds and the steady rhythm of survival—they found something deeper than either of them had known before.

It was something eternal.

Not built from romance or adrenaline.

But from faith.

And fire.

And the kind of grace that only survives when everything else has been stripped away.

One afternoon, while still in the hospital, a knock tapped softly on the door.

James stood immediately, alert.

Two detectives stepped in, their expressions grave but gentle.

"We've charged Dylan," one began, clipboard held low. "Criminal trespass. Breach of the AVO. Assault. Unlawful imprisonment. And reckless endangerment."

The other detective added, "He's currently receiving medical treatment at another facility under police guard. Once he's discharged, he'll be taken directly into custody."

Ruthie swallowed hard. "Do I... have to testify?"

"There will be a court date," the officer said gently, his voice steady with care. "The police prosecutor is building the case, and you'll be supported every step of the way. Whether you need to testify will depend on the evidence and decisions made by both the prosecution and the defence—but in cases like this, it's likely you will be asked to give evidence."

Ruthie's hands gripped the edge of her blanket. James reached across and covered one of them with his own.

"How long will this take?" Her voice was quiet, almost afraid of the answer.

The detective looked up from his notepad, his expression softening. "It depends," he said carefully. "If he pleads guilty, things could move a little faster. A few months, maybe. But if he fights it—if it goes to trial—it could take a year. Maybe more."

Ruthie swallowed, her throat dry.

"But," he added, leaning forward slightly, "the evidence we've got... it's strong. It would be very difficult for him to deny what happened."

Ruthie nodded, not quite trusting her voice. But something in her chest loosened—just a little.

The next day, Ruthie was discharged and returned to the farm.

Relief swept through her as the familiar landscape came into view—the open sky, the distant hills, the quiet hum of the land. But stepping onto the porch felt strange, almost dreamlike. Each footfall echoed in her bones, the timber groaning beneath her as if it, too, recognised the weight of what had changed.

Her wrist was still cradled in a brace, stiff and tender. Every deep breath sent a sharp ache through her ribs, and any sudden movement reminded her of what her body had endured.

But she was here.

Alive and still standing.

Naomi had been through the farmhouse earlier. Carefully. Quietly. No grand gestures. Just love in the details.

A beeswax candle waited unlit on the windowsill.

A fresh loaf of Margaret's rosemary bread sat wrapped in a linen tea towel on the counter.

The fridge was stocked with soups, pumpkin casseroles, bone broth, and jars of jam.

It all spoke of community without intrusion. Thoughtfulness without pressure.

Bear was beside himself when she arrived. He barked and whined. He paced in frantic circles, tail thrashing, nose quivering as he took her in. Then, unable to hold back any longer, he pressed himself against her good hip with a trembling body and a low, broken whimper, as if to say, You're here. Don't leave me again.

From that moment on, he shadowed her. Always at her side. Watching. Waiting. Healing too, in his own way.

James stayed close. Brought her tea. Held her hand gently when the pain flared. Read to her in the afternoons when her eyes were too tired. Kept the fire going when the nights got cold.

And every morning—

Before she even woke—

He left a small bundle of wildflowers beside her Bible.

Sometimes lavender and wattle.

Other times a few sprigs of thyme, or daisies from the hill.

No note. No explanation.

Just something alive.

Something beautiful.

Two months passed.

The leaves shifted from sunburnt summer into golden hints of autumn, and the days at the farm settled into a rhythm that felt both new and deeply familiar.

James and Ruthie spent nearly every waking moment together.

They worked side by side in the garden—him in worn boots and rolled sleeves, her hands digging into soil like it could heal things still unspoken. They cooked simple meals and ate them on the veranda, sharing stories, memories, laughter that felt lighter now.

But some things—they never spoke of.

Not the night in the overturned car.

Not the metallic scent of blood or the shriek of metal folding in on itself.

Not the moment Ruthie whispered, "I love you," while drifting between pain and panic, clinging to the sound of his voice like oxygen.

Not the way James had cradled her against his chest like she was breakable and infinite all at once—like he wasn't sure if she'd survive, but he was determined to hold her whole until she did.

They didn't need to speak it.

Because it lingered.

It lived in the way he brushed his fingers along her shoulder when passing behind her—barely there, but grounding. As if to say, I'm here.

It showed in the way she poured his tea in the morning—no longer rushing, but with intentional care, sliding the cup to him with a smile that didn't need explanation.

It was in how they sat closer now—on the porch swing, by the fire, in the truck. No words, no plans.

They didn't name it.

But it was love.

Not the fiery, dramatic kind written in poetry or shouted across stormy fields.

But the quiet kind.

The kind built from ash and endurance.

The kind rooted in survival and blooming in trust.

It lived in the space between their hands when they reached for the same trowel.

In the softness of her laugh when he tried (and failed) to make scones.

There were still hard days.

She still flinched when the wind slammed the door.

He still checked the locks twice some nights.

But healing was no longer a theory.

It was happening—in small ways.

Chapter 36: The Letter

"He has shown you, O mortal, what is good. And what does the Lord require of you? To act justly and to love mercy and to walk humbly with your God."— *Micah 6:8*

One quiet morning, the farm exhaled in golden silence. Bear lay stretched across the porch, belly to the boards, soaking in the warmth like an old rug in the sun. One ear twitched lazily at the buzz of a persistent fly. The only sounds were the soft creak of timber expanding in the heat and the whisper of gum leaves stirring overhead.

Inside, the kettle clicked off with a gentle pop, releasing a curl of steam into the still kitchen air.

James stepped in from the gravel path, brushing dust from his boots after a slow walk down to the mailbox. Ruthie was plating up breakfast—scrambled eggs, buttered toast—her movements gentle, steady. The scent of eucalyptus drifted in through the screen door.

"Thank you," James said, smiling softly as he reached for her chair and pulled it out.

She smiled back and sat down, their knees brushing briefly beneath the table. James set the mail on the worn wooden surface beside their mugs and tucked into his meal.

It wasn't until they'd finished eating, the plates pushed aside and the sunlight spilling in at a slant, that James began sifting through the small pile of envelopes.

A power bill. A farm supply catalogue.

And then—one envelope that made him pause.

It was heavier. Folded perfectly. Government-stamped. And addressed to Ruthie.

His expression shifted. Slower now, he slid it across the table toward her, fingers lingering as he let it go.

"This one's for you," he said.

Ruthie looked at it for a long moment. The seal. The insignia. The way her name was printed—so official it made her skin prickle.

She took it with both hands.

Opened it slowly.

Her eyes moved across the first few lines.

Her mouth opened, but no words came. The legal language wrapped itself around her like barbed wire. Terms she didn't understand. Sentences that felt clinical, sterile, cruel.

"I... I don't know what this means," she said, holding the letter out to James.

James sat beside her instantly, his arm resting gently along her back, anchoring her.

He took the paper. Scanned it. Read it again.

"It's a request," he said softly. "They're not asking you to give evidence. You're not being called to testify."

Ruthie's hands dropped to her lap, fingers tangled together.

"Then... what is it?" she asked.

James exhaled slowly, grounding himself before he spoke. "They're asking if you'd like to submit a statement. It says it's voluntary."

Ruthie's lips parted, confusion flashing across her face. "I don't understand... I thought I'd have to give evidence in court. What does that mean? Does it mean he'll get away with what he did?"

James shook his head gently. "You don't have to figure this out alone," he said, his voice steady and sure. "We'll ask someone—a lawyer, someone who understands how this works."

His words were kind, but they floated past Ruthie like mist.

Confusion and fear gripped her, thick and unrelenting. The words on the page, the legal jargon, the idea of choice—it all pressed in on her, heavy and disorienting.

That same afternoon, James made a few calls. He connected with a local domestic violence advocacy service—not to speak on Ruthie's behalf or to push her into anything, but simply to open a door.

They offered her a time to talk. James didn't pressure her. He just told her when they could meet and left the rest to her.

The day of the appointment came. They drove in silence.

The legal office wasn't cold or clinical like Ruthie had imagined. The solicitor greeted them with a quiet smile—no suit, just a soft cardigan and flats. She offered Ruthie a glass of water.

They sat in a small, sunlit room as the solicitor read the letter again. She spoke slowly, carefully—aware of every word.

"I've already spoken with the detectives," she said. "This isn't a subpoena. You're not being called to give evidence."

Ruthie blinked. Her voice cracked as the words stumbled out. "So... what does that mean? That he's getting away with it?"

The solicitor met her eyes. "No, he's pleading guilty. That means he's already been convicted—officially. He accepted the charges against him."

Ruthie's throat tightened.

"The detectives said the evidence was overwhelming," the solicitor continued gently. "They didn't need to put you through the trauma of testifying. But that doesn't mean you don't get to speak."

She turned the paper around slowly.

"This is about sentencing. You have the right to submit a Victim Impact Statement. It's voluntary. It tells the court—and the judge—how Dylan's actions have affected your life. It won't change the fact that he's guilty, but it can shape how the judge understands the full weight of what he's done."

Ruthie nodded faintly, absorbing the words.

"You can write it yourself," the solicitor offered. "Or we can help. You can submit it in writing... or—"

Ruthie looked up. "Or?"

"Or you can read it aloud in court. At sentencing." The solicitor's tone was steady but soft. "It's your choice. There's absolutely no pressure either way."

Silence stretched.

James didn't say a word.

Ruthie stared at the table, then slowly lifted her chin. Her voice was quiet, but it didn't waver.

"I want to read it. I want him to hear me. I want him to hear what he did."

The solicitor blinked—not out of surprise, but out of something like reverence—and gave a slow nod.

"That's your right," she said.

Ruthie exhaled. Not with ease. But with purpose.

Afterwards, James walked beside her in silence until they reached the car.

He didn't ask how she felt.

He didn't ask if, she was sure.

He just reached for her hand.

That night, back at the farmhouse, Ruthie sat curled in a tangle of blankets on the couch. Bear lay at her feet, his steady breath a quiet anchor in the hush of the room. Her mug of tea sat untouched on the side table, long gone cold.

The letter rested in her lap—folded, familiar now.

But this time, she wasn't staring at it like it was a threat.

She was considering it.

Claiming it.

Running her fingers over the date, the courtroom address, the instructions—like they belonged to her now.

James sat beside her in silence. Not trying to fix anything. Just there.

While she traced the edges of the paper, he pulled out his phone and started searching for hotels. His thumb moved slowly, scrolling. Nothing flashy—just quiet, clean places near the courthouse. Somewhere safe. Somewhere steady.

Ruthie glanced over and caught a glimpse of the screen. A modest guesthouse. A quiet apartment. Her eyes flicked up to his.

James met her gaze and offered a soft smile. "I'm just looking for somewhere for us to stay. While you give your statement."

He didn't push. Didn't explain.

"We'll do this together," he said simply.

Her face softened. A tear slid down her cheek before she could stop it.

She didn't wipe it away.

She just nodded, exhaling slowly.

Chapter 37: The Whole Truth

"Have I not commanded you? Be strong and courageous. Do not be afraid; do not be discouraged, for the Lord your God will be with you wherever you go."
— *Joshua 1:9*

The day of the court hearing had finally come.

The air was thick with tension long before they reached the courthouse.

As Ruthie and James drove into town, the silence inside the ute was more than quiet—it was suffocating. Every breath carried weight. Every glance toward the looming horizon came laced with dread. The hum of the engine murmured beneath them, steady but subdued, like even the Ute understood it wasn't just carrying them to a courtroom—it was carrying them into the heart of everything they'd survived.

Ruthie sat with her hands in her lap, fingers knotted tightly, knuckles pale. She stared straight ahead, lips pressed into a line, her jaw clenched. Not to hold back tears. But to hold herself together.

James didn't speak. He just reached across the seat and gently laced his fingers through hers. She didn't have to look at him to know he was praying.

As they pulled into the car park, the courthouse loomed—cold, austere, its concrete edges sharp against the grey morning sky. Ruthie's breath caught in her throat. She'd imagined this moment a hundred different ways, but none of them felt like this. Like stepping into a furnace with ice in her chest.

Inside, the courtroom was colder still. Not in temperature—but in tone. Everything was rigid. Orderly. Impersonal. As though trauma could be filed away neatly and bound in legal jargon. The clock ticked. The air conditioning whispered like a warning. Ruthie's skin prickled with a chill that wasn't entirely physical.

She sat beside James on the hard wooden bench, her spine straight but her shoulders rigid with effort. His thigh pressed gently against hers. Their hands remained intertwined—his thumb brushing softly over the top of her knuckles, again and again.

She could feel her heartbeat in her ears.

The clerk called her name.

And the world seemed to still.

Ruthie stood. Not fast. Not confident. Just upright—on legs that felt like stone, carrying a body that no longer felt like it belonged to her.

Each step toward the stand echoed louder than it should have. The sound of her boots on the polished floor felt intrusive in the sacred hush of the room. It wasn't just a walk. It was a passage. From who she was then—to who she had to be now.

She clutched the paper in her hand, but it trembled. Her breath, shallow. Her lips parted slightly, drawing in one more lungful of courage. The pages blurred and sharpened again beneath her eyes, as if the words themselves needed her to read them when she was ready.

She didn't look at Dylan.

Not yet.

She looked at James.

He was sitting in the front row. Upright. Still. Watching her like she was the most important thing in the room. Because she was.

His eyes didn't leave hers.

She held his gaze for a heartbeat.

Then she turned.

Only then did she lift her head toward the bench. The judge gave a slight nod.

Ruthie cleared her throat. Her fingers tightened around the edges of the paper.

And then, quietly—but without hesitation—she began to speak.

"At first."

Ruthie began. "I thought Dylan really loved me."

Her eyes were dry. Focused.

"He was attentive—remembering small details I didn't even know I'd shared. My favourite songs. How I liked my coffee. He'd check in if I had a headache. His texts each morning reminded me to drink water. To dress warmly. His kindness felt like shelter."

She paused, breath fluttering.

For a moment, her gaze drifted across the courtroom—to where Dylan sat, head bowed, staring at the floor. He wouldn't meet her eyes. That, somehow, hurt more than if he had looked straight through her.

Ruthie inhaled softly and turned her face back to the judge. Her hands tightened around the paper.

"I told myself it was protective love. Proof that I was deeply cherished—maybe even adored. I thought I was lucky."

Her voice steadied.

"But love that glows like fire can also burn."

The room stilled.

"What began as concern became control."

Her tone didn't rise. It dropped—quiet, hollow.

"'Don't talk so much,' he'd say.

'Let me know where you are at all times,' he insisted—calling it protection."

She exhaled.

"I thought it was love. But it was the beginning of the cage."

Ruthie looked at the paper briefly. But she wasn't reading. She was remembering.

"The first time he hit me," she said, her voice low but clear, "was because I said no."

She inhaled. Her chest rose with effort. Her fingers curled in her lap.

"He cried after. Said it was the stress. That he was sorry. That I'd said the wrong thing—and if I'd just been softer, it wouldn't have happened."

A pause. Then another.

"And I believed him," she whispered. "I thought it was my fault. That I'd made him do it."

The gallery held its breath.

"I believed him when he said my tone provoked him—not just that time, but every time after. I believed him when he said no other man would love me the way he did. That I was the cause of his pain. That staying with me was his act of mercy."

Her voice trembled—but it didn't break.

"Then... it got worse."

Her hands shook now.

"In January, he shoved me into the kitchen wall. I was holding a glass. It shattered in my hand and I bled—a lot. He didn't help. He just screamed at me for being dramatic and for getting blood on the tiles."

A harsh breath escaped her.

"In February, everything got darker. He'd lost hours at work and came home angrier every day. He told me I was the reason life was hard. That I made things worse and he blamed me for the money being gone—but I was barely eating. I was scared to use anything. Meanwhile, he was drinking. Gambling. Disappearing for hours."

She closed her eyes.

"I thought that was as bad as it could get. But I was wrong."

Her next words landed like glass underfoot.

"In April..." she said, voice thin, "I tried to leave. I'd packed a bag. I was ready."

She paused. A breath caught in her throat—a breath tangled in memory.

Across the room, Dylan shifted. His mouth opened slightly, a flicker of urgency sparking across his face. But his lawyer placed a hand on his arm. A subtle shake of the head. Dylan sat back down. Jaw clenched. Eyes on the floor.

"I told him I couldn't take it anymore. That I was done. I walked toward the door."

Her hands began to shake.

"I didn't make it two steps."

She blinked. Her voice cracked.

"He grabbed me and ripped the keys out of my hand. Pain shot through my wrist. And then he hit me—so hard that I dropped to the ground."

The courtroom was still.

"And then he dragged me, By the hair. Into the bedroom. I screamed. I kicked. I begged him to stop."

Her eyes shimmered, but she didn't look away.

"And then.... he forced himself on me."

The words fell into the space between them with the full, unflinching weight of truth.

"I said no, screamed and cried." Her voice was breaking now, but steady. Determined. "He told me if I was really in pain, I'd be screaming louder."

She swallowed hard, the memory scraping its way up her throat.

"He said I owed him. And just before he left the room, he put his hands around my neck..." Her fingers brushed her collarbone as if the imprint still lingered. "He told me I don't get to leave alive."

A tear slid down her cheek. She didn't wipe it away.

She let it fall.

Stillness followed—not silence, but something deeper. Something thick. Heavy. The kind of stillness that hums beneath the skin. The kind that holds its breath and waits to see what breaks first.

"I remember cleaning myself up after while he sat on the couch. Turned on the TV and ordered pizza. He acted like nothing happened."

She blinked. Swallowed.

"That's when I knew I had to leave. Not because I was brave. But because I saw the truth. I was an object to him. Something he owned."

Her voice grew firmer.

"I believed he would kill me. Maybe not that night. But eventually."

Another breath.

"But I left. I waited until he went to the pub. I walked to the train station with one small bag and fifty-three dollars in my pocket. I didn't have a plan. Just a will to survive."

She faltered—just slightly.

"But he still found me."

Her voice dimmed.

"He tracked me. I don't even know how—but he did. And I truly believe, if things had gone differently that day, I wouldn't be here now."

She straightened slightly.

"I believe God saved me through a stranger. A man in work boots. He didn't know me—but he saw me. And when I needed safety, he gave it. Not out of duty. But love. The kind that says, 'love your neighbour as yourself.'"

Her tears welled—but didn't fall.

"He gave me more than protection. He gave me a way back—to myself and to God."

Then the calm broke.

"But the pain didn't stop. I've lived through sleepless nights robbed by flashbacks. My body responded to every sound with panic, and I was trapped in fear, in trauma."

She gripped the stand tighter.

"And Dylan didn't stop. He didn't even let me choose to leave him. He tracked my phone. He found me again."

Her voice shook.

"He broke into the one place where I finally felt safe. He threatened me. And the people I had come to love."

"And then he took my freedom."

Her voice softened, but the words cut sharp.

"He kidnapped me. Hurt me in ways I still don't have words for and I honestly thought I was going to die."

She steadied herself.

"But something had shifted. He could lay hands on my body—but not my soul. That part belongs to God."

Her gaze lifted.

"I won't pretend the months that followed were easy. They weren't. I was haunted. I couldn't sleep. Couldn't breathe if someone stood too close and I lived on edge. Constantly scanning for danger."

Her grip tightened.

"And yet..."

She looked up.

"I'm standing here, and I am not his victim anymore."

She turned to Dylan. He still wouldn't meet her eyes.

"I'm not here for revenge," she said. "I'm here because truth deserves a voice."

Her shoulders lifted. Her breath deepened.

"I don't want to live in fear anymore. I want peace. I deserve peace."

Her voice softened.

"And I forgive him. Dylan, I hope you find God. I hope you heal."

She turned back to the judge.

"But I need this court to understand: this man is dangerous. I deserve safety. I deserve peace. And I cannot have that if he is free. Neither can the people who loved me when I was still a stranger. Letting him walk free won't just endanger me—it endangers every community that believes in love, in God, in goodness."

She exhaled.

"And I'm asking you now... to protect what's left. So that what was broken might still be rebuilt."

The prosecutor gave a single, solemn nod.

The judge's voice was quiet but firm. "Thank you, Miss Matthews. You may step down."

Ruthie folded the paper slowly. Her hands trembled, but her steps didn't.

Her breath deepened.

James was waiting.

He didn't say a word.

He just opened his arms.

She stepped into them.

In the hush that followed, something shifted.

Not in the courtroom.

In her.

Chapter 38: After the Echo

"The Lord your God is with you, the Mighty Warrior who saves. He will take great delight in you; in His love He will no longer rebuke you, but will rejoice over you with singing." – Zephaniah 3:17

James and Ruthie made their way back to the small apartment in silence. The air between them felt thick—not with distance, but with everything that had just been spoken in the courtroom. It clung to them like ash after a fire.

James watched as Ruthie walked in first, her steps slow, almost detached. She placed her bag on the table with trembling hands.

She didn't speak.

Didn't cry.

Didn't collapse.

She just turned and walked into the bedroom, closing the door softly behind her.

James stood frozen in the middle of the living room, his heart aching with a helplessness he couldn't explain. He wanted so badly to rush after her, to hold her, to somehow take all the pain and the memories and the horror and undo it. But he knew better. Some wounds needed silence. Some griefs required space to breathe.

He sank onto the couch and stared blankly at the TV screen, flipping it on just for the noise. Something mindless played—lights, colours, sound—but it might as well have been static. His eyes didn't focus. His mind didn't follow.

All he could see was Ruthie—standing in that courtroom, her voice shaking but strong, her hands trembling but held high. Speaking truth, no woman should ever have to speak.

James rubbed his palms over his face, eyes burning.

He thought of Ellie. Of the things she never got to say. The things he never got to hear. His sister had suffered too—and she'd carried it alone until it killed her.

And here was Ruthie—fragile but unbroken. Wounded, yes, but standing. Telling the truth for every woman who'd been silenced. And in doing so, showing a kind of strength that James had no words for. It undid him.

He dropped his head into his hands.

He whispered a solemn prayer "God, please cover her. Please hold her heart. Wrap her in the kind of peace only You can give."

He sat there, hands clasped, elbows on his knees—not praying fancy words, just being in God's presence with his ache.

He didn't know what healing looked like from here.

He didn't know how to fix any of it.

But he knew this:

He loved her.

Not just the idea of her. Not the rescued version.

He loved all of her—the fire, the faith, the fractures.

And he would wait. He would protect. He would pray.

Because everything in him was screaming now with a truth he could no longer ignore—

He didn't just care for Ruthie.

He was in love with her.

And more than anything in the world, he wanted her to feel safe.

Ruthie sat on the edge of the bed in the apartment; the room dim but quiet. Her hands were clasped loosely in her lap, her breathing slow and steady. For the first time in what felt like years, the silence wasn't heavy. It wasn't filled with panic or dread or what-if questions. It just was.

Something had shifted in her.

She wasn't being run by fear anymore.

The courtroom, her voice, the echo of her truth—it had stripped something away. Not her softness. Not her scars. But the lie that she had to keep hiding. The lie that he still had any hold on her.

She knew the sentencing wouldn't be for another week—maybe longer. The system moved slow. But oddly... it didn't matter.

Whether it came tomorrow or a month from now, Ruthie had already made a decision. Dylan didn't get another minute of her life. He didn't get to live in her chest like a shadow. He didn't get her thoughts. Her energy. Her peace.

She stood.

Walked toward the bathroom and started the shower.

She waited for the steam to rise around her like a veil.

As the water poured over her skin, she let it become something more than just routine. She let it become release. Every drop was a shedding. Every breath was a prayer.

She lingered under the water, her hands resting against the wall, letting herself feel the warmth—not as a luxury, but as a right.

When she stepped out, she didn't wrap herself in shame or retreat into old habits. Instead, she stood a little taller. She took her time. She brushed her hair slowly. She reached for her makeup—not to hide, not to prove anything, but to honour her reflection. To soften into herself again.

For the first time in a long time, she wanted to feel at home in her body. Not perfect. Not performative. Just... hers.

She pulled on her favourite blouse—one she hadn't worn in months—and a soft pair of jeans. No frills. Just something that felt like Ruthie.

Then she stepped out into the lounge.

James looked up from the couch—and then did a double take.

Something in his chest caught. She wasn't just standing taller. She looked different. Not in the way she was dressed, but in the way she carried herself. Like something transformative had broken loose in her. Like freedom had finally taken root.

She was radiant.

"Hey," she said softly, with a small, sure smile.

James stood slowly, unsure of what to say. She was breathtaking—not because of makeup or clothes, but because of what she'd survived. Because of what she'd reclaimed.

Ruthie tilted her head and looked at him gently. "Let's go out to dinner."

James blinked. "Are you... are you sure?"

She nodded once. "Yes. Just the two of us."

There was no shakiness in her voice. No fear. Just quiet conviction.

James swallowed the emotion building in his throat. He smiled—tender, unsure, awed.

"I'd like that," he said.

And he meant it.

The city pulsed softly around them—golden lights flickering against glass, car horns distant, the smell of rain still lingering in the air from a short earlier drizzle. Ruthie and James walked side by side down a quiet street just off the main strip, the sidewalk glistening under the lamplight.

They didn't rush.

Every step felt intentional. Like time had slowed—not out of hesitation, but out of reverence.

James stole glances at her. She wasn't forcing a smile or faking confidence. She looked... present. Open. A little fragile maybe, but strong in a way that stunned him.

She caught him looking and smiled softly.

"You've been staring," she said gently.

He smiled, rubbing the back of his neck. "I know. I'm sorry. I just... I wasn't expecting you to want to go out tonight. I just wanted to make sure you were okay."

Ruthie shrugged lightly. "I wasn't expecting to feel like I could."

She paused, then added, "But something in me needed to mark the shift. Not with pain. Not with fear. With life. With something simple and good."

James nodded. "Then we'll make it good."

They turned the corner toward a small restaurant, with fairy lights strung across its windows and warm jazz humming from within.

It felt right.

Inside, they were seated near the window, where city lights spilled over their table.

Conversation started slow—small talk about the food, the music, the string of lights hanging unevenly from the ceiling. But slowly, it deepened. Ruthie talked about what it felt like to walk into that courtroom. James shared how helpless he'd felt, sitting there, listening, praying he was somehow doing enough just by being near.

They laughed once—about how awful the coffee was back at the apartment. Then they sat quiet for a few seconds that didn't feel awkward.

Just full.

At one point, Ruthie rested her hand on the table, fingers relaxed.

James hesitated.

Then gently—reverently—he placed his hand over hers.

She didn't pull away.

Her thumb brushed against his, a simple movement that carried more trust than a hundred words.

When dinner was over, they stepped back outside. The city had grown quieter, the shops beginning to close, the air cooled by the evening breeze. They walked with no real destination, just letting the night hold them.

They reached a small pedestrian bridge that overlooked the river. Lights shimmered on the water like stars stretched thin.

James stopped.

Ruthie looked up at him. "What?"

He shook his head. "Nothing. Just... I didn't think tonight would feel this right."

She bit her lip, eyes glinting in the streetlight. "You've seen me at my worst. Maybe it's time you get to see the rest."

James stepped a little closer. Not rushing. Not pressing.

Just enough that she could feel his warmth—the safe kind. Not consuming. Not demanding. Just present.

The kind of closeness that asked permission without needing words.

His voice dropped low, a gentle rumble beneath the quiet.

"Can I tell you something?"

Ruthie nodded, breath already catching before he even spoke.

"I've loved you for a while now," he said softly. "Not because of what you've survived. Not because you're strong or brave—though you are. But because of who you are when no one's watching. Because I see your tenderness. Your fire. The way you choose faith when it would be easier not to. I see you. And I'm not going anywhere."

Her breath hitched.

Her eyes shimmered beneath the streetlight, like they were holding back both history and hope.

"I don't know how to do all of this," she said. "But... I love you. So much."

The confession came out as if it surprised even her—not because it was sudden, but because it had been waiting in the wings of her heart, quietly growing.

She exhaled.

And then—slowly, deliberately—she leaned in.

Not as a performance. Not for reassurance.

But as a choice.

So did he.

Their foreheads met first—gently. As if checking for safety. As if honouring every moment that had come before.

Then James lifted his hand and brushed her hair back, his thumb grazing her cheekbone.

He cupped her jaw like she was something precious—not fragile, but sacred.

And then... they kissed.

Soft.

Steady.

Unrushed.

A meeting of two stories written with sorrow and resilience—with grief, grace, and God.

When they pulled apart, they didn't speak.

They didn't need to.

The city around them had quieted. The lights hummed. The river moved beneath their feet.

And somewhere in the space between breath and heartbeat, the night said it for them:

Something new has begun.

Chapter 39: The Visit

"But let justice roll on like a river, righteousness like a never-failing stream!"
—Amos 5:24

The city skyline blurred and slipped behind them as James guided the Ute onto the highway, Ruthie sat in the passenger seat, her gaze fixed on the window, where skyscrapers shrank to silhouettes and morning mist softened the hard edges of the road ahead.

They hadn't spoken much after packing up the apartment that morning. There hadn't been a need to.

They were leaving the city behind—not because it was over, but because it had done what it needed to. Ruthie had said what needed to be said. The court would call when it was time. But their hearts were already moving forward. Toward the farm. Toward home.

A silent breath moved through Ruthie's chest as she thought about the night before. Her fingers lifted unconsciously, grazing her lips—remembering. The way James had kissed her. Not hungrily. Not to claim. But with love and gentleness.

No one had ever kissed her like that before. No one had ever held her like a story worth unfolding.

She glanced at him now.

James had one hand on the steering wheel, the other resting near the centre console. The sun caught the slope of his forearm. His shoulders were relaxed; eyes fixed on the road — but something about the quiet told her he was remembering too.

She did love him. Of that she was certain. But love... love was a word she was still learning how to hold. Still learning how to trust. It had once meant survival. Submission. Pretending. But this? This was different. This was safe and slow and startling in its goodness.

She thought about how he'd walked her home after dinner. No pressure. No assumptions. Just his hand in hers, his presence steady. He'd made her tea. Sat beside her on the couch. Said goodnight with a smile and went to bed.

He hadn't tried to take more than she gave. He hadn't needed to.

Her hand moved before she even realised it—hovering above the centre console.

Then, gently, she placed it on his.

James looked down for a moment. A breath passed between them.

Then he turned his palm upward, lacing their fingers together without a word.

His thumb brushed hers, slow and grounding.

They drove that way for miles—fingers tangled, hearts quiet, the road unspooling before them like a new beginning.

By the time they pulled up the dusty driveway—a road they'd travelled more times than they could count—something had changed. The land was the same, the farmhouse unchanged, but the air between them buzzed with something unspoken. Hope. Love. A quiet kind of knowing.

James didn't say a word. He just started unloading the car, moving with quiet purpose. There was no need to fill the silence. He was close without pressing in—offering her room, but never far.

Their silence wasn't the kind born of discomfort anymore. A new language written in glances, gestures, breath. Grief had once sat like a weight between them, but now it had made space. Carved out a hollow that something softer could fill.

That night, they ate together at the kitchen table. No TV. No music. Just the clink of forks and the soft exhale of belonging. When Ruthie looked up and caught James watching her—not with expectation, but with that quiet reverence she was still learning how to receive—her heart twisted in a way that hurt and healed all at once.

Later, she stood at the window while the wind whispered through the trees outside, and for the first time in a long time, she felt... safe. Not just from the past. But within herself.

The next morning, the sun spilled through the kitchen window in soft golden ribbons.

Naomi had offered to bring Bear back now that James and Ruthie were home.

As Naomi's car crunched up the drive, Ruthie's heart beat a little faster. Bear jumped from the passenger seat and ran toward her, tail wagging wildly. Ruthie knelt down, arms wide, as the familiar weight of him hit her chest. His warm, earthy scent pressed into her like a homecoming. She held him tighter than she meant to, whispering, "Good boy... I missed you."

James offered Naomi a polite nod as he passed, his hand brushing gently over Ruthie's in a quiet gesture of reassurance. A soft smile tugged at his lips—fleeting but full—before he slipped out toward the shed, intuitively giving Ruthie the space she needed.

Naomi, ever perceptive, waited until they were both settled on the lounge with warm mugs of coffee before breaking the silence.

"Well," Naomi said, arching a brow with a mischievous grin, "something's definitely different. Spill. What happened between you and Mr. Farm boy?"

Ruthie flushed, colour blooming across her cheeks. A soft smile teased at the corners of her mouth, unsure at first, then growing with the kind of quiet courage that comes from stepping into something new.

"It surprised me, honestly," Ruthie began, her voice hushed but steady. "When we first got to the city, I was completely overwhelmed. All I could think about was giving my victim impact statement—getting through it, surviving it. The fear, the anxiety... it clung to me like fog. I couldn't breathe past it."

She paused, looking down at her coffee as if trying to find the right words. Naomi stayed quiet, sensing the weight of what was coming.

"But then... once I gave the statement—once I actually said it all out loud in that courtroom, something shifted inside me. It was like I'd finally laid the burden down. And in that space, that emptiness that used to be filled with fear... I could suddenly feel everything else I'd been holding back."

She looked up, eyes glistening.

"I realised how deeply I feel for James. And how safe he makes me feel—not just protected but seen. So that night... we went out. Just a simple dinner. We walked for a while, through the lights and the quiet backstreets. And then, he stopped."

Ruthie's breath caught as she relived it. Her fingers absently brushed her lips.

"He told me he loved me. That he wasn't going anywhere. And then... we kissed. Not rushed or dramatic. Just... full. Gentle."

Naomi leaned forward, eyes wide. "Okay, but give me the details. Was it full-on romantic movie kiss or more soft lighting and hand-holding kind of kiss?"

Ruthie laughed—a real laugh, full-bodied and free. "It was both, somehow. Our foreheads touched first, like we were just soaking in the moment. Then he cupped my face so tenderly, like he was holding something sacred.'"

Naomi's smile softened, voice reverent. "Ruthie... that's the kind of love that heals."

Ruthie nodded, blinking back tears she hadn't expected. "Yeah. And the best part? He didn't expect anything after."

Naomi reached across the space between them and squeezed Ruthie's hand.

"I think you've found something real."

Ruthie exhaled, voice trembling but sure. "I think I have too."

She paused before continuing.

"I think..." Ruthie's voice trembled, but she didn't stop. "I think I was terrified that letting myself love again would mean Dylan still had power over me. Like if I opened up—really opened up—I'd be vulnerable. Exposed. And I didn't want to feel small again."

She looked down at her hands, fingers twisting in her lap, and then back at Naomi. "But it's not like that. What I feel with James... it doesn't make me smaller. It makes me braver. It feels like I'm finally taking something back. Reclaiming the parts of me he tried to destroy."

Naomi's eyes shimmered with tears. She reached for Ruthie's hand, squeezing gently. "Because that's exactly what you're doing. You're taking your story back, one piece at a time."

Before either of them could say another word, the shrill ring of the landline shattered the quiet.

Ruthie flinched, then stood and crossed the room. She lifted the receiver with a steady hand.

The voice on the line was clipped and formal. "This is Claire Holden from the Melbourne Court Registry. Am I speaking with Ruthie Matthews?"

A knot tightened in Ruthie's stomach.

"Yes, this is Ruthie."

"Thank you, Miss Matthews. I'm calling to inform you that sentencing has been handed down."

Ruthie's grip on the phone tightened. Her throat felt dry.

"Okay... Thank you for calling. I'm listening."

"Dylan Watts has been sentenced to twelve years' imprisonment. A non-parole period of eight. The judge considered the depth of your victim impact statement and the consistent, ongoing nature of the abuse. He specifically acknowledged your courage in standing up and speaking your truth."

Ruthie didn't breathe. Her chest felt hollow and full all at once. Her heartbeat thundered in her ears.

But she didn't cry.

She stood taller. Straighter. Like something invisible had been cut loose inside her—and now she was standing in her own skin, unshackled.

"Thank you," she said, voice even, firm, with no trace of the girl who once flinched at shadows.

When she turned back, Naomi was already on her feet, her arms open—not to fix or soothe, but to simply be there. Present.

"Twelve years," Ruthie said, more to herself than anyone. "Eight before parole."

Naomi's eyes searched hers. "How does it feel?"

"It feels... final," she said. "Like I can't erase what happened, and yeah, the pain is still there. But now... I know I can move forward. This... this feels like the start of real healing."

Naomi stepped into her arms and pulled her into a tight embrace.

No words. No platitudes.

Just love.

Chapter 40: Washed New

"Therefore go and make disciples of all nations, baptising them in the name of the Father and of the Son and of the Holy Spirit."– Matthew 28:19

The morning air on the farm was crisp, laced with the scent of damp earth and eucalyptus. A light mist clung to the paddocks, curling low around the trees like breath made visible. Ruthie stood at the edge of the field, barefoot in the cool grass, arms wrapped around herself—not from cold, but from the weight of something stirring deep inside her.

Behind her, the screen door creaked open, and James stepped out onto the porch, his flannel shirt tugged haphazardly over his shoulders, eyes still soft with sleep.

"You're up early," he said, voice husky.

"I couldn't sleep," Ruthie replied, gaze still fixed on the horizon where the sun was just starting to rise. "But not because of nightmares."

James padded quietly across the grass to stand beside her. He didn't speak, just waited.

"I feel different now," Ruthie continued. "Lighter."

James glanced at her, eyes quietly searching her face.

"I've been thinking," Ruthie began, her voice steady but soft. "About my life... everything that's happened. How it's all unfolded. And how—looking back—I can see the moments God showed up. The quiet ones. The big ones. The ones I only recognised later, through Scripture or through the kindness of others."

She drew in a breath.

"I used to think He was absent. But now... I'm starting to see how present He's been all along. I just didn't know how to look."

James stilled, sensing something special unfolding.

"I'm ready," she said, her voice firm now. "I want to take my relationship with God to the next level."

She paused.

"I want to be baptised."

James blinked, not from shock—but from the clarity and conviction in her eyes.

"Not as a ritual," Ruthie continued. "As a declaration. I want to leave it all behind—the past, the lies he told me, the parts of myself I buried just to survive. I want to go under and rise up clean. Whole and new."

For a long moment, James said nothing. Then his face softened with something deeper than a smile—something reverent.

"That's beautiful," he said quietly. "If you'd like... we can call Pastor Luke. I'm sure he'd be honoured to walk through this with you."

Ruthie nodded, eyes misting with unshed tears. But her chin lifted, and her breath steadied. She nodded again—this time with quiet resolve—grateful for James's steady presence beside her.

That afternoon, they drove into town with the late sun flickering through the trees. Ruthie sat quietly in the passenger seat; her fingers gently laced through James's as they followed the familiar curves of the country roads. Her thumb traced slow, thoughtful circles over the back of his hand.

The radio played softly—a mix of acoustic guitar and soft vocals that neither of them really registered, more of a backdrop to the reverence settling over the day.

As they pulled into the gravel car park beside the weathered country church, Ruthie drew a slow breath. The steeple stood simple but strong against the pale blue sky—a place she'd passed many times but never entered with this kind of intention.

Pastor Luke was already outside, as if he'd been waiting—not just watching for them, but expectant in that quiet, prayerful way of his. He wiped his calloused hands on his jeans and stepped forward, his smile stretching wide beneath a silver beard that caught the morning sun like threads of grace.

"You two look different," he said, voice warm and rich like honey over tea. "Peace seems to suit you both."

"We are," Ruthie answered softly. James's hand lingered for a moment in hers, then slipped away as she took a step forward. Her boots crunched lightly on the gravel.

She paused. Then, chin lifted, voice steady, "I'd like to be baptised," she said.

Pastor Luke's eyes glistened—not with surprise, but with sacred joy, the kind that comes when prayers are answered in quiet fields and quiet hearts. A shepherd seeing one of his lambs ready to come home.

"Well then," he said, nodding deeply. "Let's prepare for Sunday."

He gestured toward the church doors, worn and sun-faded but full of welcome. Inside, the scent of wood polish and old Bibles lingered. They followed him into his office, where he rifled through a drawer, pulled out a form, and handed it gently to Ruthie.

"What I'll need you to do," he said with a soft chuckle, "is bring something simple to wear—cotton works best. The river behind the church where we do baptisms is cold this time of year, but the Holy Spirit doesn't mind a chill."

They all laughed, but Ruthie's gaze stayed steady, anchored in something deeper. There was no fear. No flinching. Just a radiant stillness blooming inside her.

Pastor Luke sat down across from her, hands folded, tone shifting into something reverent.

"Baptism," he said, "is more than just water. It's not a ritual for show, Ruthie—it's a sacred declaration. A turning point. When you go under, it's symbolic of dying to the old life—your sin, your shame, your past. And when you rise up from the water, it's resurrection. It's walking in the newness of life, joined with Christ."

He paused, letting the words settle.

"You're not just making a statement to the people watching. You're making a covenant with God. That you believe in the power of Jesus to wash you clean. That you're choosing Him—not just for a moment, but for every moment that follows."

Ruthie nodded slowly, the weight of it sinking in—but not as a burden. As freedom. As truth.

"I've carried so much," she said. "But I don't want to live from fear anymore. I want to live from faith."

James reached for her hand again, and this time she didn't let go.

Pastor Luke smiled again, soft and sure. "Then we'll meet at the river Sunday morning. You bring your faith. I'll bring the towel. And God will do the rest."

Sunday morning came with golden light, and a sky painted like a promise. A small group of church members had gathered by the river—not out of obligation, but anticipation. Word had travelled. This wasn't just a ceremony. It was a resurrection.

Ruthie stepped into the water slowly, the hem of her dress clinging to her legs. Pastor Luke stood waist-deep, smiling gently as she reached him.

"Ruthie," he said, "do you believe that Jesus Christ is the Son of God, that He died and rose again for your sins, and that you are a new creation in Him?"

"I do," she said, voice trembling—not with fear, but fullness.

"And do you choose to lay down your old life and walk in the freedom of Christ?"

"I do," she whispered, tears already sliding down her cheeks.

He placed a hand behind her back, the other over her clasped hands. "Then I baptise you in the name of the Father, the Son, and the Holy Spirit."

The water closed over her.

And then—she rose.

The crowd clapped softly. James watched from the shore, his heart swelling with something that didn't have words. Only awe.

She walked back toward him, hair soaked, eyes shining, face lifted.

"I feel... clean."

"You look like heaven touched you," he said, stepping into her space and wrapping her in a towel.

They held each other for a long moment.

That night, the fire crackled low in the fireplace, and the stars winked through the cottage windows. Ruthie curled against James on the couch, both barefoot, both wrapped in the quiet warmth of the day.

They talked softly—about childhood memories, about favourite books, about dreams that hadn't been dreamed yet.

At some point, Ruthie turned toward him.

"Thank you," she whispered.

"For what?"

"For seeing me... before I even knew how to see myself."

James reached up and gently tucked a damp strand of hair behind her ear, his fingers lingering just a second longer against her skin.

"You were never invisible to me," he murmured, voice husky with truth.

The words hung between them.

Ruthie looked up, her breath catching in her throat. There was no hiding left in her eyes. No masks. Just the ache of being seen, truly seen, and still wanted.

Their eyes locked.

And this time, neither of them looked away.

Slowly, like gravity pulling two worlds together, they leaned in. When their lips met, it wasn't rushed—it was deliberate. A kiss full of trembling reverence, like touching something eternal.

James's hands found her waist, sliding around with quiet need, and she melted into him, her own hands rising to curl around the nape of his neck. The space between them vanished. Breath tangled. Heartbeats stuttered into rhythm.

The kiss deepened—hunger rising just beneath the surface—but still, there was gentleness.

But then... Ruthie stilled.

She rested her forehead against his, breath unsteady, her chest rising and falling between them. Her fingers trembled against his collar.

"I need to tell you something," she said, voice soft but steady. "I want this. I want you. Every part of me is screaming yes. But... I've been thinking a lot about what love really means, about commitment, and faith. I never used to dream about marriage, not really. But now—I do. I want to stand before God, with you. I want that covenant. That covering. Before I give that part of myself again... I need to wait. Until marriage."

James didn't pull back.

He didn't falter.

He simply opened his eyes and looked at her like she was the most beautiful storm he'd ever survived.

"I'll wait," he said. "As long as it takes. You're worth that."

And somehow—that made her knees weaker than any kiss ever could.

James looked at her, no confusion, no frustration—just understanding. He nodded once, his hand moving from her waist to cradle her cheek.

Then, with the same reverence he'd shown since the beginning, he pulled her gently back in.

Not out of impatience. Not to convince her otherwise.

But because love can live in a kiss without rushing the rest.

Their lips met again—slower this time, soaked in emotion, in the ache of surrender. It was a promise sealed not in passion alone, but in tenderness. In restraint. In holy desire that knew its boundary and honoured it.

When they finally parted, Ruthie stayed close, her forehead resting against his again, her heart full to the brim.

She wasn't just wanted.

She was cherished.

And somehow, in that quiet knowing, she felt more whole than she ever had before.

Chapter 41: Sparks in the Distance

"Two are better than one, because they have a good return for their labor: If either of them falls down, one can help the other up." – Ecclesiastes 4:9-10

The days on the farm found a new rhythm. Morning coffee brewed slow on the stovetop. The animals responded to James's call with an ease that made Ruthie smile. She'd taken to walking barefoot again—the earth no longer something she avoided, but something she trusted.

Healing wasn't loud. It wasn't a parade. It was in the way she reached for James's hand without flinching. In the way she laughed with her whole body. In the way James watched her, as if he still couldn't believe she was real.

They read together most nights now—books Ruthie had once loved and lost. They cooked side-by-side. She burned the toast more often than not, but he kissed her cheek anyway.

Sometimes, they just sat. Not every moment needed filling.

And then there were moments like this one.

James came in from the field just as the sun was beginning to dip low, casting long golden fingers through the trees. He found Ruthie near the old swing, her legs tucked beneath her, reading. She looked up as he approached.

"You look dusty," she teased.

"You look beautiful," he replied, meaning every word.

She smiled, but her eyes were soft. "You always say the right thing."

"No," he said. "Just the true thing."

Later that night, they stood outside the barn, wrapped in each other beneath the open sky. The air was still, cool against their sun-warmed skin. Above them, the Milky Way unfurled in dazzling silence—an endless river of light arcing across the heavens.

Ruthie leaned into James, her arms looped loosely around his waist, her head resting in the crook of his neck. He held her close, one hand splayed across her back, the other gently cradling the back of her head like she was something precious—and breakable.

Neither of them spoke. Words would have only interrupted what the silence already held.

They stayed that way for hours, unmoving, just breathing in rhythm. The kind of quiet that doesn't ache but heals. His chin rested against her hair. Her fingers lightly curled into his shirt. The rise and fall of his chest anchored her, like the rhythm of waves against a familiar shore.

Above them, the stars shimmered like old prayers—unrushed, unforgotten.

"I don't want to move," she said.

"You don't have to," he murmured.

And so, they stayed—just two souls beneath the galaxies, wrapped in dust, memory, and something deeper than comfort. Something eternal.

If the earth had cracked open beneath them, they might not have noticed.

Because in that moment, they were whole.

A few days later, James met Micah at the supply shed near the northern paddock. The two men worked in companionable silence, patching an old gate and wrangling stubborn coils of fencing wire that had a mind of their own. The sun beat down in golden waves, and James paused to swipe sweat from his brow.

Micah tossed him a water bottle with a smirk. "You're awfully quiet," he remarked.

"I've got a lot on my mind, mate," James replied.

"Oh boy." Micah leaned on a shovel, squinting. "You're not about to tell me you bought another tractor off that dodgy bloke from Shepparton, are you?"

James shook his head, smiling despite himself. "No, worse." He smirked.

Micah crossed his arms. "Worse than dodgy tractor bloke?"

James looked out over the gum trees lining the ridge. His voice was low, quiet.

"I'm in love with her."

Micah blinked. "Ruthie?"

"No, Micah—the postwoman," James deadpanned, then grinned. "Yes, Ruthie."

Micah let out a dramatic sigh. "Finally. Took you long enough to admit what the rest of us could see ages ago."

James laughed, rubbing the back of his neck.

"It's different now," he said after a beat. "Deeper. She's not just someone I care for. She's it, Micah. She's the one. I think I want to spend the rest of my life with her. I think I want to marry her."

Micah's teasing faded into something softer. He stepped closer, resting a hand briefly on James's shoulder.

"But I'm scared, Micah," James admitted, voice rougher now. "She's been through so much. What if I can't be what she needs? What if I mess it up?"

Micah looked at him—really looked—then sighed dramatically and tossed the shovel aside like it had offended him.

"James," he said, stepping forward, "you built a chicken coop during a thunderstorm with one hand and a busted ankle. You taught a traumatised dog how to trust again. You made gluten-free scones that didn't taste like cardboard—for a woman who didn't even ask you to bake. And now you're worried you're not enough?"

James gave a sheepish smile, but the worry still lingered in his eyes.

Micah softened. "Look, love doesn't ask you to be perfect. It asks you to be present. To show up. To listen, to grow, and sometimes to apologise for being a stubborn mule."

He grinned. "Which you are, by the way. Stubborn as a mule with its hooves in concrete."

James chuckled. "Thanks for the vote of confidence."

"I'm serious," Micah said, his voice gentle now. "You already are what she needs, James. Not because you'll get everything right, but because you're willing to try."

There was a long pause. The breeze rustled through the trees, and a kookaburra laughed somewhere off in the distance—like even creation was in on the moment.

Micah picked up the coil of fencing wire again. "Now, go propose to the woman before I have to do it for you."

James shook his head, laughing, heart lighter. "I'm working on it."

"You better be, Because I've already started writing my best man speech—and let's just say, the stories I've got stored up for that occasion are next-level." He grinned.

James groaned, tossing his glove at him. But the smile that followed was real—full of promise.

He was ready. Almost.

And Micah would be right there beside him—steady, loyal, and just annoying enough to make sure he didn't forget it.

Chapter 42: The Sky Turned Red

"He will cover you with his feathers, and under his wings you will find refuge; his faithfulness will be your shield and rampart. You will not fear the terror of night, nor the arrow that flies by day." – Psalm 91:4-5

It began with a smell.

Faint. Acrid.

The kind that prickled the nose before the mind had time to catch up.

Ruthie stirred, her body tensing instinctively beneath the sheets. The air in the room felt strange—dry, unmoving, thick with silence. A stillness that didn't belong.

She sat up slowly. Her breath caught in her throat as the dim orange hue of dawn filtered through the curtains—too sharp, too early, like the sky had forgotten how to rise gently.

She turned toward the doorway, heart quickening. James's silhouette stood outlined in the glow of the kitchen light, phone pressed to his ear, shoulders taut—listening. Alert. The way people stand when something isn't right.

Ruthie had never lived in the country. Her life had always been framed by the soft hum of traffic, streetlights bleeding into midnight, and suburban fences drawn like borders around a world she understood. But this place—this vast, unpredictable land—was still foreign. Still unfamiliar.

James turned. Their eyes met. His face was drawn, jaw clenched.

"Yeah," he said into the phone, his voice low. "The fire's a hundred kilometres out. Moving fast. If the wind shifts, we're in the path. We'll start prep now."

He hung up and exhaled. The calm in his voice didn't match the storm in his eyes.

Ruthie's stomach flipped.

By the time she pulled on her boots and stepped outside, the world had changed. It wasn't on fire—yet—but it felt... off. The sky was veiled in a yellow-grey haze, a silent warning stretched across the horizon. The light was wrong. The air scratched her throat. And the birds—normally loud, playful—were gone.

She stood there, blinking at the sky, her chest tightening with the weight of what if. Of what now. Her hands shook.

Then arms wrapped around her from behind.

"Morning, beautiful," James whispered, pressing a kiss to her hair like it was any other Thursday.

But his body betrayed him—tense, urgent.

She felt it.

He tried to smile. "It's just a fire. We get them all the time," he said, aiming for casual, but missing. "We over-prepare most of the time. Nothing ever comes of it."

Ruthie looked up at him. Really looked.

"But what about the times it does?"

James paused. His eyes didn't flinch.

"I won't let anything happen to you," he said.

The wind had shifted again—sharp, dry, and unnerving. It whipped through the gum trees, rattling their leaves like brittle bones. The once-familiar canopy, which had so often felt like a protective cover over their land, now loomed dark and restless. The trees were no longer companions; they stood like strangers, brittle and on edge, whispering of danger.

James glanced at Ruthie, noting the tightness in her jaw, the way her fingers gripped the hem of her shirt. He reached for her hand, grounding her with a gentle squeeze.

"It's going to be okay," he said softly, trying to steady the worry rising behind her eyes. "I've written down a list—just so we don't miss anything."

He pulled a folded, slightly crumpled piece of paper from his pocket and handed it to her. Black ink, hurried and slanted, listed their fire prep in bullet points. She scanned it—troughs filled, gutters cleared, hoses uncoiled—each line a fragile attempt to stay ahead of the flames.

"We'll split up," James said, his voice steady now, tempered by action. "You take the back fence and soak the woodpile. I'll clear the brush near the eastern shed."

Ruthie nodded, tucking the list into her pocket. The urgency between them didn't need to be spoken anymore—it pulsed in the air, in the way they moved, in the way the land held its breath.

She nodded again. She didn't want to. She wanted to beg him not to leave her line of sight. But instead, she swallowed hard and nodded.

They moved.

Ruthie hauled buckets to the garden beds, her breath coming fast, her limbs tight with adrenaline. She soaked the soil until it turned dark and heavy, trying to smother panic with water. She unfurled the garden hoses, hands trembling, unwinding them like veins across the earth.

Across the paddock, James worked like a man possessed. He had already cleared a stretch of the scrub and was now boarding the south-facing windows with sheets of tin. Sweat streaked down his temple, soot smudging his arms. His muscles moved with purpose, but Ruthie could see the fear behind every swing of the hammer.

The wind changed again, hotter this time.

Ruthie turned toward the hills—and gasped.

The sky had shifted. What had been yellow haze was now a dirty orange smear creeping across the ridgeline. Smoke. Low, thick, alive.

She didn't need James to tell her what it meant.

The fire was no longer a possibility.

It was coming.

The wind picked up, sharp and sudden, whipping Ruthie's hair across her face.

James dropped a tool and stared west.

The yellow haze was darker now. A smear of smoke creeping low over the hills like a predator crouched and watching.

James stepped away, pulling out his phone with trembling fingers. Ruthie watched as he turned his back to her, his voice hushed and clipped, urgency laced into every syllable.

"...not long now... yes, just her and Bear... no, I'll stay... see you in five."

Her breath hitched. The words hit her like a fist.

She was already walking toward him, heart pounding. "What was that?"

He turned slowly. His jaw clenched, eyes shadowed with something heavy.

"Naomi's coming."

She frowned. "Okay... good. When?"

He hesitated, eyes darting toward the hills behind her. "Soon, she said she was about five minutes out."

Something in his tone—too flat, too even—set her on edge. His calm was a lie.

And suddenly she knew.

Her voice trembled. "James... why just me and Bear?"

He didn't answer.

Her chest cracked open. "No," she said, voice breaking. "Don't you dare."

"Listen please Ruthie—"

"NO!" she cried, storming toward him, voice thick with grief and fury. "How could you do this? How dare you! I love you, you fool! You don't get to send me away like I'm a suitcase to be packed and left on the porch! You don't get to stay behind like your life doesn't matter!"

James flinched. His face buckled at her words. He opened his mouth, but she didn't let him speak.

"You don't get to make that choice for me," she said. firm. "You don't get to be the hero and leave me behind! That's not love, James—that's fear pretending to be noble!"

He looked down, torn. "If something happened to you—"

"If something happened to you," she said, her voice shaking, "I wouldn't survive it either. Don't you see that?"

The wind picked up again, sharp as a blade, tearing through the dry branches. Ash drifted down like snow—silent, deadly, surreal. It clung to her hair, to his shoulders. The world was tilting, burning, and she could barely stand in it.

He reached for her. She didn't stop him. His arms wrapped around her, and she folded into him like she always had, trembling.

"I love you," James whispered hoarsely. "That's why I'm asking you to go."

She pulled back just far enough to look him in the eye. Her tears came hot and fast.

"Then act like it!" she cried. "Loving me doesn't mean dying for me, James! It means living with me. Holding my hand through gray hair and quiet mornings. It means showing up for our future—not sacrificing yourself for it! I love you, and you don't get to do this!"

Just then, the crunch of gravel broke through the storm of their emotions.

Naomi's ute pulled into the drive, tires skidding slightly as it stopped. Dust rose in thick waves behind her, mixing with the ash that fell like judgment from the sky.

The door flung open.

Naomi stepped out and immediately took in the scene—Ruthie sobbing in the dirt, Jame stiff with conflict, the firelight just beginning to taint the sky behind them.

She didn't hesitate.

She walked straight to them and grabbed James by the arm, firm and unwavering.

"No," she said sharply. "We all leave. Now."

James tried to protest, but Naomi cut him off with a glare that could melt steel.

"You have thirty seconds to grab what you need. I'm not letting you martyr yourself, James. Not today."

James looked at Ruthie. Ash clung to her lashes. Her lips trembled, but her eyes—those eyes—held a fierce, aching kind of love he didn't think he'd ever be worthy of.

He nodded slowly.

Naomi exhaled, grabbed Bear's lead, and started shouting instructions.

Ruthie wiped her face and reached for James's hand.

He held it like it was the last thing anchoring him to the earth.

And maybe, it was.

Chapter 43: When the Wind Turned

"Because of the Lord's great love we are not consumed, for his compassions never fail. They are new every morning; great is your faithfulness." – Lamentations 3:22-23

James moved with calm precision—but it was the kind of calm that comes from knowing panic would undo everything.

He flung open the shed doors, shoving aside tools and crates, his boots scraping across the concrete as he yanked the fire pump into position, hoses trailing.

Ruthie ran, breath ragged, chest burning. Naomi was beside her. Inside the house, everything felt too still—too full of memories to touch. Her hands shook as she grabbed the emergency bag, heart thudding.

She reached for the pillowcase, stuffing it with James's family photos—the ones in cracked frames and with bent corners. Then the memory box from under the bed, her fingers hesitating on the lid for half a second. It felt like stealing from the past.

Bear barked wildly at the front door, his nails clicking across the floor, spinning in tight, frantic circles. Ruthie's eyes flicked to the windows.

The sky.

The sky had turned gold, but not the kind of gold that sang of sunrise or wheat fields. This gold was thick, choking—burnt. The smoke had turned the world into an old photograph curling at the edges. Ash danced through the air like cursed snow, weightless but heavy with meaning.

Outside, James and Ruthie moved quickly, hands working on instinct. Water. First-aid kits. Tins. Blankets. Flashlights. His grandfather's worn Bible with pages soft from years of prayers. Each item flung into the back of the Ute felt like an apology to the life they were leaving behind.

James slammed the tailgate shut, and the sound cracked through the air like a gunshot. For a moment, no one spoke.

He turned back to the house.

And froze.

His eyes shimmered—not just from the smoke, but from the grief curling in his chest like the fire through the hills. He reached up and wiped his face with the back of his arm, but it was too late. The tears betrayed him.

"I know it's just land to most people," he said. "Just dirt and trees. But not to me."

His voice broke.

"This place raised me. When I had no one... when Dad died, and Mum left, and Ellie—" His breath caught. "This place held me when no one else did. Every nail in this house has their story. It's more than a house. It's home."

Ruthie stood rooted in place, her chest aching with the weight of his sorrow.

Then, gently, she stepped forward.

She cupped his face with both hands, rough with ash and sweat. She turned him to her.

"James," she said. "You have me now."

His gaze flicked to hers, confusion swimming behind the grief.

She steadied.

"You have me," she repeated, firmer. "I'm your home now. Not this land. Not these fences or trees. Me. I love you. I need you. I'm not going anywhere. I'm your safe place."

He held her then.

Held her like the world was ending.

Because maybe, it was.

And then—he kissed her.

Not out of fear. But out of surrender. Out of a desperate, a kind of love that could only be born at the edge of everything.

When they finally pulled apart, ash clinging to their lashes and lips, James whispered into her ear:

"All right. Let's go."

She nodded, tears drying on her cheeks, throat aching.

They climbed into the Ute. James clicked Bear's harness into place in the back. Ruthie settled into the passenger seat, fingers clutching the dash as he turned the key.

They didn't speak.

They just drove—windows closed to keep the smoke out, hearts pounding like war drums.

Behind them, Naomi followed in her car, steady as ever.

But none of them knew what waited on the road ahead.

Only that they would face it.

Together.

The dirt road twisted down past the dam, winding through the old gums that lined the fence like ancient sentinels, silent witnesses to generations of storms—but none like this.

The wind was no longer a whisper. It screamed now—wild, unrestrained, alive.

Inside the Ute, Ruthie gripped the edge of her seat. Bear whined behind her, trembling with each gust. Naomi followed in her Ute, headlights cutting a path through the thickening smoke.

Then James saw it.

A single eucalyptus tree—tall, noble, now engulfed. Fire licked its trunk like fingers claiming what had never asked to be taken. An ember had landed silently, as if by ghost hands, and it was already too late.

The flames had crossed the road.

James slammed the brakes. The Ute skidded, gravel spraying. Ruthie's breath caught in her throat.

"No!" she yelled.

James reversed, tyres shrieking, the world narrowing to smoke, fear, and reflex.

"Go around!" Ruthie shouted, twisting in her seat to check behind them.

"We can't!" James's voice was sharp, brittle. "That's the only access in or out!"

They spun back into the driveway, the familiar yard now drenched in smoke and dread. Naomi was already there, her door swinging open as she stepped out.

No words. Just a glance—and the shared knowledge:

They were trapped.

James leapt from the Ute. Bear jumped out behind him. Ruthie ran toward the house, legs barely obeying, lungs burning.

"What now?" she asked, eyes wide.

"We stay," James said. "We bunker in."

Ruthie stared, stunned.

Naomi nodded, voice tight. "We fight. We don't have a choice."

And just like that, the moment passed. No tears. No panic. Just action.

Ruthie sprinted toward the linen cupboard, yanking fire blankets down. Naomi began sealing windows with wet towels and filling basins. James dragged the last tin sheets to the verandah and hammered them in with hands blistered from speed and heat.

"Sprayers." James yelled.

Naomi bolted to the tank. "Pump's primed!"

"Bear—inside!" Ruthie called, and the dog obeyed, skidding into the hallway.

They moved like they were born into this moment. As if fire drills had written their muscle memory. As if some part of them had always known this day would come.

Sweat ran down James's face, mixed with ash and memories. Ruthie's palms were raw from hauling sacks of damp soil against every door gap.

The sky darkened into something ancient. A sick red. Not like a sunset. Not like dusk.

Like war.

A distant roar rolled toward them—not thunder. Not engines.

The growl of a firestorm.

The last hose kinked. Ruthie yelled, tears stinging her eyes. She slammed it against the tank. James ran, unkinked it, then grabbed her by the waist and held her for one breathless second.

They didn't speak. They didn't need to.

Bear barked from inside the house, whining. Naomi ran past them, face grim, arms soaked, shouting, "Front's coming in!"

And then—the wind shifted.

A rain of embers fell from the sky like stars falling backward. One hit the shed roof, hissing. Another landed in the dry brush by the coop. The world became sound and heat and light and dread.

Then—fire.

A sigh of death across the paddocks.

It whispered through the long grass, curled under the fence, slithered like a serpent up the trees. The air shimmered with unbearable heat. Paint blistered. Wood cracked.

"Inside!" James ordered, voice hoarse.

They retreated.

Ruthie slammed the back door. James locked the front. Naomi double-checked the seals and grabbed the emergency radio.

The three of them met in the bathroom—small, tiled, wrapped in wet towels. Bear curled at their feet, tail tucked tight.

James pulled Ruthie into his chest. Her body shook.

"I'm sorry," he said. "I should've got us out sooner."

"You stayed. You stayed with me. That's all I needed." she said, gripping him.

Naomi reached out and wrapped them both in a fierce, trembling hug. "We're together. That's all that matters."

They crouched there, the three of them, wrapped in silence and prayer.

The walls groaned.

Glass cracked.

The fire pressed against the house like a hand trying to crush its way in.

And still, they held on.

Not to the house.

To each other.

To faith.

To the belief that love could hold when everything else burned.

And in the darkest moment, with the firestorm howling around them, James leaned in close, voice shaking.

"Ruthie, if we make it through this—"

She looked up.

"—Will you spend the rest of your life with me and marry me.

Ruthie choked on a sob and nodded, pressing her forehead to his.

"Yes!" she responded. "Yes."

Inside that bathroom—through the ash and fear and trembling hearts—

there was something the fire could not reach.

Hope.

And love that did not run.

Chapter 44: Through the Flames

"Again, truly I tell you that if two of you on earth agree about anything they ask for, it will be done for them by my Father in heaven.
For where two or three gather in my name, there am I with them." — *Matthew 18:19–20*

The roar outside was no longer distant.

It was here.

A living, snarling force pressing in on every side, breathing hot against the walls of the farmhouse like a beast desperate to devour them whole. Smoke clawed through every crack. The windows glowed with an unnatural light—the breath of fire licking closer, brighter, hungrier.

Inside the bathroom, time had folded in on itself.

Ruthie clung to James, her face buried in the soaked cotton of his shirt. It smelled of smoke, sweat, and dust—evidence of everything they had fought to protect. Her breaths came shallow and uneven. Naomi was beside them, kneeling on the tiled floor, one hand gripping Ruthie's shoulder as if she could, will her strength into her. The other pressed a sodden towel tight to the base of the door, a futile line of defence against the suffocating heat outside.

Bear whimpered low, curled at their feet like a trembling shadow. His paws were muddy from pacing. His eyes darted between them.

Ruthie's hand searched for James's and gripped it hard, her fingers threading through his until she could feel the thrum of his pulse—proof that he was still there. Still hers.

And somehow, in that terrifying stillness, she was thinking about love.

About vows whispered in candlelight and promises carved in pain. About the way James held her like she mattered more than survival. About the fire they'd already walked through—just to find each other.

"We should pray," Naomi whispered. Her voice was raw. Not just from smoke—but from knowing. From faith that had lived through its own infernos.

They bowed their heads; three hearts pressed together in the hollow of fear.

Ruthie began. Her voice cracked but didn't break.

"God... You see us. You've always seen us. You know what we've walked through. You know how scared we are. We want to live, Lord—but if we can't... please, let us stay in Your presence."

James's voice followed, rough with emotion. "We're not asking because we're good. We're asking because You are."

Naomi's words came next. "Cover this house. Cover us. Be the breath in our lungs and the shelter around these walls. Let Your mercy be louder than the flames."

Then silence.

Not empty—but electric.

Holy.

A silence so thick it felt like heaven might be leaning in.

The storm outside still raged. The fire still roared. But something inside them settled. Not in safety—but in surrender.

And then—

A sound.

So small, it almost went unnoticed.

A soft tapping on the roof. Like the timid knock of grace.

Ruthie's eyes flew open. "Was that...?"

Another tap.

Then another.

Then a patter.

Then a downpour.

The sky opened with a roar of its own. Water crashed against the tin like an army of angels descending.

Naomi gasped. "Rain. Oh—God, it's rain."

James surged to his feet and flung the bathroom door open. Smoke poured in, thick and acrid—but beneath it, unmistakable—

The scent of petrichor.

Of mercy.

They ran to the back door and threw it wide.

The verandah was blackened, scorched. The air was heavy with ash. But the rain—oh, the rain—it was real. Ruthie stepped into it, blinking against the deluge. It soaked her hair, her skin, her clothes. It felt like baptism.

The eastern paddock still smouldered, glowing in angry patches. The shed roof sagged, charred. But the house—

The house still stood.

The flames had kissed its edges. Had clawed at the walls and windows. Had demanded entry.

But it had not been consumed.

Naomi stepped onto the verandah beside them, arms raised. Rain streaked her face like tears made visible. Her lips moved in silent praise. Her entire body trembled with reverence.

James turned to Ruthie, eyes wide and wild with something more than relief.

"I don't know how we made it," he whispered.

Ruthie looked up at him, rain trailing down her cheeks. Her voice shook—but her words didn't.

"I do," she said. "God."

James pulled her to him, wrapping her tight against his chest like he never wanted to let her go. Bear stepped forward onto the wet boards, gave a single bark, and pressed his head against Ruthie's knee.

Naomi dropped to her knees, overcome. Sobbing. Her hands covered her face, shoulders shaking as rain washed over her like absolution.

The world still smelled of smoke. Of scorched wood and singed dreams.

But the fire was no longer king.

The land exhaled.

Ruthie lifted her eyes to the grey sky. Water streamed down her temples, clinging to her lashes, her chin. She turned slowly in a circle, as if trying to take it all in.

And something rose up in her chest.

Not just relief. Not just awe.

But a fierce, unshakable knowing.

That they had been kept.

That they had been seen.

That they had been saved.

Her laughter broke through her sobs, wild and bright and holy.

She stepped off the verandah into the grass—wet, blackened, reborn.

James followed. Naomi stood and joined them, arms stretched wide to the heavens. Bear barked again and tore off into the yard, spinning in giddy circles.

And there, in the middle of the ruin, the four of them danced.

Tears and rain. Smoke and grace.

Hearts still trembling—

But faith standing strong.

Chapter 45: Ashes and Grace

"He will give a crown of beauty for ashes, a joyous blessing instead of mourning, festive praise instead of despair." – Isaiah 61:3

The morning after the fire didn't begin with sirens or shouting. It began with birdsong.

Soft, tentative notes in the hush of dawn. Like creation itself was holding its breath, daring to believe it had made it through the night.

The world was hushed and dripping—every leaf kissed by dew, every surface steaming with the memory of flame. Ash clung to everything like a second skin. The air was thick with the scent of burnt eucalyptus and wet earth.

And still, the birds sang.

James stepped out first. His boots pressed into the blackened soil with a solemn crunch. The deck groaned beneath him, littered with soot, flecked with ember-scars. A corner of the tin roof hung low, curled and beaten, and the gutters leaned away from the house like arms exhausted from holding on too long.

But the house—the house was still there.

It had held.

He paused, one hand on the weathered post, his throat too tight to speak.

Behind him, the door creaked open.

Ruthie stepped out barefoot, her white nightgown grey with ash, her curls still damp from the night before. She didn't speak at first. She just looked—eyes wide, mouth parted—as if the very act of seeing this place still standing was too sacred to interrupt.

Then she saw him.

"James," she whispered.

He turned to her, his face streaked with smoke and dried tears, eyes hollowed by exhaustion but filled with something more tender than she'd ever seen.

Ruthie's lips trembled. "About what you said... in the bathroom. About marrying me. I know you only said that because you thought we were going to die."

James blinked slowly. Took a step forward.

"Maybe," he said quietly. "Maybe it wasn't how I wanted to say it. Not on my knees on cold tile with fire at our backs. But Ruthie—" His voice cracked. "I meant every word. Every. Single. One."

She stared at him, frozen in the mist and silence.

"I love you," James said. "I want you by my side every day we're given. I want to grow old with you, plant things with you, build things with you. I want you when the sun shines and when it doesn't. I want to carry you when the world gets heavy, and let you carry me when I fall apart. I want it all, Ruthie. You and me. Forever."

She pressed her hand to her mouth, breath catching.

James stepped forward, took her hands in his—still blackened from ash, still trembling from the storm they'd just survived.

"Please," James whispered, his voice thick with emotion, eyes glistening with a fierce, holy kind of love. "Make me the happiest man alive. Marry me."

Ruthie's tears came in rivers now, carving clean trails down her soot-smudged cheeks. Her breath caught as her whole body trembled, heart pounding like it might burst from the sheer flood of joy.

She nodded—once, then again, and again, as if the word couldn't come fast enough.

"Yes," she choked out, her voice cracking under the weight of grace. "Yes. Yes, James. I will."

Behind them, a sudden scream shattered the stillness—not one of fear, but uncontainable delight.

Naomi, who had chosen to stay the night to help with the cleanup, had clearly overheard the exchange. She came barreling out the front door, flannel pajama pants flapping, hair wild with sleep and joy. Arms flailed like a child on Christmas morning.

"YES!" she hollered, spinning in wild, glorious circles on the damp earth. "Thank You, Jesus! HALLELUJAH!"

Her voice echoed into the trees, into the skies, into heaven itself.

James laughed, teary-eyed and breathless, while Ruthie collapsed into his arms, laughing and crying all at once. Bear barked at the commotion, tail wagging, as if he too understood the sacred celebration unfolding before him.

In the aftermath of ashes, love had bloomed.

Not just survival.

But promise.

A new beginning.

Ruthie laughed through her tears. James grinned and wrapped her up, lifting her right off the ground in a dizzying, spinning embrace, the world falling away beneath their feet.

They kissed—not like they had the night before, out of terror or urgency. But with the slow, grateful kiss of survivors. Of lovers. Of soulmates who had just been given tomorrow.

When they finally pulled apart, they walked further, hand in hand, hearts still trembling.

Past the coop—half-singed but standing.

Past the tool shed—roof scorched, but not fallen.

The fence in the west field had collapsed, tangled in charred branches. Trees lay like broken soldiers across the boundary lines, some still smouldering, their insides hollowed out by flame. The paddocks bore the marks of war. But there—through the rising mist and smoke—

The cows.

The goats.

Muddied, trembling, their eyes wide with animal memory.

But alive.

Ruthie gasped, a hand flying to her mouth. "They made it!" She yelled. "James... they made it!"

James sank to his knees right there in the wet ash. His hands dug into the blackened soil, then lifted, fingers spreading toward the grey-blue sky like a prayer without words.

"Thank You," he breathed. "Thank You."

Ruthie dropped beside him, her forehead pressing gently into his shoulder as her arms slid around him from behind.

And there they knelt—no longer afraid, no longer fleeing—just weeping in the ruin and the grace.

By midday, the wind had dropped, leaving the air still and heavy with the scent of scorched earth and eucalyptus. The sky, once choked with smoke, had cleared to a pale, washed-out blue—faded and fragile, like something freshly laundered and hung to dry.

In staggered waves, the CFA trucks rolled in—mud-caked and sun-bleached, engines humming low like the steady breath of guardians. Men and women climbed down with weary eyes and soot-streaked faces, their movements efficient but gentle, as if the land itself had become something sacred in its survival.

They moved through the property with practiced grace—checking for hotspots beneath smouldering brush, marking weakened trees with bright spray paint, offering bottled water with rough hands and soft voices. Their nods carried weight—an unspoken language of solidarity. No dramatics. No fanfare. Just the quiet acknowledgment of shared fragility and strength.

One of them paused beside James, handed him a bottle of water, and said simply, "You did well."

James nodded, throat too tight to reply.

Further down the paddock, another volunteer knelt to check on a still-glowing log, while Ruthie stood barefoot on the deck, watching them work. She felt small in the aftermath—but not weak.

Humbled.

Awakened.

Alive.

The chaos had passed. But the miracle lingered in every breath of clean air, every charred fence post left standing, every moment that ticked forward into a future they still had.

In the days that followed, James and Ruthie became more than caretakers of their land.

They became servants of something bigger.

The community around them had not fared as well.

Neil and Margaret's water tanks had melted clean through. The Miller family's orchard was scorched black. And no one could get through to old Mrs Cowen, whose property sat closest to the ignition line.

James and Ruthie loaded the Ute with fencing wire, tools, sandwiches, and two tired dogs—Bear and Naomi's retriever—and set out each day to help.

They rebuilt fences. Cleared fallen branches. Hauled water to neighbours whose tanks had burst or boiled.

Each evening, James and Ruthie came home aching, blistered, and smoke-stained.

And each evening, they found something new still standing.

A lemon tree with half its leaves intact.

A shovel handle unburnt.

One night, as the stars emerged from behind the fading smoke, Ruthie sat on the front step with a cup of tea, her legs stretched out, James beside her.

They watched the community drive past—Utes full of tools, families sharing meals across tailgates, teenagers hauling feed for animals that weren't theirs.

There was no talk of insurance yet. No rebuild schedules.

Just presence.

Just helping.

Just love, showing up in work boots and worn-out hats.

James reached over and took her hand.

"You really meant it?" he asked quietly.

Ruthie turned toward him.

"What?"

"Saying yes. Saying you'd marry me."

She smiled. "I meant it more than I've ever meant anything."

He swallowed. "Even after all this?"

"Especially after all this."

He looked down, thumb brushing over the raw skin of her knuckles.

"We'll rebuild, you know. Help everyone rebuild."

She nodded. "We already are."

And as she looked out over the darkened fields—where embers had once threatened to consume everything but hadn't—she felt something deepen inside her. Belonging was no longer just about safety or love. It was about *standing with others*, carrying what was broken *together*. The land had held her through grief. But it was the people—this messy, beautiful, growing circle of hearts—that would carry her forward.

Chapter 46: A Wedding in the Ashes

"Place me like a seal over your heart... for love is as strong as death... many waters cannot quench love; rivers cannot sweep it away." – Song of songs 8:6

It started with a shovel.

James was digging a new post hole where the old fence had burned, shirt clinging to his back, sun climbing high. Ruthie stood nearby, arms full of salvaged timber. They were quiet—just the creak of leather gloves, the scrape of wood, the occasional cough from the dust still rising from the scorched earth.

Then James leaned on the shovel and looked up at her.

"What if we just got married here?" he asked.

Ruthie blinked, half-smiling. "Here as in... right here?"

"Here as in on the land," he clarified. "Not in some hall. Just... here. Among the gum trees. The paddocks. The people who stood beside us when it all could've ended."

Her heart swelled. Not with glitter or grandeur—but something deeper. Like home. Like peace.

She set the timber down and walked over to him, dust in her hair, love in her eyes.

"I wouldn't want it anywhere else."

"Just us. And the people who matter."

By sunset, the plan had taken root like a seed in warm soil.

They would marry on the land.

The very land that had burned and lived.

The very place that had nearly broken them—and built them.

Not with crowds. Not with perfection. But with presence.

Word spread fast—because it always did in towns like theirs. One whispered conversation at the bakery, one phone call to a neighbour, and by morning, it seemed like the whole valley knew that James and Ruthie were getting married.

And with the news came offers.

Naomi, still in her muddy gumboots from helping with the fire clean-up, grinned as she held up a bundle of handmade table runners. "These somehow survived the shed," she said. "They've got singed edges, but that just adds character, right?"

Margaret beamed with a kind of youthful energy that belied her age. "I still have my old lace veil," she declared, fishing it out of a yellowed box from the back of her linen closet. "Wore it only once—about time it saw the light again! And I'm taking charge of food—no arguments!"

Neil, quiet and steady, opened a cedar box he'd kept sealed for forty years. Inside were chisels, smooth from years of use, and a blueprint for a handmade altar he'd once dreamed of building for his daughter's wedding.

"Figured it was time to finish it," he said simply. "For you two."

Micah volunteered to pick the wine and champagne, claiming he had "just the right bottle" stored under his bed from a trip to the Barossa in '09. He promised to toast until the stars came out.

And Pastor Luke? He was practically glowing.

"I get to do the ceremony," he said, eyes twinkling like a man ten years younger. "And I've got a few dozen folding chairs stacked behind the vestry. They'll do just fine."

No one asked about colour schemes.

No one asked for RSVPs or seating plans or security deposits.

They just... showed up.

With arms full and hearts open. With stories and laughter and casseroles. With wheelbarrows, bunting, handpicked wildflowers, and hymn sheets.

Because in towns like theirs, weddings weren't events.

They were offerings.

They were love in motion.

They were the sound of hammers on timber and pies in the oven and someone tuning a battered old guitar on the porch.

They were home.

The week passed like a blur—full of clinking hammers, floral donations from nearby farms, and mismatched chairs dragged from every neighbour's shed.

Ruthie stood in the middle of the paddock one afternoon, looking at the space where they'd say their vows. A ring of stones had been laid down, and someone—Naomi, probably—had tied eucalyptus and gum nuts along the outer fence.

She turned slowly, barefoot in the grass, the breeze tugging at the hem of her cotton skirt.

James approached from behind, wrapping his arms around her waist.

"Looks like a wedding," he murmured.

She leaned back against him. "Looks like grace."

He nodded. "It does."

It was a week before the wedding, and James and Ruthie had invited Naomi and Micah over for lunch.

Ruthie sat on the back step beside Naomi, a steaming cup of chamomile cupped between her palms. The night air wrapped around them like a soft shawl—cool, quiet, alive with the hum of crickets and the faint rustle of leaves. Above them, stars spilled across the sky, bright and countless, scattered like diamonds on black velvet.

"You nervous?" Naomi asked after a long stretch of silence, her voice low and reverent, like the question itself was sacred.

Ruthie took her time before answering. She watched the steam rise from her mug, curling upward in gentle spirals, like prayers lifting into the night.

Then, with a small shake of her head, she whispered, "No. Not nervous."

She paused, her thumb trailing slow, thoughtful circles around the rim of the mug.

"I'm just... full. Like I can't hold all the feelings in one chest. There's grief, joy, hope. It's all there—layered. Pressing against my ribs like it's too much and yet... just enough."

Naomi smiled softly, her eyes shining. "That's love. The real kind. It doesn't just fill you—it remakes you."

Ruthie turned to her, eyes glinting in the starlight.

"Naomi," she said, her voice thick with emotion, "I love you. I don't know what I would've done without you. You are my family. Not by blood, but by fire, by faith, and by choice."

Naomi blinked fast, her breath hitching.

"I have something I've been wanting to ask," Ruthie continued, setting her mug down.

"I want you to stand beside me on the day I say yes to forever. Will you be my bridesmaid?"

Naomi looked down, brushing an invisible speck of dust from her jeans. But it couldn't hide the tears already streaking down her cheeks.

When she lifted her face again, her smile trembled with joy.

"I would be honoured," she said, voice breaking.

Ruthie reached over, arms wide, and they pulled each other into a tight embrace—one that held years of history, months of healing, and a lifetime's worth of gratitude.

They stayed like that for a long moment, wrapped in silence, stars above, hearts open, and the kind of love that didn't need to be spoken to be understood.

Inside, the warmth of the kitchen wrapped around them like an old wool jumper. The smell of fresh timber polish lingered faintly in the air, mingling with the comforting scent of coffee brewing on the stove.

James sat at the kitchen table with Micah, a quiet sense of purpose settling between them.

"I've been thinking," James said, voice a little rough around the edges. "You've always been there. Through everything. You've seen the worst of me, and somehow you still stick around."

Micah smirked. "Someone's got to keep you out of trouble."

James let out a quiet laugh, the kind that softened the weight in the room, then looked up—his expression shifting back to something tender and true.

"I'd be honoured if you stood beside me on the day," he said. "As my groomsman."

Micah blinked, caught off guard for a moment. A flicker of emotion crossed his face—brief, but real.

"You don't have to ask me that, mate," he replied, voice low with feeling. "I was going to be standing up there next to you either way."

Their eyes met.

And then they both laughed—deep, genuine, the kind of laugh that only comes after walking through fire together and still finding joy on the other side.

That afternoon, the four of them—Naomi, Ruthie, James, and Micah—gathered outside near the old barbecue, its lid rusted in patches but still doing its job. The sky above stretched wide and blue, a soft breeze teasing the edges of the tablecloth someone had pinned down with smooth river stones.

Laughter drifted like music through the air, mingling with the sizzle of sausages and the clink of mismatched plates. Naomi passed around enamel mugs filled with ginger beer while Bear dozed in the shade, tail occasionally thumping in contentment.

They talked about nothing and everything—childhood stories, near-disasters, awkward teenage moments, and dreams for the future.

But more than that, they simply were. Together. Whole. Chosen.

There was something sacred in the simplicity of it. No titles. No roles. Just four people who had walked through fire, grief, and grace—and found each other on the other side.

Family, not by blood.

But by bond.

Chapter 47: The Day the Earth Sang

"Love is patient, love is kind. It does not envy, it does not boast, it is not proud.
It does not dishonour others, it is not self-seeking, it is not easily angered, it keeps no record of wrongs.
Love does not delight in evil but rejoices with the truth.
It always protects, always trusts, always hopes, always perseveres." - 1 Corinthians 13:4–7

The day of the wedding finally came.

The morning light filtered through smoke-scrubbed skies like gold spilling from heaven.

A hush had fallen over the land.

Birdsong drifted through the paddocks. A gentle breeze stirred the gum leaves. The land, still raw and marked by fire, breathed with life again.

And in the centre of the field that had once burned, something sacred was being prepared.

A ring of gum branches and salvaged timber formed the ceremony space. Wildflowers—most of them donated or foraged—had been tied along fence posts with old twine. There were no matching chairs, no white aisle runner, no polished sound system.

But there was music in the air.

The kind only hearts in love can hear.

Inside the house, morning light filtered softly through the gauzy curtains, casting a golden hush across the room.

Ruthie stood barefoot in front of the mirror, heart full, breath shallow, surrounded by the quiet holiness of the moment.

The lace veil Margaret had gifted her rested delicately in her curls, pinned with a small eucalyptus sprig Naomi had tucked in with care. It smelled faintly of wild things and new beginnings.

Her dress was simple—a soft cotton, slightly off-white, flowing around her like water, like grace incarnate. It clung at the waist and drifted to her ankles, brushing lightly against the wooden floorboards with every slow breath she took.

Her hands trembled—not from fear or doubt—but from something far more sacred.

Awe.

Wonder.

The weight of what it meant to stand on the threshold of forever.

Behind her, Naomi worked the final button at the back of the dress with steady fingers, her own gown a soft eucalyptus green that caught the light like dewy leaves at dawn. She stepped back slowly, taking in the sight of her dearest friend transformed.

"You look..." Naomi's voice caught, a tear sliding down her cheek. "You look radiant."

Ruthie turned to face her, eyes brimming. "Thank you," she said. Then, without hesitation, "I love you."

Naomi's breath hitched, and she stepped forward, wrapping Ruthie in a tender embrace. They stood there for a long, still moment—hearts pressed close, arms around one another—two women who had weathered fire and storm, now standing in peace.

There were no speeches.

No need for more words.

Only the deep knowing that they had found each other in this life and held each other through to joy.

Outside, the soft rustle of trees and faint sounds of arrival hinted that the day had begun.

But for now, in that room, time slowed.

And Ruthie let herself feel it all—every ache that had healed, every sorrow that had shaped her, every sliver of hope that had led to this morning of beauty, belonging, and breathtaking love.

In the back paddock, where wildflowers now dared to bloom through the blackened soil, James stood beside Micah.

The morning sun caught in his tousled hair, casting a soft golden crown over his head.

He wore a crisp white shirt, sleeves rolled to the elbows, dark trousers, and his father's old belt buckle—now polished to a gleam, as if even the past had decided to show up clean.

Micah glanced sideways, a quiet grin pulling at his mouth. "You good?"

James exhaled slowly, the breath long and full. "I've never been more sure of anything in my life."

He looked out across the property—fence posts still charred from the fire, but green shoots pressing bravely through the ash. The field was dotted with neighbours and friends. Barefoot children darted between rows. Dogs meandered under folding tables.

Micah gave his shoulder a pat. "Time to let go of what was—and walk into what is."

James nodded, and together they walked toward the ceremony site—just an open space in the paddock, where eucalyptus branches arched like a natural cathedral and Pastor Luke stood waiting beneath a makeshift altar of salvaged timber and wildflowers.

Luke took James's hand in both of his, his grip firm, eyes bright with pride. "She's coming," he said quietly.

James swallowed hard and turned.

The music began—no dramatic entrance, just the strumming of an acoustic guitar, tender and imperfect. It drifted across the field like a heartbeat.

Then Ruthie stepped through the gate.

The world stilled and James forgot to breathe as he took in her beauty.

She walked barefoot, her cotton dress swaying around her ankles, the lace veil Margaret had given her trailing behind her like a whispered story. A sprig of eucalyptus tucked into her curls caught the breeze. Her hands were open at her sides, palms facing heaven.

Naomi walked just ahead, her pale green dress brushing through the grass.

When Ruthie reached him, James reached for her hands like a man taking hold of the only thing that had ever made sense.

"You look gorgeous," he breathed.

A gentle wind stirred the trees, their leaves rustling like a thousand hands clapping in the branches.

Pastor Luke stepped forward, Bible in hand, voice steady despite the emotion thick in the air.

"We gather here," he said, "on land that was nearly lost. Among people who stood together when everything burned. We stand on ash—but also on resurrection."

Silence swept through the crowd, reverent and alive.

Pastor Luke turned to James. "James, do you take Ruthie to be your wife? To walk beside her through fire and peace, to offer your hands, your heart, and your days—all the way home?"

"I do," James said. "With everything I am."

Then Pastor Luke turned to Ruthie. "Ruthie, do you take James to be your husband? To meet him with grace, to speak the truth in love, and to be his safe place in this world?"

"I do," she responded without hesitation, smiling through tears. "Always."

They didn't read vows from a script.

They spoke them from memory—etched not on paper, but in scar tissue and hope.

"I won't run when it's hard," James said, eyes locked on hers. "I will stay. Just like you stayed."

"I won't close off," Ruthie replied, her voice trembling. "I will have faith in us and stay open to you. Because love isn't safe, but it's worth it."

James slid a simple silver ring onto her finger—engraved with a small cross, faint but unmissable. Ruthie's hand shook as she placed a handmade band onto his—a smooth circle, forged by a neighbour from melted scraps, made new.

Pastor Luke lifted his hand, heart full.

"By the power of love, and the grace of the One who holds us through flame and flood, I now pronounce you husband and wife."

A beat of silence.

"You may kiss your bride."

James didn't wait.

He pulled Ruthie close and kissed her like a man who had lost everything once—and now stood on holy ground, holding it all.

And maybe the land itself rejoiced.

Because just as their lips met, the breeze lifted the veil and the sun broke fully through the clouds.

The gum trees danced, and the ground seemed to exhale.

The crowd erupted in cheers.

Children twirled in the grass. Bear barked joyfully. Naomi whooped. Margaret sobbed.

And Ruthie, laughing, crying, trembling, held onto James like he was both the promise and the proof.

They feasted on fresh bread and stews cooked in tin pots over fire pits. There was lemonade. Scones. Fruit from neighbouring trees.

No one wore heels.

Everyone stayed long after the sun had dipped low.

James and Ruthie sat on a hay bale under the stars, hands clasped, watching the fireflies flicker between the trees.

"I think the earth sang today," Ruthie said.

James looked at her.

"It did," he said. "And it sang for us."

Chapter 48: The Quietest Hallelujah

"I will betroth you to me forever... in love and compassion. I will betroth you in faithfulness, and you will acknowledge the Lord."
– Hosea 2:19-20

That night, the house was quiet—but not empty.

Ruthie stood just inside the door, toes pressed into the wooden floorboards, veil folded in her hand, curls tumbling down her back. She wasn't sure when the laughter had faded or when the guests had slipped away. Only that now it was just them.

She watched James across the room—the man who had steadied her in firelight, who had kissed her beneath smoke-stained skies, who had promised her love with eyes full of truth.

He was moving slowly now, deliberately. As if rushing would somehow diminish the sacredness of what came next.

He unlaced his boots one by one, left them by the door, then walked toward her with bare feet and soft steps. Ruthie felt her breath catch in her throat—not from nerves, but from the enormity of what this moment meant.

"You're staring," he said gently, a smile at the edge of his voice.

"I'm memorising," she whispered.

And she was.

Every angle of his face. The way his shirt clung to his chest. The softness in his gaze, even after everything they'd survived. The man who had seen her at her most broken and never looked away.

He reached her, slowly lifting his hand to brush a strand of hair from her cheek. His fingers were calloused, roughened by work and weather, but they moved across her skin with softness.

"You're so beautiful," he said. And it wasn't just the dress or the curls or the veil now laid aside. It was her.

Ruthie smiled, a tear catching at the corner of her eye.

"So are you."

He laughed softly, cheeks flushed. "I don't think anyone's ever said that to me."

She stepped closer until their foreheads touched, until his breath mingled with hers.

"Well... someone should have."

They stood like that for a while—breathing each other in, the quiet hum of night filling the silence. Outside, the wind rustled the trees gently. The embers from the fire pit glowed low through the window, casting flickering light across the floor.

Ruthie reached for the buttons on the front of her dress, her hands trembling slightly. James gently caught her wrists.

"Let me."

His voice was steady. Not demanding. Not hurried. Just reverent.

He began with the first button, just below her collarbone, fingers working slowly. Each one undone felt like the shedding of armour, the letting go of all that had once said not yet.

When the dress slipped from her shoulders, he caught it. Carefully, respectfully, he let it fall to the floor.

She stood before him in the soft slip beneath, fabric thin but not revealing, her form outlined in lamplight. She felt the vulnerability of it all—skin and soul. But she didn't flinch. Not with him.

James stepped back just enough to unbutton his shirt. Ruthie watched as he shrugged it off, revealing skin that bore the marks of life: scars, freckles, sun-kissed lines from long days in the paddocks. She reached out and touched his chest, fingers light, as if tracing a story.

"This body," she said quietly, "carried so much pain. And still, you chose to love."

James took her hand and brought it to his lips.

"This heart," he replied, "healed mine."

They moved to the bed slowly, as though the world might stop if they moved too fast.

James pulled back the quilt. Ruthie climbed in first, legs folding under her, curls falling over her shoulders. The sheets smelled like eucalyptus and earth. Like home.

When he joined her, there was a pause—an ache so full it felt like music.

Their bodies met not with hunger, but with a kind of desperate peace. They kissed—slowly, deeply—his hand on her jaw, hers in his hair.

And when the rest of their clothes fell away, they didn't hide.

There was nothing shameful here.

No fear. No hesitation.

Only tenderness.

James touched her like she was a psalm—every inch holy, every breath worth memorising. Ruthie responded not with performance but presence—every sigh, every tremble an offering of trust.

They spoke in whispers.

Until the words weren't just language anymore—but the shape of their breath, the rhythm of their heartbeat.

When he entered her, Ruthie gasped—not from pain, but from awe.

It wasn't fireworks. It wasn't something stolen in the dark.

It was coming home.

The world didn't stop spinning, but for them—for this moment—it softened. Slowed.

His forehead against hers.

Her lips at his ear.

Their hands clasped like a vow all its own.

And when they reached that quiet, trembling place of completion, it wasn't rushed.

It wasn't frantic.

It was reverent.

Their bodies stilled, but something sacred moved between them.

A hallelujah unspoken.

A sunrise that rose behind closed eyes and settled deep in the soul.

After, they simply lay there—skin to skin, heartbeat to heartbeat.

The candle flickered low, casting gold across the ceiling.

James ran his fingers through Ruthie's hair as she traced the lines on his chest, slow and unhurried.

"You, okay?" he asked softly.

Ruthie smiled against his skin. "I am, better than okay."

He kissed her temple. "I didn't know it could be like that."

"Me neither," she said. "Not in books. Not in movies. Nothing felt like this."

He held her tighter.

Chapter 49: Something New Begins

"Therefore, if anyone is in Christ, he is a new creation. The old has passed away; behold, the new has come." – 2 Corinthians 5:17

The morning light filtered through the curtains in soft ribbons, catching the folds of the quilt and painting golden lines across the skin of two newlyweds tangled beneath it. Ruthie stirred first, her cheek resting against the rise and fall of James's chest. She didn't open her eyes right away. She didn't need to. She knew where she was—home.

Their legs remained intertwined beneath the sheets, the soft ache in her body a reminder of the night before. Their first night.

Married.

Safe.

Whole.

James stirred, his hand instinctively sliding along her spine in slow, absent-minded strokes. His voice, rough with sleep, hummed against her hair.

"Morning, wife."

She smiled into his skin. "Say that again."

My beautiful Wife," he murmured, pressing a kiss to her temple.

She sighed, a quiet sound full of contentment. "I like how that sounds."

He shifted, propping himself on one elbow to look down at her. Her curls were wild and beautiful, a halo on the pillow. His thumb traced her cheekbone, reverent, as though still unsure whether he was allowed to touch her like this, love her like this.

They kissed again—not with urgency, but with deep reverence. A kiss that said, I know you. I see you. I honour you.

Later, beneath warm quilts and morning sun, their love deepened again—slower this time. Not the clumsy rush of discovery but the unfolding of something holy. Ruthie traced the line of James's collarbone with trembling fingers. James followed the curve of her shoulder with lips that trembled too. They explored not out of hunger, but wonder.

With every whispered "I love you," they were rewriting what love meant. The sound of their laughter tangled with sighs; breaths caught between trust and release. They didn't need to speak. Their bodies spoke in tenderness, in presence, in promise. It was not perfect, but it was sacred.

After, they held each other in the stillness. James ran his fingers through her hair while Ruthie pressed a hand to his heartbeat.

They had crossed a threshold—and everything felt different now. They had become one.

Later, when Bear pawed gently at the door, James rose to let him out, bare-chested and barefoot, the waistband of his jeans riding low on his hips. Ruthie watched him move, struck again by the miracle of loving someone who loved her back so deeply. She wrapped herself in a shawl and joined him in the kitchen, her steps slow, her heart full.

There was no rush. No schedule. Only the hush of a morning that felt like it belonged to them.

They moved around each other in quiet harmony. James brewed tea while Ruthie sliced fresh bread. Occasionally, they would pause just to touch—his palm on her waist, her fingers trailing across his wrist. Small gestures that said, I'm here. I'm yours.

They ate breakfast on the front steps, watching the land breathe under a soft sky. Scorched trees stood tall, branches budding again. The garden, battered but not broken, had signs of new life. James took Ruthie's hand, holding it like something fragile and sure all at once.

They loaded the ute later that day—tools, gloves, sandwiches—ready to help the neighbours rebuild. Their honeymoon, they decided, could wait. Love wasn't a retreat from the world. It was showing up for it, together.

At Margaret and Neil's, Ruthie knelt beside lavender bushes, hands deep in soil. James worked the fence line, sweat glistening on his back. The community wove around them—Naomi dropping off scones, Micah offering help with the water tank, laughter floating across the garden like balm.

"You've brought us hope," Margaret told Ruthie as they packed up to leave.

Ruthie blinked, surprised. "Hope?"

Margaret just smiled. "After everything... you reminded us of what it looks like."

That night, they curled into the couch with tea and tired limbs. James wrapped his arm around Ruthie and held her like the world had finally gone quiet.

"I didn't know it could feel like this," he said.

"Like what?" she asked.

"Like peace. Like I'm not fighting anymore."

"You're not alone anymore," she responded.

And when they kissed again, it wasn't a beginning or an end—it was an echo of everything they had already lived, and everything they were becoming.

And later, in their bed, as rain began to patter gently on the tin roof, they moved toward each other again. Not for passion's sake, but because love is a rhythm—a return. And as James whispered promises against Ruthie's skin, and Ruthie cried softly without knowing why, something unseen stirred within her.

A seed had taken root.

Weeks passed in a haze of routine and tenderness. Ruthie began to notice a change in her body—small things at first. A flutter of nausea in the mornings. A sudden tenderness in her chest. Emotions rising without warning, like tides stirred by a full moon. She told herself it was just the adjustment of marriage, the emotional settling after all they'd endured.

But the sense grew—quiet and sure. Something was different.

One crisp morning, Naomi arrived unannounced with a basket of warm sourdough and a familiar, searching look in her eyes. She stepped through the kitchen door as though she belonged there, as though she could already feel the shift in the air.

"Brought bread," she said simply, setting the basket down. Bear thumped his tail lazily under the table, and the kettle began to whistle.

Ruthie smiled and moved to pour the tea, but Naomi's eyes didn't leave her face.

"You look pale," she said gently, stepping forward and placing a warm hand on Ruthie's. "Tired too."

Ruthie hesitated. "I've been a bit off," she admitted, voice quiet. "Nothing dramatic. Just... not quite myself. My body feels unfamiliar some days."

Naomi tilted her head slightly, her expression softening. "You think you might be pregnant?"

The word hit like a hush falling over a cathedral. Ruthie froze, the teacup trembling slightly in her hands. She hadn't said it out loud—not even to herself.

"I don't know," she replied. "Maybe. I hadn't really—" She swallowed, voice thin. "I think I was afraid to hope."

Naomi reached for her again, steady and kind. "Then let's find out."

"But I don't have a test," Ruthie said.

"I'll go into town," Naomi said, already reaching for her coat. "You sit. Drink your tea. Breathe."

And just like that, she was gone.

The minutes stretched long and strange while Ruthie waited. She sat in silence at the table, hands wrapped around her mug, heart wrapped around a maybe. The birds outside went on singing. The wind moved through the gum trees. And she sat there, wondering if her whole world was about to change again.

Nearly an hour later, Naomi returned, cheeks flushed from the drive, holding a small brown paper bag like it was something holy.

They didn't rush. Naomi placed the test gently on the bench, and they stood in the quiet kitchen for a moment, side by side, listening to the sound of their own breathing. When Ruthie nodded, they walked slowly down the hallway together. Naomi waited just outside the bathroom door while Ruthie stepped inside.

The silence while they waited was thick with breath and heartbeat and every prayer Ruthie hadn't dared to speak aloud.

And then she looked.

Two lines.

Clear. Bold. Undeniable.

Ruthie stared, hand flying to her mouth, her knees buckling slightly as she sat on the edge of the tub. A sound escaped her lips—part sob, part laugh, part unbelieving joy.

Naomi was there in a moment, kneeling in front of her and gathering her close.

"You're having a baby, sweetheart."

Ruthie didn't answer with words. She let the tears come.

Naomi held her like a sister would. Like a mother. Like a midwife to the soul.

Later, when the sky turned silver and Naomi had gone, Ruthie walked into the orchard, cradling her lower belly with both hands. The lemon trees had just begun to flower, and their scent mingled with the damp earth and the promise of rain.

She stood still, the weight of the moment anchoring her.

The wind picked up—gentle. It lifted the hair from her shoulders and kissed her cheeks.

It wasn't just wind.

It felt like presence.

Rain began to fall—light, warm, almost ceremonial. She tilted her face to the sky, letting the drops trace her skin like a benediction.

"I trust You," she whispered.

Soft footsteps soon came from behind.

James.

He wrapped his arms around her waist, pulling her into his chest. His hands slid over hers, fingers threading together.

"I knew I'd find you out here," he murmured into her hair.

"I needed to talk to God."

James kissed the top of her head. "Did He answer?"

She turned in his arms, eyes glistening, voice sure. "Yes, he did. With his presence."

James pressed his forehead to hers.

And there, in the orchard—soaked in rain and grace, cradled by the whispering trees and the grey sky above—Ruthie knew:

Something new had truly begun.

Chapter 50: Rain Like Blessing

"Children are a heritage from the Lord, offspring a reward from him." – Psalm 127:3

Ruthie watched him—her husband—his body warm and steady behind her, arms encircling her waist, their fingers still intertwined.

Her voice trembled with anticipation, breath catching as she gathered the courage to speak.

"James..." she whispered, heart pounding. "I'm pregnant."

At first, he didn't say anything. Just held her tighter.

She felt his breath catch against her shoulder, his fingers twitch slightly over her stomach as if trying to grasp the impossible truth. And then, slowly, he turned her in his arms, hands cupping her face.

"You're... you're serious?" His eyes were wide, searching hers, raw with wonder. "You're really—?"

She nodded, tears slipping down her cheeks. "I took the test this morning. Naomi brought it. It's real, James. We're going to have a baby."

He exhaled like something sacred had just entered his lungs. Then, with sudden urgency, he dropped to his knees in the wet grass, pressing his face gently to her belly, his arms wrapped around her hips like he was anchoring himself to the moment.

"Hi, little one," he whispered into the curve of her. "It's your dad."

The words hit her like a wave—so simple, so full of truth it ached. Her knees gave way, and she knelt down with him, their foreheads resting against one another, breath mingling in the rain-damp air.

Then he kissed her.

It wasn't polished or poetic. It was desperate and tender and alive. A kiss that tasted of tears and soil and eternity. A kiss that said we made something out of nothing. That said I see you.

Their clothes were soaked, their hands muddy, her hair plastered to her face, but none of it mattered. Right there beneath the lemon trees, the sky weeping soft above them, they undressed each other with trembling hands—slowly, reverently, not in passion, but in devotion.

James lay her down in the grass, his body curved around hers like a prayer. Their lovemaking was quieter this time. Not rushed, not fiery. Just... sacred.

Ruthie closed her eyes and let it wash over her—the sound of rain, the weight of his hand on her belly, the way he whispered "thank you" again and again like a man overwhelmed by grace.

When it was over, they stayed wrapped in each other, bare skin against earth, the storm around them finally stilling.

"I've never loved you more than I do right now," he whispered.

"I know," she breathed. "Me too."

The weeks that followed were both tender and tiring.

Morning sickness became a steady visitor, and Ruthie found herself gagging at odd smells and crying over empty tea canisters. Some days she felt bloated and sick and far from the glowing image she'd imagined of pregnancy. Other days, she stood in front of the mirror, hands resting on the soft rise of her stomach, whispering promises to someone she hadn't met yet but already loved with her whole being.

James was relentless in his devotion.

He warmed wheat bags for her aching back. Cooked toast at midnight when nothing else would stay down. Left love notes on the bathroom mirror—short and misspelled and utterly perfect.

You are already the best mum.

We're doing this together.

God gave her you.

He built a cradle out of old fence posts they had salvaged after the fire. Sanded it until it was smooth as silk. Painted it the colour of eucalyptus leaves.

Ruthie sat nearby each evening, rubbing peppermint oil on her temples, watching him work with tears in her eyes.

One night when doubt had washed over her, she turned to James.

"I don't know how to do this," she confessed, voice small. "What happens if I am not a good mother, it is not like I had a good role model."

James looked up from the cradle, dust on his shirt, sweat on his brow. "Neither do I."

"Doesn't that scare you?"

"Yes," he said simply. "But loving you... that doesn't. And loving our baby? That's already happening."

She broke then. Not from fear—but from relief. From the beauty of being seen in her uncertainty and still chosen anyway.

When Ruthie was fourteen weeks pregnant, they drove to town for the first ultrasound.

Ruthie's heart pounded the whole way. James held her hand on the console, knuckles white, but neither of them spoke.

The room was quiet. Clinical. Cold.

And then there it was.

A flicker.

A heartbeat.

A tiny body, curved like a comma on the screen. Fingers. Toes. A face.

The sonographer smiled. "She looks healthy. You're having a girl."

A girl.

Ruthie's whole body trembled. She reached for James without looking, and he squeezed her hand so tightly it hurt.

In the car afterward, parked beneath the gum trees behind the clinic, they stared at the black-and-white photo like it held all the answers in the world.

"A girl," Ruthie said out loud.

James nodded, silent.

"What do we name someone who's already changed everything?"

He looked at her with eyes still full of wonder.

"Eden."

She stilled. "Eden?"

"It means delight," he said.

"And beginning."

Ruthie nodded slowly, the name blooming inside her like spring. "Eden Grace."

James ran his thumb across the photo and kissed her temple.

That night, Ruthie couldn't sleep.

James snored softly beside her, one hand resting protectively on the curve of her belly, even in sleep.

She climbed out of bed and padded barefoot into the kitchen, wrapping herself in her cardigan. The farmhouse was still, except for the creak of the timber and the wind rustling outside like breath.

She lit a candle. Pulled out paper. Sat at the table where their life had quietly taken root.

And began to write.

Dear Eden...

If you are reading this, it means time has passed. You've grown. Maybe you've laughed till your belly hurt. Maybe you've cried till you forgot how to stop. Maybe you've fallen in love. Maybe you've fallen apart. Whatever the season, whatever the storm or the sunrise you're standing in—I want you to know this:

You were born from ashes and anointing. From trembling hands and holy ground. You were born in a house lit only by candlelight and the prayers of the broken who dared to believe that beauty could rise again.

You are my redemption story. My answered prayer. My garden after the fire.

Your name, Eden Grace, wasn't chosen—it was revealed. Eden, because even after loss and exile, God still plants life. Still walks with us in the cool of the evening. Still brings us back to the place of beginning. And Grace—because that's the only way I made it. Unmerited. Unearned. Undeniably God.

I was a woman running from herself when I found Jesus—or maybe, more truthfully, when He found me. I thought I was too ruined, too ashamed, too late. But He called my name like it was never broken. He met me in the wreckage. In the quiet. In the grief. And He stayed. Oh, Eden, He stayed.

You are not the start of my story. But you are the moment everything changed. The moment hope took form in a heartbeat. The moment I stopped asking if I was worthy of love and just started loving anyway.

There is something I need you to know, not just as your mother, but as a woman who once stood where you might someday stand: lost, hurting, unsure of her place in the world.

You are not a mistake.

You are not too much or not enough.

You are not invisible.

You are not unloved.

You are God's.

And you are ours.

Your father—loved me when I didn't love myself. He saw me not as damaged, but as becoming. His love helped me trust again. His hands helped build the home you were born into. A home full of laughter.

Your dad, Eden... he is an angel. Not with wings or halos, but with calloused hands and a heart that always makes room. His love has healed places in me that I thought were too far gone. He listens like it's an honour. He prays like he knows heaven is listening. He touches the earth with gentleness and brings peace wherever he goes.

And Naomi... she's the reason I ever believed it was possible. If you remember anything about her, remember that love doesn't have to share your blood to be family. She mothered me when I was motherless. She carried me through the ache. And she carried you too, long before you were born.

This world will wound you, Eden. I won't pretend otherwise. There will be moments you feel alone, unwanted, unseen. But in those places, cry out to Jesus. He is the One who stayed when others ran. The One who bled so you wouldn't have to live bound. The One who turns graves into gardens.

Let Him be your compass.

Let Him be your safe place.

Let Him tell you who you are.

And please, forgive—quickly, freely, fully. Not for them, but for your own peace. Bitterness will rot your joy from the inside out. Let go of what no longer serves your soul. Let love win, again and again.

Dance barefoot in the kitchen.

Cry when you need to.

Worship like no one's watching.

Tell the truth even when your voice shakes.

And never, ever be afraid to start again.

You were born of fire—but you are not the flames.

You were born of grace—and you carry it now.

You are our daughter.

You are God's daughter.

And that makes you unstoppable.

Wherever you go, whatever you become, come back to the garden.

Come back to the God who never left.

Come back to the love that first named you.

I will love you forever,

until breath leaves my lungs

and even beyond then, in eternity—

I will love you.

Mum

Chapter 51: Come Back to the Table

"They broke bread in their homes and ate together with glad and sincere hearts."
—Acts 2:46

The farmhouse kitchen breathed warmth.

Not just from the oven—though it worked hard, steady and faithful—but from something older, deeper. The kind of warmth that came from years of laughter and healing held within the walls. That lived in every knick in the floorboards and every window that rattled when the wind blew just right.

The scent of rosemary, garlic, and woodsmoke clung to everything. A lemon cake cooled on the windowsill, its glaze softening in the golden light.

Ruthie stood near the counter, barefoot, one hand on her belly and the other resting lightly on Bear's head. He sat close, his grey-muzzled face lifted, ever watchful. Always nearby. The quiet guardian who had held space for her long before she had the words for safety.

The baby kicked —low and steady.

Ruthie smiled, but it came with a sting behind her eyes. There was something almost unbearable about this moment. About being here. About surviving long enough to feel full.

Behind her, the screen door creaked open.

Naomi swept in, cheeks flushed from the cold, apron dusted with flour. She held a dish wrapped in an old tea towel and her braid had half-unraveled, as it always did by mid-afternoon.

James came in through the back, cheeks windburned and sleeves rolled up. Bear trotted to greet him, tail wagging with dignity. James gave him a scratch behind the ears before crossing the kitchen and pulling Ruthie into his chest.

His hand instinctively slid over her belly.

"Hi there, little one," he murmured. "You ready for your first dinner party?"

"She's been practicing her kicks all day," Ruthie said.

"She'll fit in, then. This family's nothing if not loud."

They stayed like that for a moment—just breathing. James's chin resting on her head, Bear's head nudged between their knees.

More footsteps.

Margaret entered next, slowly, wrapped in the shawl Ruthie had crocheted for her.

Micah followed in her wake.

"I brought dessert!" he declared, holding up a pack of store-bought ice cream cones with pride.

"You're officially in charge of setting the table," Naomi told him with a wink.

Bear followed him dutifully, nosing around his pockets for treats. Micah giggled and offered a biscuit from his pocket, which Bear accepted quickly.

Neil and Pastor Luke arrived not long after, one with a guitar, the other with a sourdough loaf.

The farmhouse filled slowly.

But every soul who entered brought something sacred with them—something more than the food or the music or the stories.

They brought memory.

Forgiveness.

Restoration.

James had built a new table that was long and sturdy—oak and pine salvaged from storm-felled trees. Ruthie had sanded it herself, running her palms over every rough spot until it was smooth enough to hold plates and elbows and the weight of stories unspoken.

Tonight, the table was full.

Full of warm bread and soft butter, roast lamb carved thick, chutneys spiced and sweet, golden honey, lemon cake still fragrant from the oven, and mugs of tea steeped strong and familiar.

It was messy.

Imperfect.

Holy.

When every dish had found its place and each person had taken their seat, a gentle hush settled over the room.

Pastor Luke looked around the table, eyes soft with reverence, and asked quietly—

"Shall we pray?"

James stood slowly, clearing his throat. His hand rested lightly on Ruthie's shoulder as he looked around the table. Mugs were set down. Even Bear seemed to settle at his feet.

"Would it be okay for me to speak this one?" James asked.

No one objected.

James looked around at the faces before him—weathered, radiant, flawed, beloved. Each one part of the story. Each one a thread in the tapestry that had somehow, against all odds, been woven back together.

He bowed his head.

"Lord," he began, voice thick with emotion, "thank You. Thank You for this table, and for every soul seated around it. For the food before us, but more than that—for the hands that prepared it, the laughter that carried it, the grace that made space for it.

"Thank You for second chances, for homecomings, for the kind of love that doesn't need to be earned but welcomes us anyway. Thank You for Ruthie... for her strength, her softness, her courage. For the little life growing within her. For Bear, who reminds us that loyalty doesn't need words. For friends who became family, and family who chose to stay.

"Thank You for Naomi—steadfast, wise, and loyal. For the way she speaks truth with gentleness and holds space like a sister.

"For Micah—his wonder, his joy, his messy enthusiasm that reminds us what it means to live with open hearts.

"For Margaret—whose quiet presence and faithful hands have mended more than clothes and warmed more than tea. For the wisdom she carries and the love she gives freely.

"For Neil—who shows up without needing words, whose presence alone steadies the room.

"And for Pastor Luke—who listens more than he speaks and reminds us what it means to walk humbly, love deeply, and serve without needing the spotlight.

"Lord may this home always be a place of peace. A place of gathering. A place where the lost are found, where broken hearts find rest, and where no story is too far gone for redemption.

"We honour You, Lord. You've been here—in the fire, in the flood, in the silence, in the song. You are the reason this table is full again.

"Bless this meal.

Bless this family.

And bless the days to come."

He opened his eyes to a hush that didn't need words.

And then—

Naomi passed the bread. Micah clanged a spoon against his cup. Margaret asked if someone could pass the lamb before it got cold. The room stirred back to life.

Ruthie smiled as she watched it all unfold—plates passed, stories swapped, tears and laughter mingling freely. James's hand found hers beneath the table, their fingers lacing like always.

There was no performance here.

No pretending.

Only love.

Only grace.

Epilogue: The Quiet Things

"The boundary lines have fallen for me in pleasant places; surely I have a delightful inheritance."—Psalm 16:6

The grass was tall and soft, whispering against their legs as they walked through the paddock behind the house. Wildflowers stretched lazily toward the sun—golden buttons, paper daisies, bluebells. The sky above was an open canvas of pale blue, scattered with slow-moving clouds that didn't threaten rain or storm—only shade, softness, time.

Ruthie spread the old woollen picnic blanket near the base of the gum tree. It was worn at the corners and still smelled faintly of eucalyptus and summer dust. She eased herself down with a sigh, knees brushing over the ground, and smiled as Bear trotted past her—his greying coat still thick and warm, his gait slower now, but steady.

James dropped the basket beside her and flopped down with a groan, stretching out beside her in the sun.

"Still think we should've brought the proper chairs," he said, shielding his eyes.

"And miss this view?" Ruthie teased, nudging him with her foot.

He turned to look—not at the wild hills or the distant lines of trees, but at her.

"No. Wouldn't trade this for anything."

A delighted shriek pierced the quiet, followed by the sound of fast, unsteady footsteps thudding through the grass.

Eden.

Their daughter.

Golden curls wild and tangled. Cheeks smudged with fig jam from lunch. Her tiny arms flung wide as she ran toward Bear, who patiently tolerated her hugs and tugs and love-offerings of small rocks and half-eaten fruit.

"Bear!" she shouted joyfully, as if she hadn't seen him every hour of every day of her life.

He looked up from where he'd flopped in the grass, gave a single thump of his tail, and allowed her to crawl into the curve of his belly as though she belonged there—which, of course, she did.

Ruthie's hand moved instinctively to her chest.

She still hadn't grown used to the way her body reacted to moments like this. How it stored them like sacred memory. How it felt like her bones sighed with gratitude.

"You okay?" James asked softly, sitting up now, elbow resting on his knee.

She nodded, unable to speak just yet.

Because how do you explain to someone that this—*this*—was the thing you never knew how to hope for? That watching your daughter chase sunlight through a paddock while your husband watched *you* like you hung it in the sky—that this was what healing looked like, long after the crisis passed?

She reached for his hand.

They sat that way for a while—watching Eden spin in circles, picking flowers, giggling at bugs, and yelling "COW!" even though there wasn't a cow in sight.

Bear followed her, never too far behind. Still her shadow. Still Ruthie's. A quiet keeper of the years.

"She's got your determination," James said, squinting as he watched Eden try to scale a tree stump.

"And your stubborn streak," Ruthie added with a smirk.

They fell quiet again.

The kind of quiet that doesn't need filling. The kind you only get after you've faced down storms together and come out the other side still holding hands.

Ruthie leaned into him, head on his shoulder.

"She'll never know that fear," she whispered. "She'll never have to unlearn the lie that she's unworthy."

James kissed the top of her head. "She'll only know love."

Ruthie's eyes burned, but she didn't cry. Not this time.

Just let the moment wash over her.

The warm breeze.

The sound of Eden squealing with delight as Bear rolled in the grass beside her.

The weight of James's hand on her thigh.

The distant hum of bees.

The land held them gently.

And Ruthie knew in the marrow of her bones: she was no longer surviving.

She was living.

Really living.

Not looking over her shoulder. Not bracing for loss. Not waiting for the other shoe to drop.

Just breathing.

Just being.

Just loved.

James handed her a slice of apple from the basket, and she bit into it absently, never taking her eyes off Eden.

"She's going to change the world," she said quietly.

James smiled. "She already changed ours."

Bear gave a low, contented sigh and flopped on his side, Eden sprawled across him now, drowsy in the sun.

Ruthie reached into the basket and pulled out her journal. The same one she used to write prayers in when words didn't come easy.

She flipped to the back, tore out a page, and wrote two lines:
We came back to the garden.
And it was still here.

Then she folded the page, tucked it under the corner of the blanket, and lay back with her head on James's chest.

Above them, the sky stretched wide and steady.

And below them, life—quiet and full—unfolded in golden threads across the earth.

About the Author

Melissa Baker is a storyteller, counsellor, and follower of Jesus who writes from the quiet conviction that no life is too broken for redemption. With a heart for women who have lived through trauma, abuse, and shame, Melissa's writing weaves together truth, tenderness, and faith—pointing always to the God who heals, restores, and stays.

She believes stories carry light. That even fiction can become a form of testimony. And that through the power of words, we can remind each other that hope is not lost, and grace is never out of reach.

Melissa lives in Australia, where she spends her time writing, counselling, and encouraging others in their walk with Christ. Her greatest desire is that this book would not only move you—but draw you closer to the One who saves.

More than anything, Melissa longs to use her words to spread the Gospel—to whisper the name of Jesus into the places where silence, shame, and sorrow once lived.

We'd love to hear from you!

To connect, collaborate, or explore how we can share stories of healing and faith together, reach out via email:

admin@thewaypublishing.com.au

Or visit our Facebook community:

facebook.com/thewaypublishingAus[1]

---

1. https://www.facebook.com/thewaypublishingAus